THE
UNWANTED

THE
UNWANTED

A NOVEL

PETER CLENOTT

First published by Level Best Books/Historia 2022

First edition

ISBN: 978-1-68512-078-8

Cover art by Level Best Designs

This book was professionally typeset on Reedsy.
Find out more at reedsy.com

To my parents, now deceased, Martin and Esther Clenott, who stood behind me for many years and to my children Leah, Stephen and William who, I hope, will stand with me for many years to come.

I

BOOK 1

Chapter One

September 1939

L ate summer. The first day of September, to be precise. And, to a young girl about to die, time, running out, matters above everything. In the past, on a fine day such as this, this girl, now hunched over her notepad in the back seat of a BMW, might have visited a museum in Berlin. She might have crossbred flowers with her grandmother, studied her precious textbooks, hiked through her native Bavarian forest looking for plant samples. But this first day of September in 1939 is an unusual day. At 4:45 AM this very morning, the German army under General von Rundstedt and General von Bock have invaded Poland. World War II has begun.

Does she even care, this girl? She's only fourteen years old. Mind on lock-down, does she notice the forests passing by on either side of her grandfather's car? The war is distant. Turbulence at home is daily. Does she hear the radio playing, already touting the magnificence of Der Fuhrer's lightning strike? Does she hear her grandfather's satisfied grunt... 'Hitler is right. Fire and iron is making Germany great again'...or catch his eye as he darts a worried look toward the female creature, whose blood he denies is akin to his?

No. She's too intent on her notepad to notice anything. Writing with a manic intensity that neither of her male attendants understands, she is bent over her paper as if some weight is forcing her down, never taking her eyes off her work, keeping her creations a secret from the world.

"Esh-vie-zet-vie-geh-vie. Esh-vie-zet-vie-geh-vie."

She mumbles this rhythmic chant over and over, "Esh-vie-zet-vie-geh-vie" until her grandfather Friedrich can no longer tolerate it and turns the knob of the radio to raise the sound, to drown out her existence.

She's crazy, this one, her grandfather is thinking. *Not of my blood. I've a clear conscience about this. Not of my blood.*

Her name is Hana Ziegler. And while she does have a family, grandparents, and two uncles, Edward and Walter, she is very much alone in the world. Mother deceased, father an unknown, she has borne her existence through her intellect, her studies of a world that her family apparently does not want her to inhabit much longer.

"Esh-vie-zet-vie-geh-vie."

Her lone suitcase sits at her feet, her few possessions thrown in at the last minute. Papers, schoolbooks, gnawed pencils, an eraser, and a sharpener. The sun had barely risen three hours earlier when she was rousted from her bed by her family's maid Hilda. Money is not the problem for the Zieglers. Hana is.

"I'm sorry. Time to get up, *liebschen.* Time to get ready." The maid had wept silent, angry tears. "These people. So early. Such a hurry. No time to eat. Not even a good-bye. Their own child."

It was Hilda, tears unrestrained, who bothered to neatly fold and pack a change of clothes and some toilet items in the only suitcase Hana would be allowed to carry with her to the Hollenschloss Institute. Hana herself acted as if still asleep, muttering under her breath, talking to some spectral entity, chanting what Hilda interpreted as a Catholic prayer though, in truth, was anything but.

Esh-vie-zet-vie-geh-vie.

From the moment Hilda pulled Hana from slumber, the mind of the outcast was borne into a parallel realm, another sort of dream world, though one of asphalt and steel that require Hana to coexist with people who mistake her for insane.

Her grandfather believes she is just engaged in ridiculous doodling, a meaningless, childish release of whatever mush exists in her brain.

"Scribble, scribble, scribble. What sort of nonsense is that?"

If he could reach far enough behind him, he would rip her notepad from her lap, crumple it up and toss it in her face. His question is not aimed at Hana but at the driver of his car, Hana's treating psychiatrist, Lorenz Koerner.

"You hear her? Is that singing or babbling? It's enough to want to make you throw her from the car onto the highway. An accident. Who would question it? What do you make of it, Koerner?"

"She may be self-comforting," Koerner replies. His hands grip the steering wheel, but his eyes move back and forth from the road ahead to the rearview mirror where he can see Hana, a mechanism of madness, driving her pencil into making strange figures on her notepad. In a way, he thinks, as she does so, she seems rather to be praying. Davening, the Jews call it. Her back is gently rocking. Her lips are moving, but Koerner can't quite make out what she is saying. And what deity would listen or understand such madness?

Whether or not she is comforted by it, the older man, Hana's grandfather, is not. Hatred is not too small a word. He has intentionally turned the radio up even louder to try to drown out the noise coming from his distasteful grandchild.

"Now you understand why we are doing this, Herr Doctor," the old man says, disgusted.

Actually, Koerner isn't entirely sure. There are several obvious possibilities. The neurological one. Hana is manic-depressive, oddly compulsive, unnerving to the average person, like now in the backseat as she chants and scribbles madness in her notebook. Then there are the political and economic rationales. The Nazis have been making it plain for some time that they do not want the imperfect to be able to procreate. The crippled and feeble-minded should be sterilized, prevented from passing on their illnesses to future generations. More recently, Hitler has secretly approved of harsher measures, expecting casualties from war, needing the hospital space currently taken up by the sick and infirm, the physically malformed and the mentally deranged. Why should money be spent on the psychotic, the retarded, when hard-working people struggle to put food on the table? This is not a caretaker country. Germany has to be purified. Only by being strong, will it make itself great again. People like Hana, even babies, if they are helpless, if their lives are *lebensunwertes leben*, lives unworthy of life, must be removed. Euthanized. At places like Hollenschloss.

"You do agree, don't you, Koerner?" Friedrich asks, as if he has a conscience and needs reassuring.

Koerner, at least, has a sense of shame not to openly engage the old man in a discussion of his granddaughter's fate right in front of her, right in front of her though he has co-signed the papers with little hesitation that are not only institutionalizing her at the Hollenschloss but that have designated her ultimate fate.

"Numbers," Friedrich says, risking a peek behind at what Hana is up to. He doesn't like being cooped up in this car with his granddaughter. He should have assigned Ilse, his wife, Hana's grandmother, this responsibility, or left it to Koerner. Walter, his youngest son, had talked him into this, to make sure that the thing was done right. They are practically alone driving on this two-lane road to the small Bavarian village that is the end of their trip. It won't end fast enough.

"*Juden*, **they** like numbers, too. They're very good with numbers. Bankers. Loan sharks. Too good. You get my point, Koerner?"

The psychiatrist doesn't. He can't help listening to Hana even though her chant is muted by the German broadcaster.

Esh-vie-zet-vie-get-vie. Esh-vie-zet-vie-geh-vie. Hana's foot is on the accelerator, the rapidity of her gibberish picking up energy as they approach the place from which she will not return.

"Why, just look at her," Friedrich says, not looking at her. "My people are pure Aryan stock. She's dark. The hair. The eyes. Her people, they rock backwards and forwards when they pray, don't they?"

"Her people?"

"We never knew who her father was. My daughter, her mother, lived in Berlin, hung around with the theatre crowd. Jews, you see now? We always suspected her father was one of them. And what would the SS do if they

6

found out that we were harboring in our own house, a…a…? Our bloodline corrupted. We have no choice, you understand, Koerner. None at all."

Koerner's eyes turn to the rearview mirror. If Hana is hearing any of this conversation, she isn't exhibiting any resentment. She is like a wind-up monkey except Koerner knows she can go on like this for hours at a time. Koerner is a much younger man than Ziegler. Herr Ziegler is so old, he can still rhapsodize over Bismarck and the Kaiser. He is a stolid stalwart German of the previous century. An industrialist who prides himself on his business acumen. Koerner prides himself on being a more modern man, a follower of Freud, himself a Jew. Who could say what years of analysis would do for a girl like Hana? But the pity of the world and of the times they are living in is that there is no tolerance and no time for analysis. While at this very moment, the Poles are feeling the brutality of *Blitzkrieg*, Koerner knows full well that German children like Hana will suffer the consequences just as inevitably. And yet, he signed the papers.

"How will they do it?"

"What?"

Koerner's attention has briefly been diverted to a van passing along the other side of the road. It has come from Hollenschloss. It is empty now. In a few days, it won't be. Gas enters through a hose. The passengers never leave their seats.

"How will they do it? You know what I mean."

Ziegler prods Koerner. The grandfather, the patriarch of a very rich family, is utterly tactless. Koerner pretends not to understand. He looks back at Hana with a smile.

"Your grandfather means how will we process the paperwork at Hollenschloss? We Germans love bureaucracy. But time is of the essence. And we don't want to keep you waiting forever. At Hollenschloss, our motto is quick and painless."

"Esh-vie-zet-vie-geh-vie. Esh-vie-zet-vie-geh-vie."

If anything. Koerner's attempt at making light of Ziegler's contempt for Hana has only ratcheted up the girl's response. Her writing hand is now moving so quickly over her notepad, it is a wonder she doesn't tear a hole

7

through it and send the tip of her pencil into her leg. Her chant has become an annoying drone, the buzzing of an angry hive of bees locked inside the car, windows rolled down, with three anxious people vying to escape. Who is mad now?

Koerner says, "I was in your room at the institute the other day, Hana. It's really quite nice. On the second floor with a balcony view. Neat. Clean. You'll have a roommate. Siggie. She's about your age, the daughter of Herr Haefner, one of our major donors. I think you might get along quite nicely, eh, Hana?"

"Esh-vie-zet-vie-geh-vie. Esh-vie-zet-vie-geh-vie."

"There's a window looking out onto a beautiful garden. A fountain with a statue and water bubbling out of its mouth. And flowers. Your grandmother insisted there be flowers. She grows them herself, doesn't she? Pretty flowers. The smell even this time of year is intoxicating."

Hana pays Koerner no mind. In fact, it appears that she is about to burst, her shaking body ready to explode into smoke and flame.

But Koerner, unlike the muttering older man, persists with nonchalance. "We are almost there, Hana. You see? Over the treetops on the very top of the hill overlooking the town. You can just make out the turrets if you look. An old castle. Quite elegantly turned up, I must say. A fairy tale castle for two fairytale princesses, eh, Hana? Not so bad. Not so bad at all."

"Esh-vie-zet-vie-geh-vie. Esh-vie- zet-vie-geh-vie. Esh-vie- zet-..."

In an instant, the rocking stops. The chanting. The manic writing. Hana freezes. If her psychotic manifestations are unsettling to the two men, her abrupt silence is worse. The wealthy industrialist Ziegler has faced down many a politician and business adversary in his time but has no idea how to handle this fourteen-year-old mental deviant. Koerner, trained at the finest European university under the tutelage of the most renowned specialists in his chosen field, has no inkling of what he has said to cause this momentous turn of events.

Hana keeps them waiting, then says, "One question, Herr Doctor Koerner, *bitte.*"

"Of course, Hana. Anything."

When at last she raises her eyes to the two men, much older and wiser than she, who have determined her fate without her knowledge, she does so with complete innocence. At least, that is what they believe.

"How **will** they do it?"

Chapter Two

May 1947

The driver of the car doesn't particularly like his passenger, but that is the nature of this business transaction. It isn't the first he has negotiated. It won't be the last, though it is getting harder each day to keep the bargains made over cash.

Post-war Germany is a mess. It is violated. It is bankrupt, deservedly so. In peace, it is still a battleground. It is an open sore on the face of Europe. It is a place fought over by four-star generals and weasels in trench coats. Trials are being conducted. Former leaders of the master race are being hung. On the one side, the Allies, America, England, and France. On the other, the Ivans, the Slavs, the Communists. For the multitude, the survivors, there is nothing to eat, no comfortable place to sleep. For the clever, there is money to be made. A lot of it. In this particular case, however, the driver wasn't paid in cash, a fact which made him hesitate until his customer explained.

"The brooch itself is worth a thousand American dollars," was the customer's claim. "The necklace was in the family two centuries."

"**Your** family?"

"Does it matter?"

"The provenance of such items is quite important."

"Some provenances are best-kept secret."

"Ah." Now the driver understands. The items belonged to some rich Jewish family, now deceased. Still, who would ever know? "There's more?"

"I have to support myself somehow," the passenger had negotiated. "You want it all?"

The driver gave it some thought. They had rendezvoused at a farm in Bavaria. The passenger has been hiding out for two years with a family called Voss, making connections finally with a mutual American friend. He looked like he had been sleeping in the barn with the horses. Walls were closing in. Escape routes were being cut off. He had to be desperate. Nooses liked former members of the SS. The driver was of a mind to push for as much as he could get. Then again, this ragged former Nazi looked like he had reached his limit, and the driver decided to be kind.

"Get in," he said.

"You have my credentials?"

"I do. Perhaps you should get into something more appropriate. Don't you have any other clothes?"

"Will you wait for me?"

"Not all day."

The driver glanced at his wristwatch, pulled out a Marlboro, smoked four no-filter, before his customer returned, not only better dressed but washed and clean-shaven.

"Well, well," the driver said, crushing his final cigarette underfoot. "Now you look American."

He and the driver of the car, flying two American flags on either side of the hood, are both young, in their thirties. They would both be considered good prospects for some gorgeous young debutante. They are good-looking, well-educated, charming in a way that is clinical, professional. The uninitiated wouldn't be able to tell if they were naturally gifted or just putting them on. In the movies, one would have been played by Olivier, the other by Errol Flynn. They might have been friends at Harvard, Oxford, or even Berlin. Fraternity brothers sharing wine, women, and song. In the car, as they drive toward the German border with Switzerland, they chat as young men might in a world that knows only the best of everything.

"The day is looking good."

"Better all the time."

11

"I should think. In your shoes."

The sun, in fact, is rising at the beginning of a warm late spring day. To either side, farmland. Ahead, mountains, the Swiss Alps. Pristine country unpeopled by monsters. The passenger has packed a flask of whiskey which he offers the driver. The driver passes. His eyes check the rearview mirror. It is not uncommon on this road to see military vehicles. Civilian traffic is limited except by tractor or horse. It will take much time, many years, for Germany and the Germans to recover.

What interests the driver is a car traveling behind them. He had noticed it at first as he was driving up an incline and the other car was just topping a hill behind, moving quickly. Now driving on a straightway, he can see the following car slow down only about fifty meters behind. His passenger doesn't notice. Taking a swig from his flask, he watches the road ahead. Switzerland, the first stop on his way to freedom.

"I've never been across the Atlantic," he says. "Strange to say, I've never even been on an airplane."

"It can take getting used to. The taking off. As long as you don't run into any turbulence, you should be fine. The girls in Buenos Aires, I understand…"

"Yes. Absolutely. Something to look forward to."

The passenger lifts his flask in salute to good days ahead. The driver eyes the car behind, a relic from the early 30s, he guesses, a German make. Definitely not military.

"Does it ever cross your mind?" the driver wonders.

"What?"

"The things you did. You know."

"The things I did? What things do you think I did?"

"The camps. The Jews."

The driver takes another worried peek behind. The other car is being driven by a man. In the passenger seat, a woman. Husband and wife? Boyfriend and girlfriend? Difficult to say how old they are. But why would they be out on this road, at this time of day, heading in this direction with no indication that they're Red Cross or with the United Nations Relief and

Rehabilitation Administration, the driver's employer? His job in this chaotic free-for-all in Germany is to help resettle the homeless, which, in a sense, is what his mission is today.

"I choose not to think about what you might have done," he says.

"Then why did you ask?"

The driver doesn't respond. The car behind is closing in.

"If it's a relief to your conscience," the passenger says, "I was a minor functionary. SS, yes, but nothing to do with the camps. Have you heard of the BDM? The *Bund Deutscher Madel*?"

The driver makes a grunting sound which could be a 'yes' or a 'no'. His attention has clearly been diverted as the car behind picks up speed and appears ready to pass.

His passenger is oblivious. He is happy, garrulous, and getting high. "Hitler's girls. The future of the Aryan race. I was Baldur von Schirach's aide. I could have had any one of them. Any one of them at any time. And did, I must admit. I have a daughter even. Yes, me. I operated the Lebensborn Program. I knew Goebbels, yes, but only in passing, in certain social settings. After all, we needed strong babies to replace the unpure."

Now the old-time auto has pulled up alongside the driver's car, such that the United Nations man can clearly see the two people in the front seat. Because he is looking in their direction, he misses the road sign that alerts motorists to Hollenberg and the Hollenschloss Institute, two kilometers away.

His passenger is still rambling on about his harmless escapades with the female version of the Hitler Youth, in particular this girl named Silke, a real beauty, he claims, when the car to the side, rather than attempt to pass, purposefully sideswipes the car with the American flags. This jolts the passenger into the present.

"What the fuck?" the driver yells.

"What is going on?"

Red-faced with anger, the driver points to his glove compartment. "Open it," he orders his passenger. "Give me the gun."

Another metallic sideswipe sends the driver's car off the road onto the shoulder. He maintains control, but barely.

"What are they doing?" the passenger shouts. He has spilled his whiskey all over his clean and pressed new clothes. Pushed against the driver with the last hit, he manages a glance in the direction of the attacking car. *"Scheise!"*

He recognizes the woman in the car. Yes! Yes! It is definitely her. And the man. The passenger knows him, as well. He rolls down his window to scream at them. But before he can utter a sound, the Relief and Rehabilitation man, holding onto the steering wheel with one hand, raises his gun with the other.

"Sit back!" he yells and aims his weapon at the colliding vehicle.

"But I know these people!" the passenger yells.

That is when the exchange of gunfire begins on this sunny German autobahn, surrounded by pastureland and picturesque mountains. The driver's shot misses its target, the other man driving the second vehicle. His bullet pings off the roof of the pursuer. The next shot that is fired comes from the pistol held by the woman. It creases von Schirach's aide but strikes the American driver in the forehead.

The woman knows how to shoot. The resettlement specialist is dead with the first shot, his blood and brains further contaminating his passenger's disguise. He lets go of the steering wheel, and the car careens out of control off the road where it flips over and skids on its roof into a ditch.

The passenger with the harmless SS record is bounced and thrown against the driver, against the dashboard, and comes to rest at last on the roof. It takes him several minutes to recover his senses. His first thought is to locate the gun his business partner fired. His next thought is to squeeze through his open window and get the hell out of the car before it explodes or catches fire. He knows the two people in the other automobile. He will deal with them when he is free of the wreck. The jewels. Perhaps they will accept the jewels.

He staggers out bleeding and muddy. The world is still spinning when he sees the woman and man descend into the ditch. Their faces are a blur to him. But he can hear the man speaking. He at least seems reasonable, someone like himself, who can moderate his feelings even in the most catastrophic of

14

circumstances. Someone who knows the art of negotiation. Someone who, like most Germans of their generation, can and must put the past behind them.

The woman, however, is another matter.

"Children!" she screams.

"What? What children?"

She breaks free of her companion's restraining hand.

"Children, just children!"

The SS man is still dizzy. He is not quite understanding her. He raises his hand in protest as if his bare palm can resist a bullet, but it is too late. She has taken dead aim. Protest is pointless. She is unmoved. She is crazy. And she rarely misses.

The bullet that ends the life of von Schirach's aide hits him square in his handsome face. He topples into the drainage gully. The second shot is aimed lower though it is unfelt, the man already being dead. Only when the woman has emptied her revolver, however, does she stop firing. Then she stands over the corpse and spits on it.

"For the children," she says.

So much for Buenos Aires.

Chapter Three

For Silke Hartenstein, the journey to the Hollenschloss Institute isn't a final one. American teenagers would call it a field trip, a chance to escape the confining walls of the local high school to adventure out into the adult world to learn something about the life they would come to know more intimately once they graduate. It is a learning experience made so much more important because she is a member of the BDM and the future of the Fatherland depends upon girls like her, the pure-bred Aryan mothers of the eternal Reich.

She is not alone. Eleven other girls, accompanied by two adult chaperones, are traveling to the institute to see for themselves why they have been chosen to become the Fatherland's perfect mothers. The girls, between the ages of ten and sixteen, are expected to sit quietly in their seats, demurely, backs straight, hands folded in their laps. It isn't a comfortable ride, but life, they are taught, isn't always comfortable. The German woman can cope with anything. She is strong, resilient, and the perfect mate to the German man.

All the girls wear the same BDM uniform: a brown jacket over a white shirt with a black tie and a black skirt. On the sleeves of the jackets, the girls wear the triangular insignia of their unit, in this instance, the Sud Schwaben. Beneath the unit insignia is the red and white diamond Nazi symbol with a black Swastika set in the middle. Their hair is done up in braids tied by two white ribbons. They are feminine and they are strong. They are the backbone of the nation. Let none of them ever doubt it.

Silke doesn't. She has, however, an unfortunate habit. She tends to giggle at the most inappropriate of occasions. At roll call. During an intense lecture on the merits of sterilization. Whenever she's being reprimanded. Someday, she has been warned, your unbridled hilarity is going to come back and bite you in the arse. Her worried parents believe her disposition is more suited to the stage than to the front lines. She is beautiful. Make no mistake about that. Her perfect countenance, her mother and father figure, is her saving grace. She is the quintessential German woman. Blonde. Blue-eyed. Athletic. Tall for her age, which is sixteen. She can throw the javelin forty meters. That would have been a women's world record a decade ago. She rides horses and loves to watch Charlie Chaplin movies. Men who should know better want to take her to bed. Her mother will not allow this, of course. Silke is a virgin and will wait for the right circumstance to procreate with the right German man.

Six months ago, her face appeared on the cover of a German magazine fronting an article meant for the entire nation to read on the absolute beauty of the German female. Photographers from Berlin had spent an entire week following her around snapping pictures of her in her BDM uniform, in a swimming suit, on horseback, helping her mother with the housework, helping her father in his job as a groundskeeper. She even posed with her javelin. Perspiration, one young photographer assured her, was ideal. Not only did it show she was unafraid of hard work, but it was sexy. He said this with a wink that made her giggle.

Even now, sitting in the very back of the bus next to her comrade Dora Voss, she is showing off a black and white picture from that article. Smoothed out on her lap, hidden from view of the chaperones by the seat in front of her, it shows her being congratulated by, of all people, Nazi propaganda minister Josef Goebbels. In the photograph, she is smiling broadly. They are shaking hands. Goebbels seems to be telling her something that is about to make her laugh. Silke is proud of the picture. Her father told her that Goebbels himself had selected her out of thousands of girls across Germany. In France, in America, in far-off Australia, people

17

would know who Silke is and by relationship who the Hartensteins are.

"You think that will get you special treatment?" Dora says, back stiff, eyes dead ahead, fingers clasped together.

"There's nothing bad about being noticed. If Herr Goebbels can help my family, what's the harm?"

The girls whisper, not wanting to be heard. One of their chaperones, the extremely stiff Frau Zoeller, has turned on the radio so that everyone can monitor the German army's advances into Poland. Everyone is supposed to listen because Frau Zoeller will question them once they get off the bus which generals are leading which armies through which Polish towns.

"My brother has noticed you," Dora says. "He told me he wants to hug you."

"I doubt that."

"And kiss you."

"Ugh."

"And kiss your bottom."

Silke snorts. It is one of those moments of hilarity that she tries to stifle. Dora is always doing that to her, trying to get her in trouble. "You have a dirty mind, Dora," she says, just managing to control her giggles. "He says no such thing. Karl's only twelve years old."

"Perhaps Minister Goebbels then. I bet he wanted to lick your arse. That's why he chose you. It's not your face, Silke. It's your damned fat arse every man wants."

This time, Silke can't stay a guffaw that she quickly turns into a series of coughs when one of the alerted chaperones looks around. The scowl on Frau Zoeller's face is enough, Silke thinks, to turn her arse to stone. The image of which forces Silke to have to utter a louder series of coughs and bury her head in her lap to keep from belting out the most inappropriate of laughs.

"Are we all right, ladies?" Frau Zoeller calls out.

The other girls on the bus are tempted to look around, but none of them do.

"Just dust," Silke manages to sputter. "Fumes from the bus."

"Did you fart?" Dora wonders.

"Stop it."

Silke pinches Dora's leg then manages to get herself under control picturing herself, as she does whenever similar circumstances have aroused her amusement, standing before a firing squad. She has been told that that is what they do to traitors, and she is very afraid of being branded a traitor to the Fatherland. She has also heard, though she thinks this is just a rumor meant to frighten people, that people are killed in buses like this one. They are shoved inside, doors are locked behind them, then gas is pumped inside. Within minutes all are dead. Dora has told her they do that very thing at Hollenschloss Institute.

"You go in one of these," she says, "you don't come out."

Silke doesn't trust Dora. If truth be told, she doesn't like Dora. Or, for that matter, the BDM. But these days everyone in Germany is forced to make sacrifices. Silke isn't afraid to do her share. She just doesn't care for the images that seem to fascinate Dora so.

Dora really is a low-life, Silke thinks, as their bus passes through the stone gates of the Hollenschloss. Built as the estate of a seventeenth-century Bavarian count, the institute has served a variety of purposes including as a hospital for soldiers wounded during the first world war, then as an orphanage for children bereft of parents through the deprivations of Germany post-war. Now it is a psychiatric center for mentally deranged people who have little or no hope at all of ever living a normal life.

The bus follows a circular drive, past well-manicured gardens. The grounds are beautifully maintained. The shrubbery is neatly trimmed. The lawns are newly mowed. Not a speck of litter lies on the roadway. Silke appreciates the hard work that goes into managing a large estate's grounds. She often helps her father, who works for the Haefner family, who are the primary financial backers of this institution. Silke's mother is the Haefner family cook. Her father is the Haefner groundskeeper. The Hartensteins are a proper middle-class German family.

"We're going to take a tour of the facility now," Frau Zoeller says as the twelve girls line up in two rows outside the bus. Silke stands head and shoulders above them all. "Stay in line. Don't speak to any of the patients. No matter what you see, understand that it is for the good of the nation. You are not to think of these children as unfortunates, for God has other plans for them. Understand only that your role in the future of our country is to produce children who are whole and healthy, the torch bearers of our Aryan race for the next thousand years."

Silke is a typical sixteen-year-old who thinks about sex. Not constantly, but enough to be distracted by a cute face and a healthy physique, girl or boy. As the BDM girls march in line to the entry into the main building of Hollenschloss, she can see some boys and young men, patients in grey institutional clothing, working the grounds. Her eyes shouldn't wander, but she can't help wondering what will happen to these boys if they don't recover soon. Will they end up, like Dora says, in a locked bus, windows darkened so no one in the outside world can see inside, as the gas slowly fills the lightless interior? What is it like? Do they smell the gas? Do they wonder what is happening? Are they scared? Do they try to break out? Do they scream for help that won't come? What is it like to die when you are young and your whole life lies ahead?

A pleasant-looking middle-aged man, a doctor in a white smock, greets Frau Zoeller and introduces himself to the BDM girls. "I'm Doctor Grosbach," he says with a smile. "I run the children's unit. The boys live in one wing of the building. The girls live in the one you are about to visit. Not only do they come from Germany, but we have girls here from Austria and Czechoslovakia. Their parents have sent them to us to build up their bodies and minds so that they can go home again strong and healthy."

"Will they all go home?" one of the younger BDM girls asks.

It is an innocent enough question. But Silke catches the doctor hesitate before answering.

"That is our hope," he says at last. When he turns around to begin the tour, Frau Zoeller gives the ten-year-old who asked the question a rough clap on the arm.

The girls march in single file. Because Silke is the oldest and tallest of the girls, she walks in the very back behind Dora and in front of the second chaperone, Frau Goedeler. The smell of the facility is the first thing she notices. Antiseptic, scrubbed down, and bleached. That is until they reach the first ward. Then in an instant, the odor becomes one of unclean bodies and urine. The impact of the change is potent enough to make one or two of the girls emit shocked squeaks that compels Frau Zoeller to order them to be still.

Doctor Grosbach is well aware of the reaction. He says, "Children come to us in different states of well-being. Some, those you might have seen on the grounds, are allowed to work outside, earn money even. We feel it is the best way toward preparing them to return home. Robust sun. Hard work. Other children need more attention. In some cases, let us be honest, the children need almost constant care. They are physically unable to perform the simplest task. Some were born this way. Others, unfortunately, suffered illnesses or accidents after birth that their families can't manage. So, they send them here where they get the best care possible. There are children here and adults in our adult wings, who left alone will sit in the darkness or lie in their beds soiling themselves and never moving or uttering a recognizable sound. They have to be fed. They have to have their clothes and bedding constantly changed. It is very difficult on our staff, as you can imagine, keeping up with it all. Especially in wartime when we now have to focus on our brave wounded soldiers. That is why you may smell odors that are unpleasant. But have no doubt, we maintain as high a standard of healthcare as any in Europe."

Silke, in fact, is horrified by what she sees. While it is true, the floors and walls of the ward are sparkling with cleanser and the bedding on many of the beds has been recently washed, it is the condition of the patients that has Silke wanting to cry. Her grandmother had been a nurse, and Silke is certain that her *grossmutter*, would be shocked by what she sees. Children as young as one or two lying two to a bed in soiled linen, wide-eyed but silent, barely moving. Older girls whose hair Silke would have liked to take a brush to. Some mumble or mutter to themselves. One girl sits in a wheelchair by herself in a dark alcove. There is an open book in her lap, but she clearly is uninterested in reading it.

Silke wants to ask, 'What's the matter with her?' But Frau Goedeler pushes her forward.

"No staring," Frau Goedeler orders. "It isn't polite."

Silke is never so happy as when the tour finally comes to an end and she is able to smell the clean air outside the main building. There are four units in all, each containing forty to sixty patients. She can't imagine what the others are like if the one she has witnessed is the best.

As the girls line up waiting for the return of their bus, Silke lifts her head and takes an audible breath of a fresh breeze that could have come all the way from the neighboring Alps.

"I don't see why they don't just kill them all," Dora whispers. "I mean, did you see the one in the wheelchair? What's the point of living like that?"

"Maybe it doesn't have to be like that," Silke argues.

She turns her eyes to a black BMW just coming to a stop at the entrance to the main building. The first person out of the car is the driver who hurries around to open the door for his passenger, an old man in a black suit and homburg, lighting up a cigar. It is the passenger in the back seat who captures Silke's full attention. A girl around Silke's age, slender, dark, wearing what looks like hand-me-downs. Her long black hair has fallen loose down to her shoulders. She is clutching a notebook to her chest as the driver of the car reaches into the interior to grab a worn suitcase. The gruff old man is looking around at everything except the girl as if he wants to pretend she isn't there.

But she is there, old man, Silke thinks. For whatever reason, she can't explain it herself, she is angered when the old man gives the girl a shove. He snaps at her, but the girl doesn't cry. She is trying to force something into the hands of the other man. A piece of paper. She is insisting he take it. He won't because he is afraid of upsetting the old man.

The girl pleads. Her anguish only intensifies Silke's rage. Herr Doctor Grosbach has joined in the fray so that now three bigger men are surrounding the girl who is only trying to hand one of them her piece of paper. The squabble has drawn the attention of everyone in the courtyard from staff to patients to boys tending the grounds to Silke's companions.

The BDM girl in Silke tells her to remain calm, ignore what is none of her business. Her parents would advise her not to make other peoples' problems hers. Frau Zoeller and Frau Goedeler are harrumphing and muttering something about, "Here's another one."

It is then that fate intervenes in the form of a breeze, if not from heaven, then from Switzerland. It grabs hold of the paper that the dark-haired girl has been holding, rips it from her hand, and sends it floating in the direction of Frau Zoeller. But before Frau Zoeller can stoop to pick it up and probably toss it away, Silke jumps in front of her unit commander and grabs the precious document.

What she reads in the brief moment she is in possession of it both puzzles and frightens her. Much of the paper is taken up by a single phrase, scribbled and written repeatedly with very disturbed handwriting. *Es-y-zet-y-geh-y.* Over and over again. In the margins, across the top and bottom, diagonally, vertically, horizontally. A phrase or word that somehow Silke knows or thinks she knows from somewhere. What is clear to her is that this was not the girl's original intent. Because the paper begins as if she were going to write a friend a letter. It opens with an address in the United States and a name: *My dearest Peggy, I am in dire need of your help.*

Before Silke can hope to decipher the crazy scrawl, Frau Zoeller grabs the letter from her, makes one quick perusal, then makes a show of displaying it to all of her charges.

"See, here," she says, "this is what I am talking about. This is the impurity that threatens us all." Then she crumples the paper up and slaps Silke across the face. "You will learn no matter what it takes even if you are Goebbels' baby doll."

Silke is sorely tempted to strike back. But this is not the way of a BDM girl. You strike the enemy, not your own. If you get slapped in the face, you accept it and move on. What is Frau Zoeller after all but a bully in a uniform? Instead, Silke's eyes turn from the ugly face of her group leader to that of the fragile girl.

Hana Ziegler senses something different. From across the driveway, surrounded by three frustrated men, she looks up. Hope is rekindled. And

23

in the moment that their eyes lock, their destinies are sealed.

In the background, Silke can hear Dora say, "Why bother, Silke? The girl no longer exists."

Oh, but she does, Silke thinks, and she knows things that no one else can.

What is the worst of all? It is the sound coming from all around her now. Even Frau Zoeller and Frau Goedeler are joining in as the hapless girl from the black BMW is escorted into the Hollenschloss Institute. It is a sound Silke is all too familiar with. Only this time, she is the only one who isn't laughing.

Chapter Four

September 1939

Peggy McAuliffe has several things in common with Hana Ziegler even though they live thousands of miles apart. Peggy is a little older, twenty-two. But she has a family and she comes from wealth. She likes to draw. She is good with pen and pencil, particularly landscapes. She is gangly, awkward, and, according to her parents, mentally challenged.

The family story is that she lay in her mother's birth canal far too long. Father and Mother should have sued the doctors at Maine Medical, but the discovery of her mental instability wasn't made until she hit puberty. Up until then, the family just accepted that Peg was a little behind the other children in her crowd. A little awkward. A little, how should we put this, inappropriate. Unpleasant, perhaps, but tolerable. A series of private schools kept her differences from becoming the object of social gossip in and around Cape Elizabeth and Boston where the McAuliffes maintain their chosen circle of friends. But you can't keep your daughter at a distance forever. Can you?

Peggy has a twin brother Charlie. That is the complication here. Harold McAuliffe, who took the wealth inherited from his father and increased it tenfold, has plans for his eldest son. While youngest son David is bound for Harvard Law, Charlie is going to be the first Catholic president of the United States. But if the nation suspects that what one twin has, the other must also, that is problematic. Charlie must be kept well and clear of his twin sister's dilemma. Harold says as much at a family dinner on the very night the Nazis have invaded Poland.

"A war hero, a dashing war hero," he says to his gathered family over a salmon casserole with corn on the cob and Maine potatoes served with garlic, "has a leg up on the rest of the mob. He's photogenic. He's charming. Who can resist him? Certainly not the female voters. With money backing him up, he's a shoo-in. Unless, of course, well, we don't need any screw-ups, do we?"

"You think war is inevitable, Papa?" Harold's wife Elizabeth 'Liz' McAuliffe asks.

"Now it is. It's just a matter of time before Roosevelt pushes the button."

Harold is the American ambassador to Denmark recently brought home to discuss with other members of the diplomatic corps the prospects in Europe. At first a supporter of Hitler's strengthening of Germany because of its economic benefits to American businessmen, Harold is now convinced that here is the way to ensure Charlie's ascendency to the White House.

"Herr Hitler," he intones, "is like any other global capitalist although he has little or no business acumen. Why be satisfied owning one company, when you can have them all? He is pushing too hard, too fast. Poland today. He's said he wants the world. Wait until he goads Stalin. Then you'll see what happens."

"America can't stand apart forever," Charlie says, sitting at his father's right. "Hitler won't let the Atlantic get in the way. We're as strong as he is, or could be if Roosy doesn't sit on his hands. At some point down the road, Hitler has to come for us. And I, for one, won't let us down."

Harold pats his prized son on the cheek. The McAuliffes have seven children in all. But in the hierarchy of things only two matter. Unfortunately, Peg was born a girl. And retarded. Otherwise, could have had a McAuliffe vice president. Wouldn't that have been something?

"I know you won't," says the ambassador chewing on a bite of fish. "No slip-ups. Hitler is like a child who, having won one game of marbles, wants to win them all. It will be up to us then. Must come down a peg or two, pardon the pun, my dear."

At the far end of the table, sitting between David and Liz McAuliffe, Peg doesn't reply. She hasn't been paying her father the slightest attention. The same thing can be said of her meal. The McAuliffes are renowned for the food they serve at their hosted events. But Peg, who tops in at almost six feet, is rail thin at slightly over one hundred pounds. That is one of her many 'quirks'. She eats like a bird. What she likes to do and, frankly, does quite well, is draw. Unfortunately, on any viable material close to hand. She is doing this now with a ballpoint pen on a napkin to her brother David's amusement. Rather than respect his father's opinions, the second oldest son, himself eventually headed for Harvard Law, chuckles.

"Is there something funny down at the southern latitudes?" Harold asks, wiping his mouth on a cloth napkin.

"No, nothing, sorry, Dad," David says blushing. "Go on, Peggity, show Dad what you drew."

Peg seems hesitant to do so, leaving it up to David to hold her artwork up for the family to appreciate. An amazing likeness of Herr Hitler, arm outstretched in the Nazi salute. His stiff hand is covering the earth. Acceptable enough, except that what is visible of his hand is the middle finger pointed at the moment right at Harold McAuliffe.

The other McAuliffe children snigger. Even Charlie claps. "Frame it!" he shouts. "We'll post it in my dorm in Cambridge."

"I should hope not," Liz says. From one end of the table to the other, Mother and Father share a quick look.

Harold chuckles it off. "Well," he says, "at least she's not Jewish."

After dinner, the family likes to unwind playing volleyball in the court behind their lavish oceanside estate. From their backyard, they can see Portland Light and hear the Atlantic crashing against the rocks near their private beach. Theirs is the most exclusive property in Maine. They will often entertain here, lights held aloft by ancient oak and elm. Select neighbors are invited to the most special occasions, but the ordinary folk are invited, too. If you're going to run as a Democrat, Harold's theory is, you better invite the everyday people, the voters, to your home once in a while. Show them what life could be like if they vote for the right man.

On the following evening, after a day of sailing in Portland harbor, the McAuliffes set out a spread for their neighbors to feast upon. A band out of Boston has been hired to play. Harold speaks of events in Europe and what he feels they may lead to. He makes sure Charlie, Charles, has his turn, too. Practice, they say, makes perfect.

"We don't know what FDR's plans are," Charlie says. "We know there are a lot of hard feelings about helping Europe out yet again. But we don't think Hitler will give us the opportunity to stay unbloodied. If the time comes when we must declare war, then I, for one, will be first in line."

There are cheers aplenty for Charlie's brave stand. 'First in Line'. That will be his campaign motto when the war ends and the local congressional seat comes up. David is two years behind but expects to have to accelerate his courses to graduate early. Harold sees him as Charlie's right-hand man and possibly a future Attorney General of the United States. This evening, however, as people mingle, eat, drink, dance, flirt, David keeps an eye on Peggity who wanders about the crowd seemingly lost and alone. He takes her hand.

"Steady," he says. "No drinking."

"Can I have a smoke?"

"No."

"Why?"

"It's not healthy."

"Can I dance?"

"With me. I'll have the band play 'Beer Barrel Polka'."

"There are other boys here." She giggles.

"Hands off, Peg. Ladies wait to be asked."

Peg seems whimsical tonight, David thinks. He's a handsome twenty-year-old. Then again, all the McAuliffe's are known for their looks, their charm. Except Peggy of whom many of the neighbors secretly have come to the conclusion that she's retarded. Poor thing. Money can't fix everything. We all have our crosses to bear. She often drifts off into her own world, talks to herself, seems to be chatting with other people, carrying on dialogues with spectral fairytale princes. The McAuliffes employ a visiting nurse they trust to maintain their privacy and dole out the necessary medication to keep Peg in line. But when Mrs. Butler is unavailable, the task falls to David who, alone of Peg's siblings, feels bad for her.

"I want..." she begins to say as they walk amongst their neighbors and school chums.

"Yes?"

Peg covers up a giggle.

David smiles. "What?"

Peg laughs more openly as her eyes rove the crowd and she spots a boy she is attracted to.

"Oh," David says. "Probably not a good idea." He steers her away from a couple of Charlie's Harvard classmates. Bill Sorensen and Bobby Krebs. Preppies with reps. Bright futures. Money and power. Good luck to the women who marry them. "I'm going to get your pills and sit you down beside the RCA with a drawing pad, and you're going to draw me a picture of Hitler, Stalin and Dad and we'll call them Groucho, Chico, and Harpo."

"I don't want my pills. They make me sleepy. I don't want to sleep."

"But you're going to have them. With tea and a slice of chocolate cake."

"I want to get laid." Peg laughs out loud, snorts out the mucus-like part of her supper that went up her nose. She doesn't care who notices. When Sorensen and Krebs look her way, she flips her skirt up, showing too much leg.

"Cut it out, Peg. You don't want to get laid. At least, not now. Not here. Not them. Maybe I can find you someone. To date. Not to...get laid. Jeez, you want Dad to lock you away? He will."

David worries. At one time, he had even considered the priesthood as a vocation until both parents explained the political illogic of being considered too Catholic. He has heard of other parents doing things like that to children they can't control. Cold storage. A hideaway in a distant state. He doesn't want that for his sister, but, Christ, ever since she hit puberty, it's like she's become another person. Thank God he has confiscated the drawings she's made of penises and vaginas. At least, he hopes he's gotten rid of all of them. That would be the last straw for his parents. But how can he help her, how

29

can he keep an eye on her, how can he keep her safe when he is away at school?

He leads her into the family den, sits her down in a comfortable red leather chair. "I will get you a boy," he says.

"You will?" No. But the lie will keep her from disappearing on him. Her eyes light up. She is pretty, or would be if she ate more and took better care of her personal hygiene. There is always a smell about her that David finds distasteful but ignores. He figures maybe she just doesn't clean herself, you know, down there.

He heads out having no intention of finding a boy. At the door to the den, she says something that gets his attention.

"S-y-z-y-g-y. S-y-z-y-g-y."

"What?"

"S-y-z-y-g-y. A girl taught me that. The one from Copenhagen. Remember? Hana."

"Really?"

"S-y-z-y-g-y. I liked her. She says it blanks out her mind. A boy raped her, and she said that is what she was thinking the whole time he was in her. I just like the sound."

"Good."

"S-y-z-y-g-y."

David closes the door on her singsongy rhyme. He wishes he could lock it, but runs upstairs to find her sedatives. Peggy has seen many specialists. She's been to Boston many times. But none of the doctors seem to know how to help her. The sedatives don't help. They knock her out, but how long can you treat her that way? It isn't humane.

David doesn't stay away for long. In his heart, he knows there will be no happy ending. He knows trouble lies ahead and his sister's future is dismal indeed. But when he returns he never expects to find her naked in the den, dress off, shoes off, a lustful smile on her face as she sways still humming that crazy tune, s-y-z-y-g-y. Only, now she is doing it for an audience. Bill Sorensen and Bobby Krebs. Krebs is merely singing along, but Sorensen is on his knees caressing Peggy's buttocks and moving his hand lasciviously between her legs.

"You fuckers!" David screams. He tosses the sedatives aside and lunges at Sorensen, punching him and kicking him. He has to fend off his own sister who, rather than support his efforts, actively fights him.

"I want! I want!" she yells.

David has to shove her down onto the leather chair. He would pursue Sorensen, beat him till he bleeds, but both of Charlie's Harvard classmates race out laughing, mimicking Peggy. S-y-z-y-g-y. S-y-z-y-g-y. They don't even recognize Harold McAuliffe as they bolt past him. David does. But what can he do? Peggy is fondling herself now, moaning, trying to bring herself to completion.

Closing the den doors behind him, Harold McAuliffe doesn't utter a word of reprimand. Rather, he eyes his son David, his family fixer, and says, "Get her dressed. Give her her medicine. Put her to bed. Tomorrow she is going away. Your mother and I have had enough."

Chapter Five

September 1939

Hana's room is clean. Doctor Koerner is right about that. On the second floor with a single window looking out onto a garden centered by a statue of a figure Hana believes to be Athena, the goddess of wisdom. There is no water trickling out of her mouth, however, nor out of any other orifice. The basin the Greek goddess is standing in is dry, filled rather with the first leaves of autumn. There are flowers, yes, but wilted. Worker patients are sweeping the walkways of fallen debris and depositing the dead life into wheelbarrows. There is a distinct lethargy about their movements, but at least they are functioning, increasing the odds that they will escape Hollenschloss with their lives.

Doctor Koerner drops Hana's suitcase on the bed closest to the window. The gray blanket is tucked in. There is a single pillow over which, on the wall, hangs a picture of Adolf Hitler. Koerner doesn't bother to salute it. He presents a smile to Hana.

"Well, is it not how I described it? The garden. The statue. The flowers."

Hana stands at the window staring out.

She has ceased muttering her cursed rhyme. That, at least, thinks the eminent psychiatrist, is a good thing. Left to himself, he would not have marked her off for death. He believes she is salvageable. But her family insists. And the family is well-connected. If the officials of T-4 say she has to go, what can he do but make her life as comfortable as possible until that moment...well, he chooses not to think of it. She understands. That is the problem. How she does, he can't say. But clearly, she knows what is in store for her.

"I will do what I can," he says. "Of course."

Still, she doesn't move.

"I am not a bad man," he feels the need to say. "And who knows...?" He pauses, uncomfortable in her presence, hoping for some excuse to leave her. He sits on her hard bed and gazes at the notebook that she still clutches to her slender frame. "Those symbols," he says, pointing to the notebook. "What do they mean? I know they mean something to you. You write as a means of escaping this world, I get that. But your drawing reminds me of a chemistry class I once took at university. And, I must admit, chemistry was never one of my strong subjects."

Hana doesn't bother to respond. Her mind is on a girl, a tall, beautiful blonde girl in a uniform. The one who didn't laugh. The one who understands her. Hana is only fourteen. She has never been in love. This would be a strange and inopportune time to have such feelings, but she can't keep this girl's face out of her mind. Her eyes. Her sorrow. She does understand me, Hana thinks. Too bad. Too late.

"I know you're quite a clever young woman," Koerner says. He rises from her bed, hands thrust inside his pants pockets. There is a commotion outside the room. It distracts him until he notices Hana make a move away from the window, which is open to allow in a fresh breeze. She takes a step toward her psychiatrist, then extends her hand with the notebook in it.

"Keep it," she says, then, in an instant, before Koerner can move a muscle to stop her, she leaps out the opening.

"Hana!" Koerner screams. "Hana!" But her slender childlike body has allowed her to fly through the window without interference. "Jesus! Fuck!"

He rushes to the opening, looks down, expecting the worst. But Hana has jumped not to her death. She has fallen into a bush, rolled off its newly trimmed branches, and landed at the feet of a stunned gardener. After a moment, she is even able to rise unaided, brush herself off and look back up toward Koerner who is leaning out. She reaches her hand to him.

"Herr Doctor Koerner, *bitte*, can I have my notebook back?"

* * *

It is evening now. The German divisions under von Rundstedt and von Bock are deep inside Poland and still advancing. Apparently, the Russians are moving in from the East and soon Poland, carved up like a game bird, will cease to exist.

Hana is sitting on her bed. She has been bathed. Her old clothes have been taken away and she is now covered in the gray institutional uniform of a Hollenschloss mental patient. Her feet are bare. Her hair is still damp and uncombed. She is writing calmly in her notebook, composing a letter to someone named Peg McAuliffe, when the door to her room opens and her roommate is wheeled in. It is the same girl Silke saw in the dark alcove with an unread open book in her lap.

The nurse pushing the girl's chair says with a cheerful smile, "Here is your roommate Sigrid. You see, she likes to read, too."

"I'm not reading," Hana says. "I'm writing."

"Is there a difference?"

"The reader reads what the writer writes," says Hana. She is not being impolite. She is just being straightforward. She continues composing her SOS without looking up.

Behind the nurse and Sigrid comes a cart containing trays of food being dropped off from room to room to the various patients. Each dinner is hidden by a cover hiding the prescribed meal along with the patient's name taped to the top. Hana doesn't lift the cover to her plate when it is placed beside her on the bed. She looks up only when the nurse and the meal transporter have left Hana and Sigrid alone.

She is curious regarding Sigrid whose name Doctor Koerner mentioned in the car, Princess *Nummer Zvei*. Sigrid is quite thin. That is the first thing Hana notices. Not just thin. Bony. She has light brown hair that someone has been kind enough to braid. She is a child. Hana recalls that Koerner said Sigrid was twelve. But it is hard to judge. The girl is looking back at Hana, blue eyes wide, just staring. Her fingers move on the arms of her wheelchair. Nothing else.

Hana says, "Can you talk?"

Maybe, but when Sigrid opens her mouth, garble comes out.

"Can you move? Anything?"

Sigrid seems to understand. At least, her eyes swivel toward her covered dinner plate.

"Doesn't someone help feed you?"

Sigrid's reply is an extended grunt.

Hana sits still for a moment wondering whether she should get up or not. Helping this other girl could end up being a mistake, a bad habit. Sigrid will expect Hana to keep doing it, and Hana's not sure that she wants that responsibility.

"I jumped out that window this morning," she says, pointing. "Doctor Koerner thinks I was trying to commit suicide, but I wasn't. I was just trying to get transferred to another hospital, one where they don't, you know..."

Realistically speaking, Sigrid probably doesn't know. What's more, she probably doesn't understand a thing Hana is saying to her. So, why keep up a friendly conversation with her, Hana wonders? What's the point? Yet, Hana leaves her bed and walks over to the bedroom door. She peeks out to see if any staff person is coming to assist Sigrid. No one is.

"How do they expect you to eat? Hey! Someone!" she calls. "We need help here."

Halfway down the hall, a nurse looks up. She is deep in discussion with a doctor. His attention is on a chart he is holding fastened to a clipboard. Neither makes a move to respond to Hana. A door opens and a dead patient is taken out on a gurney covered by a sheet. The doctor makes a brief note on his chart, and Hana can hear him say, "We'll tell the parents tuberculosis." Hana doesn't know this, but the body of the dead child will now be cremated. A formal letter will be sent to the parents telling them that their son or daughter died of TB though he/she had only arrived at the hospital a week ago without any symptoms. Perhaps the parents will care. Perhaps they won't. Perhaps that was their hope all along. That is life in Germany today.

"This is supposed to be a hospital," Hana yells at the nurse and the doctor, but they pretend not to hear. "We're all marked for death. You could at least be kind. We're just children."

She closes the door.

"They really do intend to kill us," she says to herself as if she hadn't quite believed it before. Well, will it be that sad? She can be with her mother in heaven. Better than life with her grandparents and Uncle Walter. She looks around as Sigrid has shifted in her chair. The younger girl is reaching for a spoon, but her movement is so spastic, she knocks the utensil on the tile floor, threatening to take her entire meal with it.

"Oh, all right," Hana says.

Sliding in her bare feet across the floor, she takes hold of Sigrid's handlebars and pushes her roommate to the bed.

"There." Sitting so that she is facing Sigrid, she lifts the cover to her own meal and is disgusted. "Beets and, what is this, soup? With two pieces of potato? The bread and butter I'll eat. Even if it is stale. But no meat? No dessert? What did they give you? Maybe we can trade."

Not likely. If Hana is disappointed at her own supper, she is appalled at what the hospital has given Sigrid. A thin porridge and two crackers. Tea to drink.

"We aren't mice. Are they trying to starve us to death? No wonder you're all bones. I wouldn't..."

It is only then, looking into Sigrid's eyes and seeing tears running down the other girl's cheeks, that Hana truly does understand now the plight they are both in. Yes, indeed, Hollenschloss, Doctor Koerner, her grandfather and grandmother, her uncles Edward and Walter: they **are** trying to starve them to death. **This** is how they will do it. The concept is so horrifying, Hana breaks down. She slumps on her bed and sobs.

Sigrid can do little but watch. After a while, though, the younger girl manages to raise a foot. She rubs it against Hana's leg. It takes a couple more taps of her toe upon Hana's bare shin before Hana realizes something's amiss. Afoot, actually. Surprised, Hana stifles her tears, sniffles, wipes the sleeve of her patient outfit across her nose, and sits up. She is pleased by this unexpected development and gifts Sigrid with a smile and a friendly pat on the knee.

"You **can** communicate," she says. "I'm glad. That means we won't be so lonely. We'll make the most of it while we can."

She takes Sigrid's spoon and feeds her twelve-year-old crippled roommate the porridge and the crackers. Does it matter if half of it dribbles down her chin? No. With a shrug of her shoulders, she feeds Sigrid her own supper, as well.

* * *

Hospitals are never silent. Nurses and doctors work the night shift at Hollenschloss as they do anywhere else in the world. Sick people, mentally disturbed people, don't keep track of time the way others do. They don't know that their fellow patients may want silence in order to sleep, so they roll over in bed and moan or cry out for attention. This is especially true of the children's ward.

Hana isn't able to go to sleep right away, so she sits up in bed, with the lamp on, writing in her notebook. She kept a diary at home, but that is probably out with the trash now. She would focus on her favorite escape subject, science, if her mind weren't so preoccupied with other things. Where she came from. How she came to be where she is now. Is there life beyond what she knows on planet earth, or is this the end? She doesn't know. Her family is Catholic but only by tradition. They don't go to church. Hilda, her maid, has taken her once in a while on Easter and other important Christian holidays, and Hana liked going. But she absorbed little of the spiritual aspect that so enrapt Hilda. Hana supposes she thinks too much and rejects too much. She thinks she should be like most of the other children she has known in passing who believe in Father Christmas. She has tried to believe it, but the world she has experienced is more fundamental, more scientific. More real.

Sigrid stirs. The nurses have put her to bed. Hana wonders if her new friend is ever comfortable. If she wasn't born this way, if she is here due to some catastrophic injury, what must be going on inside her head? Friedrich Ziegler would have had her strangled years ago.

Hana leaves her writing and tiptoes to where Sigrid is lying, half-in, half-out of her bed.

"Sigrid? Are you awake?"

Sigrid's eyes open. She utters a sound and reaches out her hand for Hana to touch.

"I love you, too," Hana says. "I wish neither of us were here. You want to get up? I can't sleep. We can talk, if you like. I'll read to you if you want."

Sigrid responds by reaching out both of her arms. Maybe she wants a hug. Maybe she wants Hana to lift her out of the bed and take her away somewhere. Hana decides to do both. With a hug and a kiss on the cheek, Hana struggles, but manages to lift Sigrid out of her bed.

"Let's get you in your wheelchair," she says. "Maybe we can get outside. Hey, maybe we can even find a way out of this place. Should we give it a try?"

Hana takes Sigrid's grunt as a 'yes' and pushes her out of their room into the main corridor. "You would think there'd be an elevator," she says. "Let's try down this way."

Hana turns to the right. The hall is empty. She passes two rooms on her way to a staircase. Someone is yelling in one of them. "Schnell! Schnell! Schnell! I will eat you if you don't go faster!"

She ignores the screaming and every other night noise that would scare her to death if she let them. Instead, determined, she turns Sigrid's wheelchair about and descends the staircase backwards, taking the full weight of Sigrid and her chair on her small body.

"Don't worry," she tells Sigrid, huffing and grunting with every step down. "We'll make it. We'll get there. Down the rabbit hole, through the dreaded forest past the ogre, just you and me."

By the time she reaches the first floor, Hana is so spent, she has to pause to catch her breath. She kneels and lays her head on Sigrid's lap. She almost falls asleep.

"We who are about to die," she mumbles, "salute you. The gladiators in ancient Rome used to say that, did you know that, Sigrid? Athena lived in ancient Greece. I'd go there if I could, but only for a visit."

A sudden, startling crash down the hall awakens her. Hana's head jumps off Sigrid's lap in fright until she reorients herself.

"Did you hear that, Sigrid? Oh, wow. It came from down that way. Should we check it out? Maybe someone's hurt."

Pushing herself to her bare feet, Hana maneuvers Sigrid down the hall. You would think that someone would be coming on the run to see what's going on, Hana thinks. The thing is, it's not that none of the staff aren't racing to investigate the noise. They're already there.

When Hana, still out in the corridor behind Sigrid's chair, peaks into the room where the noise is coming from, she sees two doctors and a nurse struggling with a boy, age uncertain, but large enough to be causing trouble. The boy's legs are still jerking but the doctors have pinned down his shoulders. Hana can see the boy's head, which is directed toward the doorway. It is banging against the hard floor in futile rebellion. There are five other beds in the room, all with occupants. But, strangely, none of them is stirring.

"I don't want to go to sleep! I don't want to go to sleep!" the boy yells just before the nurse jabs him with a needle. "I don't...I don't..." He lets out one final frustrated muffled cry. And that's it.

"There," the nurse says, "that'll do it."

One of the doctors stands up, panting. The other keeps the boy down until the floundering subsides. Then, rising, he writes notes onto a patient sheet. "An accidental fall, that's what we'll put on the death certificate," he says. Then for the first time, all three medical staffers realize they're being watched.

"Hey! What are you two doing out there?"

Hana is petrified. She can't move. Sigrid is making a wailing noise and crying.

"What do you think you're looking at?" the nurse yells.

More calmly, the first doctor, the one without the medical chart, approaches Hana with a smile. "We just helped the poor boy get to sleep, that's all," he says. "That's what you saw. Nothing to be alarmed about. If you're having trouble getting to sleep, we can help you, too."

Hana is too young and too scared to know if the doctor is being facetious. Without a word, she spins Sigrid's chair around and takes off at a gallop. She doesn't hear the laughter behind her nor the nurse ask, "Is that all for tonight?"

* * *

It is late night now, very early morning. It took a very strong sedative to knock her out. Hana is dreaming. She is four years old. It is October 1929 only hours before the stock market crash. It is her earliest remaining memory and, for many reasons, the one most often played out in dream.

She is sitting in a bathtub with her mother. The tub is filled to the rim with soap bubbles. Somewhere in the cloud of perfumed soap, a rubber duck swims between mother and child. Ursula Ziegler had Hana when she was sixteen years old. Now she is twenty. Her family told her to get an abortion. She refused. Her family told her to put the child up for adoption. She refused. Ursula said she would keep her baby even if it meant running away and living on her own. Her family laughed at her.

"You're just a baby yourself," Ilse Ziegler told her only daughter.

"What do you know of the world?" Friedrich Ziegler said. "All day all you do is sing in front of a mirror admiring your looks."

"I'll do it," said her older brother Walter. "Like the Spartans used to. Put it out for the wolves to eat."

Her oldest brother Edward, who was a budding playwright, said, "Give Ursula a chance. I think she can do it if she puts her mind to it."

Ursula definitely had a mind to do it if only to spite her parents. Her father, Hana's grandfather Friedrich, was on the money when he called Ursula spoiled. Then again, who spoiled her? As a child, she had been sent to study in Paris where, rather than mathematics and literature, she was taught eurhythmics, music and dance, French, and cooking. Back in Berlin, she enrolls in acting classes, where her beauty and her dancing catch the eye of a famed German choreographer. From there, still only a teenager, she enters the world of the Berlin theatre, performing in cabarets and even at the Wintergarten.

That is how Hana comes to be. After all, self-promotion in a world of props and lighting lends itself to flirtation and promiscuity. Nine months after debuting at the Wintergarten, Ursula is forced to make a bargain with her staunchly German Catholic parents. You can keep the child, but you are solely responsible for her. If you are not going to marry the man, if you even know who he is, then the child is never to meet him. The child may visit her grandparents, but they will never love her.

Hana remembers nothing of her first four years of life. Maybe a misty recollection or two. Of horses and sailboats. Of the loud noise of the cabarets and the dimming of the lights at the theatre. Her mother apparently liked to share everything with her. But what keeps coming back to her is this one special evening in the bathtub with her mother. Just two girls having fun splashing one another until Ursula suddenly picks her daughter up out of the water and caresses her to her bosom.

"On the night you were born," she says, "the sky was filled with stars. I chose the brightest one I could find, pulled it down from the heavens, and put it in my belly. Then out you came, *mein kleine sternchen*, my little star. Bright as all the heavens combined. The world awaits you."

She coughs then. Ursula is a heavy smoker. Smoking, drinking, are also part of the performance, part of being in her crowd. Only, this cough turns into a deep spluttering, phlegm-producing jag that ends with blood trickling down her cheek. Hana remembers being scared and crying out and a man answering, rushing into the bathroom with a drink of some kind to heal her mother's cough.

"I keep telling you to see a doctor," this man says.

"Doctors," is Ursula's skeptical reply. "We should drop by Max's place tomorrow. He's casting for a film. I want in. It could be our ticket to Hollywood, Louis."

"You can't travel when you're unwell," Louis says. "What about Hanaschen? She can't travel with you. She's too young. Your parents won't allow it."

"My parents can fuck themselves."

"Fuck' is a word Hana remembers. It is one of the first she ever spoke. That and 'l'chaim.' A word she got from Louis. He is ten years older than her mother, a worrier, a former actor, who has gone into the law and now acts as her agent. He may not be Hana's father, but he sometimes acts like it. He is the one man her mother comes to whenever she is in Berlin. Comes to whenever she is lonely.

Ursula steps out of the tub, dripping wet. Hana remembers this clearly, sleeping or awake. She will likely die with the memory. Ursula is holding the drink in one hand and her daughter's hand in the other. When Hana makes a playful leap from the tub to the floor, she lands slipping on a bath mat, causing her mother to lose her balance, too. Ursula's head strikes the rim of the iron tub. She utters a soft grunt. And while there seems to be a smile on her face, she never gets up.

Louis grabs Hana, picks her up, and hustles her out into the hall then returns to the bathroom. The door slams shut. Hana drips on the carpet. She is waiting, still wet and naked, by herself in the hallway, for how long who knows, when she hears the man cry out her mother's name. That is the last thing she remembers. Then darkness.

When Hana wakes up, she is bathed in pale flickering institutional light. She is lying in a strange bed. She can hear Sigrid moaning in sleep. Somewhere a baby is crying, and dawn birds are alerting her that her last day on earth may be awakening with them. Hitler stares down from the wall above her head and she can hear the rumble of a motor as a van pulls into the drive beyond her building.

She rises, leaving her bed to gaze out the window, now locked tight since her half-gainer the previous morning. She watches as the driver of the van gets out to be met by three men. She recognizes Doctor Grosbach. She doesn't know the other two, but she recognizes the red SS armband with the black swastika. They are all very interested in a large metal canister that the driver of the van is showing them.

Hana doesn't need to be able to read the labeling. She doesn't need to know what company manufactured the contents or why the men are sniffing around it like hunting dogs. She knows enough, enough certainly to say the first word after 'mama' she had ever learned.

"Fuck."

Chapter Six

May 1947

By the time Major Thomas Pershing Adams reaches the scene of the double homicide, the entire roadway on both sides has been blocked off by a half dozen military vehicles and helmeted members of the U.S. Constabulary.

He is a brusque man, a New Englander from Chelsea, Massachusetts; born to men who served their nation at the Turtle Gut Inlet, Gettysburg, the Marne; matriculated at West Point with honors and entered the military as a lieutenant five years before the war began. Class of '36, a senior the year Army tied Notre Dame 6-6. He had been the right tackle on offence and middle linebacker on defense. Tough, smart, and not happy to have been pulled away from his German sweetheart.

Salutes follow him wherever he goes, which is directly from his vehicle to the ditch where the two victims are still posed in death.

"How long have we had a presence here, Lieutenant?" he asks the young man following him stride for determined stride.

"Seventy-seven minutes, sir." The lieutenant checks his watch to make sure.

"That's it?"

"You made good time, sir."

"Had to."

Trousers pulled up, zipped, and belted, Adams had given the twenty-year-

44

old blonde he had rescued from an internment camp a quick kiss before jumping into his own vehicle to make the three-quarter-hour ride out of Nuremberg to get here. He certainly wasn't going to diddle around waiting for the MPs to pick him up at the digs where he stashed Lina. A man such as himself has the right to a life on the side, a little nibble here and there. Just so long as the fly is zipped.

He stands at the top of the ditch, hands on hips, staring down at the car flipped over and at the body of a man lying on his back, flies already conducting their own investigation.

"I assume no one's touched a thing," he says to the lieutenant.

"First thing we did was cordon off the road. I told my people to steer clear until you got here, Sir. Can't keep the damned flies from sticking their noses in. All we did was check for signs of life."

"There were none."

"No, Sir. Whoever pumped lead into that fella down there made sure of that. No face. Could be Hitler for all I know."

Adams lets out a mumbled retort, something the lieutenant can't quite make out though it sounds to him like, "Musta been his ex." Then he heads down into the gully.

"The driver?"

"Just as dead. Didn't take a close look. Wanted to wait for you."

Adams stops at the bottom, looks up toward the road, then studies the path the upturned car made on its way to its rest against a tree. He bends to look. "American flags on the hood. That's why we were called in and not the locals. Somebody killed an American official. We'll want to keep this one close to the vest, Lieutenant."

"Yes, sir. Understood."

Adams's posting in Germany is as an officer in the Criminal Investigation Command of the U.S. Constabulary, meant to provide order in the American sector of Germany. It is a job that keeps him busy. Thousands of German civilians and soldiers are still imprisoned in internment camps around the country. Eisenhower's Nightmare, they're called. Starving people steal. Desperate people kill. Untold thousands of German women have been

45

raped, not only by the vengeful Commies but by the soldiers of France, England, and the United States. Abortions are conducted in pastures and rubble-strewn alleyways by impoverished capitalists. Babies galore are being left on the steps of churches and cathedrals. Germany in the aftermath of defeat is fair game for anyone who wants to take advantage. This generates quite the workload for the police. But killing an American: that is something special. That is crossing the line. Especially if it is done by a German.

Adams kneels by the first body, the one outside the car. Reaching into the man's jacket pocket, he retrieves identification papers.

"Well, I would say the picture matches the face, only, as you said, Lieutenant, there is no face. There is a name, however. John Joseph Harding. Related to the former president?"

Adams is a distant relative of The Adamses. But he doubts that John Joseph is related to Warren Gamaliel. He studies the body for any other obvious signs, any evidence on who John Joseph Harding was. Fancy clothes but no rings, no watch, no cross medallion, and, more interesting, no money in his wallet.

"Sir! Officer! Man in charge!"

Adams tries to ignore the shouting coming from the road above and behind him. Once he is focused on an investigation, he dislikes interruption of any kind. But the intruder persists such that Adams has to rise and surrender his attention.

"Yes. What is it? Who is that man?"

That man who apparently has defied the MPs and has made his way to the edge of the gully doesn't seem to warrant any attention at all. Number one, he's a civilian. Number two, he speaks with an accent. German. Number three, he's dressed like a vagrant. Six foot, scrawny, bearded. He could be forty years old. He could be sixty. He could be eighty. One thing is clear to Adams: the man has no business being here.

"How did he get by you people?"

"Sir, we..."

"May I introduce myself, Herr Officer." The man is polite. He doffs his worn hat and bows his head, lowering his eyes to the ground. "Avi Kreisler," he says. "Not too long ago I was a resident of one of the local pleasure palaces. Dachau. Perhaps you've heard of it."

Adams relents. Not only has he heard of the Dachau concentration camp, he was a member of the U.S. Seventh Army, the 42nd Rainbow Division, that liberated the camp. The horrors he witnessed are beyond words. Protestant New England Yankee though he is, down to his calloused feet, he had been so enraged that he had turned a blind eye to the killing of many of the SS guards who had been foolish enough not to flee. Killed by the freed prisoners. Killed by his own troops. Serves ya right, was his attitude.

"I've heard of it, sir," Adams says in regard for what Herr Kreisler has suffered.

"Then may I join you? I may be of some help."

Adams doubts it. But once he has relented, he feels he must give the young/middle-aged/old man an ear.

Kreisler takes the slope on the arm of one of the MPs. He lets go as he approaches the body of the dead man named Harding. "I was a police officer myself, you see, sir," he says. "In another life." He lifts one of the dead man's hands, pushes up the muddied sleeve of his shirt all the way to the armpit, then repeats the process with the other hand before stating, "SS."

"What? How can you say that?"

"He has the fingers of a woman. He is a hedonist. His hands have never lifted anything heavier than a comb. He spends all the summer months indoors, perhaps in hiding, keeping to the shadows. His skin is pale white, like snow. What he does, he does in secret. Others do the dirty work. Once they are done, he collects the trinkets."

Kreisler rises with a grunt. The crack of his knees is audible to Adams who maintains his silence as the Jewish concentration camp survivor, former police detective, surveys the bloody scene. "A woman was the shooter," he says.

"How the hell do you make that assessment, Herr Kreisler?"

"Avi. *Herr* is for Germans."

Kreisler steps back a few paces before crouching again. He points to the ground. "She is a good marksman, or should I say markswoman. She shot him square in the forehead from ten meters."

"Footprints?"

"Slippers, I think," Kreisler says. "Not a man's shoe. Those tracks are behind her. She came with a man. But she was the one with the gun. Perhaps she dressed in a hurry. She finds out these men are on the road and races to catch up. Is the man as anxious as she is? Who can say? He sideswipes this car and runs it into the ditch. The driver is already dead. This man gets out hoping to make an escape. Ah, but he doesn't appreciate the anger which confronts him."

"A survivor," Adams guesses. "Like yourself? But this man has American i.d. Harding. He could be an employee of the State. Pulling thirteen-hour days indoors, he might have missed the sunlight. Son of a State Department muckety-muck, he wouldn't have a workingman's hands."

Kreisler shrugs, needs Adams's help to stand. As he walks back toward the car, he tells the Lieutenant with Adams to lift the dead man's arms and raise the left sleeve up to the armpit again.

"You will notice," Kreisler instructs, "this man attempted to remove a tattoo. It is barely perceptible. No one would think to look for it. It is a mark of the Waffen-SS. Blood type in case a transfusion is required." Kreisler points to his own eyes. "Much was taken from me at Dachau, but not this."

He limps to the upturned car, a thoroughly impressed Adams willingly taking a subsidiary role.

"Head shot," Kreisler says about the dead man inside. Obviously. "Again, the work of a markswoman. Unless she was aiming for the fellow outside and hit the driver by error. I suppose that's a possibility."

Adams takes his own close look. "I know this man," he says. Blood soaks the windshield, dashboard, steering wheel, seat cover, and side window. Adams isn't certain right away of the man's identity because the shot that killed him caved in one side of his face. But enough is left for recognition. "A resettlement guy. Connected. You ever hear of Harry McAuliffe?"

"Can't say as I have, Major."

"You will. His son, in any case."

And soon, Adams is thinking. Politics is never far off when an American, a local boy, is killed. Another reason to close this case as fast as possible. "An unfortunate innocent victim," he says.

"Perhaps."

"I hate to be the one to have to tell his family."

"Yes, well…" Kreisler steps away from the car. Suddenly, he appears to grow intensely weary. He has to brace his hands on his knees to keep from falling.

"You all right, Herr…Avi? You want something to drink?"

Kreisler shakes his head. After a moment, he lifts his eyes to the sky above, cloudy, ominous. "I wouldn't tell his family anything just yet," he says.

"You don't think he's an innocent victim?"

"Driving a former SS officer toward the Swiss border? Check his pockets for cash before you judge him innocent."

Kreisler removes a handkerchief from a coat pocket, coughs and spits into it. Then he offers his arm to Adams to escort him back up the side of the gully.

"You're a suspicious man, Mr. Kreisler," Adams said. "Former cop."

Kreisler grunts off the suggestion. "When I was a cop," he says, "if you offered me a large enough bribe, I would have grabbed it out of your fist and demanded more. I was not such a good man. The camps change people. I have outlived millions of my fellow Jews, most of whom were far better people than I was or ever will be. I have outlived my entire family. Parents, brothers, sisters, cousins. I never married. A good thing, or they'd all be dead, too. Why me, I ask myself? Of all people. Who can account for such absurdity?"

Adams, the devout Calvinist, thinks he knows the answer. "God?" he surmises.

Kreisler, the Jew, laughs. "God? For all the good He has done, let him keep on sleeping."

Chapter Seven

September 1939

On the night she returns from the Hollenschloss Institute, Silke can't sleep. No nightmare can supplant what she has experienced in real life. She can't get that girl out of her mind, that poor thing, stuck in a place that treats its patients worse than farm animals who are at least well-fed before they are executed.

In the morning, she consults with her fifteen-year-old brother Georg who is a proud member of the Hitler Youth. "It's none of your business," he tells her.

"Don't be a nit," Silke replies. "Whose business is it, then?"

"Der Fuhrer's. He knows what's best."

The siblings, the only children of Vitor and Gertrud Hartenstein, are scrubbing two of Herr Graf von Haefner's favorite mares. He intends to ride today with his new bride Gretchen and he wants them to look fresh. Silke spent all of the past evening trying to convince her parents that someone should intervene on behalf of that girl at the institute. No one budged in their firm commitment to the Nazi way of doing things.

"We need the beds for our wounded soldiers." "Why pay so much to feed the dying when our own neighbors can't afford to feed their children?" "What kind of life can these people expect anyway? It's a mercy to let them go to God." The arguments Silke withstood could well have been plagiarized from any of Propaganda Minister Goebbels' pamphlets or fliers or copied from radio broadcasts that the family religiously listens to each night. Goebbels has made sure that every German family can afford a radio. In the cities, there are loudspeakers to blare out the daily news. But out in the country, the radio reaches people who otherwise would be left in the dark as to why schizophrenic adolescents should be starved to death.

Frustrated, Silke can think of only one other person who might intervene for her. Someone with the right standing. Someone with influence. Someone who, with the flick of a finger, can command immediate obedience. Someone like Ernst Rudolf Graf von Haefner. Besides being the scion of Bavarian nobility, a man of consummate class and education, a man who owns property and burgeoning corporations, he is also the man who employs her parents. And, most important of all, he is a man whose own daughter resides in the Hollenschloss.

"Don't bother them while they're at breakfast," Georg warns her. "His wife is a little flighty. She won't like you butting in. She's the jealous type."

"Why would she be jealous of me?"

Georg smirks. "Seriously? Silke, you're on the cover of *Jugend* and *Volk und Welt* Magazines. Every German man is in love with your breasts."

"According to Dora, it's my arse."

"In either case, don't show them to Herr von Haefner today."

Well, today is just exactly the day she intends to show them. As far as Silke is concerned, her brother is a sweet young man who, like so many other German kids, is being fed a lot of crap. Georg is a German boy, purebred Aryan, blonde and blue-eyed like her. He fully believes that Germany was punished after World War I, that his people suffered unnecessary hardships as a result, that the Jews and communists are to blame, and that Adolph Hitler has all the answers to making Germany not only great again but great forever. It is his duty, the sworn duty of every German kid, to do whatever is necessary, to make any sacrifice needed, to make sure that this Third Reich is successful in whatever it sets out to do. Whatever.

But Silke is no fool. She may be only sixteen, but she is old enough to remember a time when Hitler was a nobody, when her father had his own horticultural business and they could vacation in the summer anywhere in Europe they wanted to go. She remembers having Jewish friends. She remembers one of her closest classmates admitting that she liked another girl and that Silke was that girl. She remembers when her family had enough money that, whenever they passed a beggar on the streets of Nuremberg or Munich, her mother would insist they contribute some money into the proffered hat. Nobody should go without, her parents had said back then. Nobody should be without a home and a comfortable bed. There should be no such thing as an orphan. Every child should have a home and parents who love them. Silke remembers all of this. These are memories not to be swept aside by bold promises and unsympathetic methods.

Silke intends to save that girl, no matter what. So, when Ernst Rudolph Graf von Haefner emerges in full riding gear with his bride Gretchen, who Silke has to admit is no Marlene Dietrich, she refuses to let go of the reins of Gretchen's horse even after the mildly contemptuous bride is square in the saddle.

"Herr von Haefner, if you will pardon me," Silke begins. Haefner is a tall man, an elegant aristocrat in his forties. He would never call himself a Nazi, never willingly associate with any of them, but if they purchase his pharmaceuticals and order his chemicals and in doing so can make him a profit…

"Now is not the time," Gretchen tells Silke. "You're a Bund Deutsche girl, aren't you?"

"Yes, ma'am, but you see…"

"And obedience is part of your motto, isn't it?"

"Yes, it is, but…"

"Then…"

With a nudge from her booted foot, Gretchen lightly kicks Silke away and trots out of the Haefner stalls. With a courtly tip of his head, Haefner follows. But that is not the end of it. Halfway down the dirt path to the grazing area, Gretchen, who is not a professional horsewoman, is startled to see the girl run past her horse which has been moving at a trot. Breathless though she is, Silke manages to catch up to Haefner.

"They are killing children, Herr von Haefner. Children! You have to stop them. Your own hospital."

"My own hospital?"

A lifetime of successful maneuvering against Germany's ever-perilous political rivalries has not let Haefner down yet. Changes in government have not cost him anything in German society. But he has never been confronted by a child before. Not in this fashion. Not in front of the woman he has just married. He is upset but cautious enough not to show it.

"I own no hospitals. I contribute. Who exactly are you, my dear? Do I know you?"

"My parents are Vitor and Gertrud Hartenstein."

"Ah, yes. Of course. Now I remember. And you're the girl who has graced a few magazine covers."

He knows exactly who she is but won't admit it in front of Gretchen.

Silke says, "I went with my troop to the Hollenschloss Institute yesterday. We went on a tour. I saw everything. It really was terrible. I think they starve the children until they're dead. And there was this girl. She was with her father or something. She was crying. You could tell she didn't want to be there."

"Ernst, can't this wait?" Gretchen says.

Silke ignores the impatient tone. She is practically on her knees in her skirt begging Haefner to act. "I'm only asking about this one girl," she says. "One girl. Here. Look for yourself."

On the morning of her visit to the institute, a fortuitous wind had blown Hana Ziegler's paper in the direction of Silke. Frau Zoeller had confiscated it and tossed it into the bushes. But while her back was turned, Silke had retrieved the disturbingly penned writings of the dark-haired girl Silke is set on saving.

Haefner reaches down from the saddle and takes the crumpled paper. "What is this?" he asks.

"She is begging for help. You can read it yourself."

"And the rest of this mess? To me, it looks like evidence in her own handwriting that she is where she belongs."

Haefner is about to return it to Silke when something else catches his eye. Something etched in the border. A symbol or something. With letters attached to it, like little bugs stuck to fly paperflypaper. Why does this matter? What is he thinking?

"Look at this, my dear." He shows the writings of a mad child to his bride. He does this not to be polite but because he thinks Gretchen might be interested. He is a chemist by training. So is she. In fact, she has something Haefner doesn't have. A Ph.D. in neurobiology.

"Insanity," she says. "Just what you'd expect."

But Haefner isn't so sure. The strange symbols strike a curious chord in him. "Who is this girl?" he asks Silke. "What do you know about her?"

"Only that," Silke admits.

"Her family?"

"I don't know, sir. They treat her poorly, I can say that."

"Poorly. Well. Such is the way of the world. I have a daughter…"

Haefner catches himself. He studies the paper, focuses on the symbol that has been drawn. A curved ladder? Leading where? To a Nobel Prize if it is what he thinks it could be. Whatever it is, it has caught Haefner's trained eye. Enough to silently work the gears in his head. No one must ever know what he is thinking. Not Gretchen. Not even Hitler. Dropping the paper to the ground as if it matters nothing to him, he kicks his horse forward. Smug Gretchen follows.

"I will look into it later," he promises Silke.

"*Danke*, Herr Haefner."

At least Silke can hope.

* * *

The next morning, Haefner is driving to Hollenschloss. He is at the wheel of his Mercedes. In the passenger seat is his attorney Reinhardt Froeling, forty-seven, with an open dossier in his lap. In the back seat, quiet and attentive, is Froeling's eighteen-year-old son Otto.

Froeling wants his son to follow in his shoes. Being a corporate attorney for someone as wealthy and powerful as Haefner has made Froeling, in his own litigious niche, just as wealthy and powerful. As Froeling's only son, Otto should be appreciative of the opportunities his father is giving him, especially since, as a university freshman Otto is just beginning his pre-law studies. But Otto isn't listening to his parent or to his parent's single client. Back stiff, pretending to be interested, he is actually meditating on a girl he has fallen in love with. It's foolish, he knows. He hasn't even met this girl. She doesn't know he exists. All he knows of her is what all of Germany knows of her. That Silke Hartenstein poses in swimsuits for magazine covers.

"Starving them to death," Haefner is saying with some anger to his attorney. "Appalling. Someone should be taken up on charges."

"Who? Hitler? Himmler? I'd like to meet the lawyer who takes that case." Froeling is sifting through the dossier which includes an inch-thick medical treatment record of one Hana Ziegler. "Besides, you have nothing against the killing, as I understand it. It is the method you disapprove of."

"Yes, yes, the method, of course. Barbaric. Sadistic. Cruel. Is this how the Master Race manages its patient overload? By watching its sub-units waste away as it calculates the number of calories it will take to kill a ninety-pound twelve-year-old? This is science? No, sir. This is sheer clumsiness, laziness, of the highest magnitude."

Froeling shrugs, flipping through the Ziegler file. Behind him, Otto is wondering what Silke Hartenstein looks like without anything on.

"If you're afraid of any legal ramifications against you, lawsuits," Froeling says, "you shouldn't. You have distanced yourself completely from the workings of the institute. Yes, your company is the sole provider of the medicines they use...to dispatch in a very compassionate way...the unfortunates who are bound for the other side eventually anyway. But you aren't telling them how to use the medicines. You're providing the syringes. You're not telling them where to stick them."

"That's not the point, Reinhardt."

Haefner pushes his foot down on the accelerator, not because he needs to be somewhere but because he enjoys speed. It calms him down.

"You don't have to kill us, Ernst," Reinhardt says.

"I want to run the cyanide test first thing tomorrow morning," Haefner says. "T-4 is very interested in seeing how it works on large groups of people. How effective it is. How economic. There is competition and we must win it."

"Gas," says Otto. It is the first word he has spoken since getting in Herr Haefner's car.

"Yes. You disapprove, Otto?" Haefner asks.

"Otto doesn't disapprove. Otto doesn't understand." Reinhardt glances back at his son. "First lesson in law, my boy. Whether or not you disapprove doesn't matter. Understanding is another thing. But that will come in time. Once you understand what is at stake and what your client wants you to accomplish, you simply act on behalf of your client."

Otto says nothing. His face gives nothing away. If he were the type of son to talk back to his father, this is what he would say in response: the first rule of law is, give nothing away.

Silke's intervention has triggered a response. That very morning after his ride, an intrigued Haefner placed a call to the institute to which he gives a great deal of charitable money. He asked about a girl who arrived with two men yesterday morning, was given a name, then demanded her entire medical record. This he received from the girl's psychiatrist who seemed reluctant to admit his part but more than willing to surrender her private records.

Haefner is not the clinical director at Hollenschloss, but he behaves like it when he greets Doctor Grosbach in the director's office. He drops Hana Ziegler's file on Grosbach's desk. "Stop starving the children," he orders.

"But..."

"It's disgraceful."

"But your own instructions regarding Sigrid..."

"I never expected you to starve her. Is that what you're doing?"

"Well..."

"What do you know about this girl?"

Haefner cuts off any excuses, reasonable though they would be. He shows Grosbach the crumpled paper Silke Hartenstein gave him yesterday morning.

"Oh, this."

"Well?"

"The creation of a schizophrenic mind."

"Really?" Haefner shows the artwork to Reinhardt and Otto Froeling. "What do you think, gentlemen?"

Froeling doesn't know what to think. "I agree with Doctor Grosbach. Chaos."

"Otto?" Haefner asks. The son doesn't speak. If he has an answer, he is keeping it to himself. To Grosbach, Haefner says, "Have you read her medical history, her background?" Grosbach can only stutter an embarrassed what amounts to a negative. "And these markings, not only on this paper here but on this one and this. She has made it a number of times. And the word s-y-z-y-g-y. You studied medicine, did you not, Grosbach?"

Another stuttered non-answer.

"Take me to the girl. I want to see her," Haefner says.

Grosbach, naturally, is in a hurry to comply, leading the three other men outside, across a manicured lawn to the main building where Hana is being 'treated'.

"You read through her file?" Haefner asks Froeling who is huffing and puffing to keep up. Otto trails, hat in hand, admiring the flowers. "This child took the exams for entry into university when she was twelve years old. Twelve. And scored higher than anyone. My Gretchen could tell you. My God. Sometimes what appears to be insanity is rather brilliance misunderstood. Did you see what her primary interest appears to be? Genetics. My field."

Grosbach is certain he will find Hana in her room on the second floor, where morning sun filtering through her window will give her plenty of light to write by. He has viewed her history, seen her crazy squiggles, and dismissed everything. He hopes he hasn't made a mistake. Herr Ziegler, Hana's grandfather, wants the whole matter dealt with right away. No starvation diet. An injection. "Quick and painless. Isn't that your motto?" the old man had said to the psychiatrist Koerner. What's the hold-up?

But Hana is not in her room. Neither is Sigrid Haefner. Grosbach is taken aback, further embarrassed.

"You don't keep track of your patients, Herr Grosbach?" Haefner says.

"We do, but…"

No one seems to know where the two girls have gone to, which leads to a great deal of scurrying around of staff being yelled at by Grosbach. Otto alone isn't distracted by the confusion. Standing beside the single window in the room, he calls for attention then points outside where he watches Hana pushing Sigrid's wheelchair toward the gate to the institute.

"They seem to be making a break for it," Otto says. He, for one, is in no hurry to intercept. He is thinking, 'You're almost there. Don't stop.'

Haefner leads the charge outside. Otto is the only one who can keep up with him. Grosbach and half of his staff and Froeling trail behind.

"Young lady! Young lady!" Haefner calls as he hits the driveway heading for the gate.

Either Hana doesn't hear or she isn't paying any attention. She continues to push Sigrid toward the gate at a leisurely pace as if their expedition is the most normal thing in the world. Haefner catches them just as they are about to leave the grounds unattended. Otto is right behind. He notices Hana panting for breath. Her pace wasn't leisurely. She is struggling with the weight of the wheelchair. The moment she sees Haefner and Otto, she lets out a startled gasp and begins prattling.

"Esh-vie-zet-vie-geh-vie. Esh-vie-zet-vie-geh-vie."

Sigrid raises a hand and reaches for Hana's. Her eyes when they alight on Haefner show intense fear. Drool trails from her mouth in accompaniment with sounds that cannot be translated except as fear.

Haefner ignores his daughter. He has kept in his hand Hana's crumpled artwork. He shows it to her.

"Young lady. Hana, is that your name? Don't be afraid."

"This is all very regrettable," Grosbach says.

"Shut up."

"Esh-vie-zet-vie-geh-vie. Esh-vie-zet-vie-geh-vie."

"You see what you've done, Grosbach?" Haefner kneels, braces himself

58

on Sigrid's wheelchair. "These symbols on your paper. This is your writing, Hana. I find it quite intriguing. Tell me what it is, can you?"

"Esh-vie-zet-vie-geh-vie."

"Spirals with letters and sometimes even numbers. You are working something out in your mind. I can tell. But what? I want to know."

"Esh-vie-esh-vie-esh vie..."

Haefner stands. Spotting a white wooden bench surrounded by flowers, he takes Hana's hand and forces her to follow him. At the bench, he sits her down and sits beside her. Fascinated, Otto comes to stand quietly behind them. His father keeps a polite distance while Grosbach orders Sigrid to be wheeled back to her room.

"I read your medical file, your history, Hana," Haefner says. "Do you know, my focus of study at university was genetics. In my day, it was a rather new field. How do we inherit what we inherit? I mean, at the cellular level. We know so little. But the possibilities are fantastic. You have befriended my daughter Sigrid. What if we could prevent such illnesses from ever happening? What if, by modifying the genes somehow, we can make sure that only strong genes are allowed to pass from one generation to the next. Weak ones are cut out, eliminated. That, in a very real sense, is what Nazi eugenics is all about. Perfecting humanity."

"Esh-vie-esh-vie-esh vie."

Hana is still chanting her rhythmic sedative but more quietly. She is listening. She is thinking. She is plotting. Haefner doesn't know this, but she is seeing another way out through those gates. Otto has placed his hands on her shoulders thinking he can calm her with his kind touch. He doesn't realize that she is already calm.

"These symbols, Hana," Haefner presses on. "When that girl showed me them, I was immediately intrigued. I can't explain why. It was like seeing an idea I have had suddenly borne to light. Are we thinking the same thing? Can it be possible?"

Hana ceases mumbling, but she doesn't raise her eyes from her lap. Softly, she says, "S-y-z-y-g-y. Cells dividing. I like the way it sounds."

"I do, too, Hana. I do, too."

Haefner stands. Froeling has seen that hungry look in his client's eyes before. Haefner has made up his mind about something, and once this has happened, there is no turning back. "Tomorrow morning," he tells Grosbach, "I will be back. I want a trial run of the gas, you understand? Have a van prepared. We must get this done. In the meantime, Herr Froeling, my attorney, will prepare other paperwork regards Fraulein Ziegler. I will see you first thing in the morning, yes, Herr Doctor?"

"Yes, Herr Haefner," Grosbach grovels. "Everything will be ready. We will make the selections right away."

"Good. No mistakes this time."

And so, like that, it is done. Tomorrow morning children will not die by starvation or injection, but by gas.

* * *

Hana spends the evening taking care of Sigrid. "I have it all worked out," she says before their bedtime medication is served. "Your father will take me out. He thinks I can help him. But I will not help him unless he takes you out, too."

Hana kisses Sigrid on the cheek. In the short time that they have roomed together, Hana has learned that Sigrid can communicate. Not verbally, but using her eyes and her fingers and even her toes. It seems as though Sigrid was not always like this. She wasn't born a cripple. There was a car accident that killed her mother and injured her in this awful way. Hana promises that once they are both free of this place, she will help Sigrid. She will show the girl's family that there is more to their daughter than a vegetable with eyes.

"This other girl tried to help me," Hana says. She has wheeled Sigrid to the window so they can both gaze out at a full moon and the quiet garden below. "She's very beautiful and very brave. Older than us, I think. Very tall for a girl. She stood up for me when no one else did. I think we should be like the Three Musketeers. All for one, one for all."

Hana knows her voice has a soothing effect on Sigrid. She doesn't mind that the conversation is one-sided or that she is babbling. At home, her grandfather didn't like hearing her talk. And Uncle Walter, he is something else Hana doesn't want to talk about at all. Only her grandmother showed any real feelings toward her once in a while. Then again, her grandmother Ilse has secrets, too. Hana knows. Ilse doesn't know she knows. Secrets that would make her grandfather quite displeased if he knew of them.

Hana and Sigrid hold hands in the moonlight despite Hitler's presence above their beds. They were both even served full meals tonight, so they are both happy, bellies full, ready for bed, and a much brighter day tomorrow.

"Your father has a lab. I can stay with him and work. I don't want to see my family again, except maybe for my grandmother. Edward isn't too bad either. He's a playwright. I think he and my mother would have gotten along if, well, I don't like to think about that." Hana feels a squeeze. This is Sigrid's way of saying basically, 'Go on. I want to hear more.'

So, despite feeling very tired post-medicine and yawning, Hana continues. "I have a father somewhere. I haven't seen him for so long, I wouldn't know what he looks like. Jewish. I think he might be Jewish. At least, that's what my grandparents think. Louis. That name might be his. One of the reasons I became so interested in genetics was I thought that might be a way for me to find him. You see, our genes are like fingerprints. I have only one mom and one dad, and their fingerprints are all over me."

This time, Hana's yawn is much deeper. She can barely keep her eyes open. She is drifting off but doesn't care. Tomorrow both she and Sigrid will be leaving Hollenschloss for good. She wheels her friend over to her bed and helps her get under the covers. The nurses at Hollenschloss are useless. Then, with a final kiss on Sigrid's cheek, Hana slips under her own unwashed sheet. Tonight, even the hard mattress and the thin pillow feel homey. Sleep is coming very, very quickly. Deep and long. But before she succumbs to it, she remembers one last thing. Turning over to face Sigrid, she calls out, "*L'chaim.*"

* * *

The sedatives the good doctors and nurses of the Hollenschloss give to their patients are intended to be strong. The longer the pests sleep, the easier. Hana drifts off and wakes with no memory of having dreamt at all. She is still groggy when someone shakes her by the arm.

"Time to get up, Hana. We've a long drive ahead of us. There are many things I want to show you."

It is Herr Haefner, and she is surprised to see him standing over her bed, hat in hand as if she is someone to be held in esteem. Behind him is a smiling Doctor Grosbach writing something on his clipboard.

"The paperwork is completed," Grosbach says. "Your attorney is very thorough. He made sure, as they say, all the T's were crossed and the I's dotted. She is free to go anytime you're ready."

"Good. Good. I've purchased some clothing for you, Hana. You didn't pack much, so I spent the whole day yesterday with the help of my wife getting you ready to move in with us. I spoke to your grandfather. I explained everything. He was...understanding."

Understanding? That hardly seems likely. Hana yawns, stretches. There is sunlight streaming in through her window, and that is odd, because she is used to waking up to darkness.

Suddenly, she is in a panic. "What time is it?"

"Why, almost eleven o'clock," Haefner says. "We didn't want to wake you prematurely. There was other business that needed attending to first. Now that that is done, you can try on your new clothes. I hope they fit. We just guessed the sizes."

Before Hana had stirred from her sedative-induced slumber, asylum staff had deposited a half dozen boxes of clothing that Haefner was now poking into. Hana has no interest in the clothes. Scrambling from her sheets, she notices for the first time that Sigrid's bed is empty. It is made up now as if no one had ever slept there. Her wheelchair is gone.

"Where is Sigrid?" she shouts.

"She's been transferred to another facility," Grosbach says. "One that can take better care of her."

Hana doesn't buy a word of it. She looks into the faces of both men. "Tell me the truth!"

"We are. Why should we lie to you? A better place, with ramps for her wheelchair."

"No, you killed her! You murdered her!"

"No, Hana, no."

"The gas. You didn't wake me. You didn't want me to know."

Hana screams. Words are so insufficient to how she feels. Betrayed. Violated in the worst possible way.

"Hana, it is easier that way."

"Esh-vie-zet-vie-geh-vie. Esh-vie-zet-vie-geh-vie."

"Calm down, Hana."

"Esh-vie-zet-vie-geh-vie."

Hana collapses to the floor. Haefner tries lifting her, but she is dead weight and won't move.

"Are you sure about this, Herr Haefner?" Grosbach asks. "One injection…"

"Shut up, you fool. A sedative. That's all. Once I get her back to my place, she'll recover."

It takes the two men and two nurses to lift Hana and put her back on her bed. Held down, she can't fight the injection of the sedative in her arm. In a moment or two, she is completely under. Only then can a breathless Haefner order the boxes of clothes to be carried to his car. Hana is put on a gurney and rolled out. In that way, at least, she doesn't see the windowless van with its bolted metal door or the lines that lead the gas into the back. She is unaware that twelve children have served as guinea pigs for the cyanide experiment which, by the way, worked to perfection. Nor is she aware that she would have been number twelve if Sigrid hadn't taken her place.

Haefner slides into the back seat of his Mercedes beside the slumped-over Hana. It is Otto Froeling who sticks the key in the ignition and begins Hana's ride to freedom.

"You didn't have to come with me, Otto," Haefner says to him. "I could have managed this myself."

Otto glances in the rearview mirror. He sees Hana's innocent face now resting against Haefner's shoulder. "No, Herr Haefner," he says, detestation for the man completely hidden. "It was my duty."

Chapter Eight

Summer 1937

I lse Ziegler is not a woman to underestimate, though underestimating women is a common enough activity, certainly in the Age of the Victorians into which Ilse had been born forty-seven years before.

Her people, the Ullrichs, supported the unification of Germany, supported its greatest exponent Bismarck and its last ruler, Wilhelm II. Their bridge into the German aristocracy was by way of warfare to the extent that her great-grandfather Ludwig invented the Ullrich rifle which was used by German fighting men in wars, so far, in two centuries. Unification with the Ziegler family in the form of a marriage at the tender age of nineteen made sense. While the Ullrichs provided the weaponry, the Zieglers manufactured the spare parts, ball bearings, and engine parts for cars, trains, planes, and, more recently, tanks and canons.

Her husband Friedrich likes to boast that without the Zieglers everyone in Germany would be stuck having to walk wherever they went. "We make Germany go," is his favorite motto.

Of course, people could always ride horses. Ilse likes riding. It gets her out of the house. It gets her away from Friedrich whom she has grown, at best, to tolerate. Barely. She is twenty years younger than he is. What she really enjoys is nurturing flowers. She has her own greenhouse and is allowed to bring to market many of her prized crossbred roses and tulips. She also grows oranges, pears, and apricots. She has never been educated in the science of plant genetics. It is just something that comes natural to her. It is the one pleasure she shares with her granddaughter Hana, age twelve.

"Which is why," she tells her daughter's daughter, "we have come to Copenhagen. Not as your uncle Walter supposes to hobnob with Americans. Let him and your grandfather hobnob. We'll look at the pretty flowers."

Hana and her grandmother dress very much like matching flowers in blue dresses with a faux flower design, puffy at the shoulders, belted, with white gloves and blue-ribboned straw hats to keep the sun out of their eyes. Low heels. Hana is a very quiet, very studious, child. She rarely speaks, and when she does, it is hardly over a whisper. Friedrich detests her. Ilse's oldest son Edward is too busy writing to pay her any attention. Younger brother Walter calls her 'our Jew' and warns Ilse that they'll have to do something with her or she'll bring down the whole family tree. Ilse is admittedly conflicted. She loved her daughter Ursula with all her heart. Ursula was her favorite child, the one who most resembled what Ilse thought she might have become if circumstances had been different. Friedrich blames her liberality for Ursula's untimely demise in a bathtub. Ilse secretly blames Hana. Yet, she can't help feeling sorry for Hana either. Hana is like one of her floral experiments gone awry. A crossbreed that has wilted rather than flourished. Something that should be loved despite the fact that she is doomed.

This bright summer morning, they are sightseeing in the University of Copenhagen's Botanical Garden inside one of its beautiful glass greenhouses. While Ilse never studied Latin, she knows the name of every flower they pass.

"That yellow bloom is *Senna occidentalis* from India. *Catharanthus roseus* is the purple flower. African. More specifically from Madagascar. You've seen them in my garden. The leaves of the *Camellia sinensis* produce a sweet tea. The name tells you from whence it comes."

"China."

"Yes, my dear. Your memory shines."

To Hana, the intense smells are almost too overpowering. She is constantly rubbing her nose with the sleeve of her dress and Ilse is constantly offering her a silk handkerchief in its stead.

"One can almost lose oneself in here," Ilse remarks. "It is so beautiful. So peaceful. Like we are in another world. Your mother loved flowers. Especially this one special orchid I created. It wasn't quite purple. It wasn't quite blue. If I remember correctly, she was about your age. A birthday present. Oh, well. I've never been able to produce another one like it."

Hana is not so much interested in the flowers themselves but in the process of creating them. Ilse has shown her the techniques she uses to produce her changelings meticulously passing the pollen of one flower's stamen to the stigma of another. Hana has grown quite good at it, carefully cataloguing everything she does in thick notebooks of data, though recently she has shown a great reluctance to accompany her grandmother to her greenhouse. That is the place where Uncle Walter first raped her. This visit to the glassed-in Palm House isn't just a getaway for Ilse. It is her attempt to regenerate her granddaughter's interest in the world of flowers.

"You've grown very quiet as of late, my dear," Ilse tells her as they stroll down the aisles. "Hilda has remarked on it and, as they say, who knows you better than your help?"

Hana looks about at the great glass house and the tropical worlds it encompasses. Hilda Schoenweis is her grandmother's help, Hana's nanny, who has stayed in Germany on a family emergency leaving Hana in her grandmother's half-hearted care.

"You're young yet," Ilse continues, pausing to lift the leaf of an *Impatiens walleriana* and smell its red flower. "But not too young to understand what is going on in the world. We have to be careful, you see. Rich though we may be, our business connections important to the economy of the land, we are in a precarious position. Herr Hitler does not trust us Catholics. Many of our acquaintances have been arrested. We are treading a very thin line. We are always under watch, and everything we do comes under the strictest scrutiny. Do you understand?"

"*Ja, Grossmutter.*"

"What? You speak so softly. Can't you raise your voice a bit?"

"Yes, *Grossmutter.*"

"That's better. Your situation makes things only harder. I do wish you would try to moderate your behaviors. It irritates your grandfather to no end. You may not think it, but I do try to defend you when I can."

"Yes, *Grossmutter*."

Hana nods obedience, wipes her nose, jumps like a scared cat as a voice calls to them from behind.

"There you are, Mother. We've been searching for you for days."

It is Walter, Hana's twenty-three-year-old uncle.

"Stop exaggerating," Ilse tells him. "You've probably only just got here. Is there somewhere else you'd rather be?"

Walter is trim and good-looking. He could grace the covers of a magazine. He is the type of young man who likes to pretend he is not rich so he can fuck girls far below his station. He doesn't bother to notice Hana. With him are two other young men, equally physically gifted who look enough alike for Ilse to guess that they are brothers. But she doesn't have to guess. She has seen their photographs. She knows their father. Quite well.

"You're not alone," she says. She has a smile for the other boys, several years Walter's junior. She thinks, but would never say, they look a lot like Harold. "Be polite. Introduce us."

The first boy, the elder by the looks of him, extends a hand first to Ilse then to Hana. He speaks a learner's German. "Charlie McAuliffe. My father is the American ambassador."

"Yes, I know. We would have joined you earlier to meet your mother, but, well, Hana here was feeling out of sorts so I thought to bring her here to calm her down. My apologies to your parents."

"No problem."

Next to offer his hand is David McAuliffe. His smile is charming and he even offers to kiss the hands of both females. Hana blushes, pulls her hand away.

"Lovely place, these gardens," he says. His German is better than Charlie's. "We have a sister, too. Maybe you two would like to meet. I bet you'd get along. Her name is Margaret, but we all call her Peg."

Hana nods. Her hands are shaking. She never looks at Walter. Once David rises, no one looks at her.

Walter says, "Well, now that we've all been introduced, shall we return to the embassy? Hana might not eat anything, but I'm sure the rest of us are famished."

"How about it, Hana?" David says. He is eighteen. His wavy brown hair with a youthful attempt at trying to grow a moustache makes him look like a teenage Clark Gable. Hana isn't taken in. She shrugs.

"That's about as much as you'll ever get out of her," says Walter, whose English is as correct as David's German.

They leave the botanical gardens crossing a bridge to get to the far side of the Sortedams So, one of three lakes strung out like a necklace in the middle of the Danish capital. Both the American embassy and the palatial home the McAuliffes are using while in Copenhagen are a puff of wind away from the beautiful gardens and parks in the city center. The air is warm. The sky is lovely. It is a summer day such as the McAuliffes would enjoy in the waters off Cape Elizabeth or the Zieglers would appreciate in the woods of Bavaria. But today they are on neutral ground, though it will be invaded by Germany in three short years on the Nazis' way to Norway and the world.

Ilse is nervous though she does not appear to be even remotely anxious to any of her young companions. Hana would never guess that her efficient grandmother could be nervous about anything. But Hana isn't the real reason Ilse has delayed meeting the McAuliffes.

"I will need a shower and a change of clothes before I meet anyone," she says. The Zieglers have been invited to stay with the McAuliffes at their place on Stockholmsgade, the boulevard that fronts the lakes. But Ilse had convinced her husband to book rooms at the fabulous two-hundred-year-old D'Angleterre Hotel instead. "I'll take a cab. Hana, you can go with the boys."

"But…"

If Hana has any trepidations about being left alone with the three older males, no one cares. Ilse seems so preoccupied, she doesn't even kiss her granddaughter's cheeks as Walter hails a cab for her. As soon as Ilse has departed, Walter wraps an arm around the shoulders of his two American mates and leaves Hana to do whatever she wills. Hana follows. She has little choice. But she does so at a distance that might have grown had David not turned to look for her.

"Hey," he says to her. "You want some company?"

"Let her alone," Walter says. He doesn't bother to look behind. "She's…" He makes a circle around his ear with a finger.

"Oh?"

"My sister's kid. We think she did something to her. Don't know her father. Probably a Jew."

Charlie stops along with David now, forcing an exasperated groan out of Walter. Hana has stopped, too. Her eyes are focused on the lake to her right, but she is clearly trembling and David thinks he can hear her mumbling something.

"You guys can go ahead," he says. "I'll see what's up."

"Suit yourself. You can drown her if you want."

Walter heads off, and in a moment both he and Charlie are in hysterics over something older brother has asked. David hears something about 'the girls of Copenhagen' before he crouches in front of Hana with a sympathetic smile.

"What's up?" he asks. "You're not afraid of me, are you?"

"Esh-vie-esh-vie-esh-vie."

"What? Is that German? Do you know any English? I've just taken a few classes at my school, but I'm a pretty quick learner if you want to go at it in Nazi, I mean, German."

Hana's chanting comes to a stop. But it takes a few more moments of deep breathing before she dares to look him square in the eye. "Walter raped me," she whispers.

"What?"

"He's done it a lot. You better watch out for your sister."

David is thunderstruck. He doesn't know what to think. Rape? This is a concept so out of his experience, he isn't quite sure he even understands what the twelve-year-old girl means. Does rape mean they had sex? Harold McAuliffe has never spoken about sex to his sons. He assumes that they will learn on their own. David would be embarrassed to admit he has little knowledge of the opposite sex let alone something like this. Is she telling the truth? Is she making it up? Is she, as Walter indicated, nuts?

"I'm sure he didn't mean anything by it," David says at last. "Walter seems a good sport." David looks behind him as Walter and Charlie continue on their merry way enjoying each other's company. "I mean, what do you mean, he raped you?"

David doesn't really want to have this conversation. Not on the sidewalk of a busy street with people strolling by to right and left. He is such an innocent, Charlie calls him Father David. But he is drawn in by this girl. She is pretty, he thinks, doesn't deserve the rap Walter gives her. There is an intensity to her eyes when she stares into his. A darkness. She knows things she will only reveal to people she trusts. But she trusts no one. Bottled up inside her, her secretive world makes her slight body tremble and makes her utter strange sounds, but she is not crazy.

David has to look away briefly toward the lake and the distant botanical gardens on the far side, otherwise, he risks being sucked into whatever mystery this girl is writing. The color of her hair, the shape of her face, David thinks she is nothing like Walter or her grandmother. He has the sudden urge to kiss her on the cheek, to show her that her trust is well-placed. At the same time, he wants to give himself a good smack for thinking such a thing about such a young girl in such a place at such a time. But there you go. These are the types of secrets people never let on to anyone else.

"Have you told anyone? Your grandmother?"

Hana shakes her head. Her tears upset David. He takes her hand. "You want to go for a walk?"

"No," she says. "I want to meet your sister."

"Why?"

Stiffening her puffed-up shoulders, Hana wipes her nose on one of her gloves. "Because," she says, "you need to watch out for your brother."

* * *

The McAuliffes hold nothing in reserve. This is Harold's first diplomatic

71

post, and it is an important one, right on Germany's doorstep. FDR may not know it, but it is also the first step in Charlie's political rise. Charlie is going to finish at Harvard and join the army, but first, he will spend the summer in Copenhagen learning something about foreign affairs and making important European contacts. Among those, of course, will be German luminaries such as Foreign Minister von Ribbentrop and industrialists like Fritz Thyssen and Alfried Krupp. Friedrich Ziegler and Ernst von Haefner may be second tier, but if their businesses flourish, so do the economic fortunes of American investors like the McAuliffes. One hand washes the other.

Dinner is set up in the spacious first-floor parlor, chandeliered and crackling with good humor and political gossip. Liz McAuliffe has chosen the menu which includes lobster brought from their home state of Maine. It might be amusing for Ilse to watch the uninitiated try to break open the hard shells without splattering themselves with the lobster's insides, but her attention drifts from her plate to that of Harold McAuliffe. His hands are skilled. He is very adept at managing his meal. Many years ago, on a visit to Boston, he taught her how to break open the claws and pull out the insides. Forcing others to look foolish is a clever way, she is thinking, for him to reign supreme over his illustrious guests. And she likes cleverness in a man.

There are two long tables covered by white cloths. Servants come and go from the kitchen in the back of the house. The adults, composed of fourteen people from six families, sit at one table, Harold and Liz at opposite ends. A table closer to the kitchen entry is surrounded by the children. Hana sits here with quiet, shy sons and daughters who don't speak each other's language. Hana would appear to be the second oldest. The oldest by far is Peggy McAuliffe, who at age twenty should have been sitting with her brothers at the adult table. She is the awkward girl at the dance who no one wants to dance with, the one whose growth spurt has left her classmates to marvel at her but not in an enlightened way.

This is exactly why Hana immediately takes to her. Peg doesn't seem to mind that the younger children, brought up to show good manners, are gawking at the way she cracks open a claw and doesn't care if she drips melted butter on her lap. When they snicker, Hana gives them the eye.

"Are you any better?" she says.

Peg notices Hana for the first time. Up to now, her attention appears to be on two things: her food and that handsome boy sitting beside Charlie: Walter Ziegler.

"What's your name?" she asks.

"Hana."

Peg mulls over the name. "You're pretty," she says. "Do you have a brother?"

"No."

"Oh. Then who is that?"

"My uncle. If he were a lobster, I would crack his skull first then declaw him with a fork."

Guffawing, Peg loses to the floor a piece of tender Maine lobster which she immediately picks up and swallows. She is amused by Hana's remark, but says, "Not me. That's not what I'd do."

From that point forward, Hana's antennae are up full height. She will not take her eyes off Peg no matter what. Even after the dinner is over and she is tired and just wants to go to bed, she makes sure not to leave Peg's side. She has been furtively watching Walter. She has seen him look Peg's way several times. She knows what's on his mind.

"Show me your house," she says to the older girl. Peg isn't paying attention. Her eyes have lodged on Walter who is standing with his father and mother and the McAuliffe men. Friedrich is doing a lot of nodding. Ilse is doing a lot of smiling, something Hana would have thought beneath her.

The McAuliffe's Danish 'house' is a four-story eighteenth-century Georgian townhouse of stone facing the lake from the far side of the boulevard. The living quarters are on the upper floors. Hana has already been there earlier in the evening. David brought her there to bathe and calm down. He had ceased probing her about her accusations and instead wanted to introduce her to his sister. But Hana could hear Mrs. McAuliffe lecturing her daughter on issues of behavior, so the introductions had been delayed.

Peg is reluctant to leave the adults and wander off with her new friend. Several times, she shakes loose of Hana's insistent grip until David joins them and helps with the subterfuge. They head upstairs away from the smoke and chatter. Hana's clothes are the same she wore to the botanical garden. They are dirty, but she hasn't had time to change them and her grandmother hadn't thought to bring a fresh outfit. She enjoys walking barefoot, though, on the thick carpet in Peg's bedroom. Peg's bed is canopied. Hana also enjoys bouncing up and down on it. It is a childish activity, and Hana has to remind herself that she isn't a child anymore, that she has a purpose for being where she is.

"You have to write me and keep in touch with me," she tells Peg who is tuning in a radio trying to find music she likes to dance to. "I'll give you my address. Will you promise to write me if I write you?"

"Peg doesn't like to write," David says. He is posted at the door, which is shut.

"I do so."

"You like to draw," David counters. "Why don't you show Hana some of the things you've drawn since we've been in Copenhagen?"

"I'd like that," Hana says. "I draw, too. Flowers and things."

Peg shrugs, points toward a desk. She is humming along with some Danish chanteuse, her hips swaying to the music. She is not paying attention to either David or Hana.

"Why is she like that?" Hana asks David.

"Like what?"

"You know."

"You mean like…" David imitates the circular finger motion Walter had made that afternoon regarding Hana's mental well-being.

"That's not very nice."

"That's what your brother thinks of you."

"He's not my brother. He's my uncle. How can you think I'm crazy after what I've told you?"

"Maybe I don't believe you."

Sliding open a drawer of Peg's desk, David discovers a drawing of his sister, naked, entwined with a male who looks distinctly like one of his classmates back home. Immediately, he grabs the graphic picture, stuffs it in a pocket, and shuts the drawer. "Well," he says, "I guess we can skip the artwork for tonight."

* * *

Hana and Peg have one other thing in common. Neither was supposed to accompany their families to Copenhagen. Peg was bound for a summer camp in upstate New York until an outbreak of measles caused last-minute rearrangements. In Hana's case, it was her grandmother who wanted to leave Hana behind. Hilda Schoenweis, the Ziegler's durable and reliable maid-slash-nanny, had a family emergency that forced Ilse to give way. Luckily for Ilse, Hilda placed a phone call to the L'Angleterre Hotel and said that her father wasn't dying after all, and she could take the next train to Copenhagen to see to Hana.

Ilse's delight went unremarked by the male members of her family. Hana wonders about it during the cab ride to the Copenhagen train station. She has never heard her grandmother sing before. It reminds her of Peg's swaying to the radio the night before.

At the station, Hana is greeted with a respectful nod by Fraulein Hilda. Hilda carries one lone bulky suitcase. She is more than a match for its weight, as she is a large woman from the country, the quintessential farmer's daughter. She is only thirty-six but already considers herself an old maid. The Zieglers took her on to help out Hilda's father whose finances floundered after the Great War. She became a boon companion to Hana's mother Ursula. And when Ursula passed, the role of surrogate mother naturally fell to her.

"We've decided to prolong our stay in the city," Ilse tells Hilda. "Father has important business to conduct with the American ambassador. I am to befriend his wife and I'm afraid we would bore poor Hana. She likes the museums. You'll have plenty of money, and the weather is so fine. You should get out and walk a bit. You can use the exercise, Hilda, if you don't mind my saying so. And Hana loves the parks, don't you, my dear."

"Ja, Grossmutter."

"What?"

"*Ja, Grossmutter!*"

But Hana is not without her own wiles. She has asked for Peg to come along with them, and the McAuliffes are only too happy to give the go-ahead. David is willing to accompany them, and so, after Hilda has dropped off her suitcase at L'Angleterre, the four head out into the city.

Along the Stockholmsgade, Hana insists that they stop by an art supply store. Drawing can be very therapeutic, a way to make human connections. She carefully chooses the materials she wants and helps Peg select paper and pencils.

"You have a way about you," David tells Hana. They speak in English, so Hana has to translate into German for Hilda. "Peg follows you around like a cocker spaniel."

"My Hana," says Hilda in broken English, "good girl."

Fully supplied, off they go. David makes his own detour once he sees his sister is in capable hands. While the three females locate a spot by the Sortedams, he purchases a picnic lunch. By the time he finds them sitting on a vast expanse of lawn outside the botanical gardens, Hana and Peg are already comparing their sketches, Hana of two flowers, a rose, and a tulip, entwined, and Peg of a tree with a girl's legs dangling from a branch.

It's a very benign scene, the three ladies quite relaxed and at peace with one another. Hilda is reading a book. A bible. She comes from a very religious background. She is reading to herself though every once in a while when she finds a passage that moves her, she shares it with the others.

"'This is what the Lord says to me,'" she reads aloud. "'I will remain quiet and will look on from my dwelling place, like shimmering heat in the sunshine, like a cloud of dew in the heat of harvest. For, before the harvest, when the blossom is gone and the flower becomes a ripening grape, he will cut off the shoots with pruning knives, and cut down and take away the spreading branches.'" She looks over at Hana with concern on her face.

"Are you Catholic or Protestant?" David asks her in German. He can see a cross necklace around her neck that she plays with as she reads.

"Catholic," she replies and puts a finger to her lips as if to tell David to keep her faith a secret.

David says, "People think there'll be a Jewish president of Germany before there'll be a Catholic president of the United States. That makes my dad all the more determined to see Charlie go all the way. What do you think that passage means?"

Hilda's watchful gaze stays on Hana who is concentrating on her spiraling flowers connected by their leaves. Hilda's anxious face is like that of a mother who has read her unfortunate daughter's future in the book she is reading. "It seems to say," she says, "that the young ones will be taken before their time while God merely watches."

Hana looks up at that moment and gifts her nanny with a smile. "I know you think I'm Jewish." She studies her finished artwork with uncertainty then looks at David. "She always reads the bible to me. She wants to convert me, but I'm already Catholic."

"Are you?" David asks.

"My mother was."

"And your father?"

"We don't talk about that," Hilda says, closing her bible and reaching for a sandwich that David has prepared.

"What else do you talk about?" David wonders. He is thinking about what Hana told him the day before about her and Walter. Does Hilda know? Has Hana told her?

"We talk about better days ahead," Hilda says.

"War? You think it's coming to that?"

"Who can say? We put our faith and trust in der Fuhrer. That is all we can do."

David hands a sandwich to Peg. has to nudge her to look up from her work on which she has added a second pair of legs up in the tree.

"We hear…" David is reluctant to say it. "…that you Germans…your Jews… "

He glances at Hana, who doesn't bite. She seems upset by what she has drawn, displeased by it for some reason.

"You needn't worry, my young American friend," Hilda says, her eyes lighting on Hana again, too. "I grew up on a farm. If I have to, I will sit on

that egg until the earth gives way to the eternal."

Hana folds up her finished drawing with a sigh. Something is wrong. Something is missing. She just can't focus hard enough. Peg has finished her picture, too, which she proudly holds up for everyone to see. She and Hana are sitting together on a tree overlooking a body of water about to jump in, completely naked. David is embarrassed by it. So is Hilda who, nevertheless, diplomatically praises the work. Hana likes it so much, she promises Peg she will frame it and put it up on the wall of her bedroom.

"Your grandmother will love that," Hilda says.

As they rise, Hana reaches for Peggy's hand. She slips the older girl a note. "Here is my address. Write me when you can and I will write back."

"Do you think I could visit you?"

"If we are ever back in America," Hilda interrupts.

David walks beside her while the two girls walk ahead. It is late afternoon now, early evening. Both Liz McAuliffe and Ilse Ziegler have assured David and Hilda that it is okay to keep the girls out as late as they want.

David says to Hilda, "Seriously, aren't you worried? If Hana is part Jewish?"

"I worry about many things. Hana is my, is my Liebchen."

"Anything else?" A lawyer-in-waiting, David wants to probe, doesn't quite know how.

"Like what?"

"You treat her like she's your own child."

"So? She is my own child."

'Or might as well be, for all the others care,' she is thinking.

"What about Walter?"

"Her uncle?"

"I guess. Does she talk about him at all?"

"In what way?"

David is reluctant to say and Hilda seems defensive. What if Hana is making it all up? What if she is like Peg? He doesn't want to ruin the relationship his father is building with Friedrich Ziegler. Money. Financial backing for Charlie's political future. Charlie's apparent friendship with Walter. He doesn't want to disrupt all that for a girl he hardly knows.

"Never mind," he says. If Hana wants to tell her nanny or keep things a secret from her, that's her business, not his.

At the McAuliffe home, David and Peg depart, Peg promising to write, David giving Hana the McAuliffe home address in Cape Elizabeth, Maine. When Hilda starts to hail a taxi, Hana stops her.

"I want to walk. Can we stop off somewhere and get something to eat? I'm hungry."

Hana doesn't want to return to l'Angleterre right away. With her grandparents socializing and Walter free to roam Copenhagen with Charlie McAuliffe, Hana would rather not go back to her room by herself.

"Can I stay with you tonight?" she asks Hilda.

"You want to stay with me? My room is not as comfortable as yours."

"Even so. You can read from the bible if you like."

"You might listen?"

"I might."

"I don't believe you. You have too much of your father's blood in you. What do they say? *Oy gevalt.*"

They stop for dinner not because the café they come to is the best in town. It is just the first they reach. Hana doesn't talk much. She lays her flower drawing on the table and studies it, occasionally making edits with her pencil. Hilda has no idea what her charge is doing but suspects it is something amazing. *Her father's blood*, she is thinking. *Yes, for all they say the Jews are terrible creatures, they are smart. But what good will that do my Liebchen? Oh, Ursula, why did you have to go and die?*

"This David," she says as their food is brought to the table. "You like him?" Hana shrugs. "Your Uncle Walter, you said something to this David about him, *ja?*"

"I don't remember. Maybe."

"You would tell me, wouldn't you, if anything was wrong?"

"Of course. Don't I tell you everything?"

Hilda isn't so sure. As much as she has come to love this child, the only one she will ever love as a daughter, she knows too well how clever Hana is, or thinks she is. Diabolical in her way. Jewish. There, she has said it. She has admitted it finally. This is the one thing, the one barrier, foolish though it may be, that keeps these two from trusting one another completely.

"Well, I will say this, my girl, just this once. Don't try to be too clever. In this world, the only thing that cleverness gets you is trouble."

Hilda will say no more. She will not bring up Walter anymore. There are many things she keeps to herself, secrets she stores away like a summer animal preparing for a long cold winter. In some circumstances, secrets are money. In others, they are weapons. She knows full well why Hana's *grossmutter* wants Hana out of the way tonight. She knows full well why she, Hilda, has been relegated to a second-floor room at the grandest hotel in Copenhagen. And while she doesn't know but can only assume, what Ambassador Harold McAuliffe will be up to in the early hours of the evening, she knows he won't be spending it alone or with his handsome American wife.

Worrying about what is to come, Hilda bides her time.

Chapter Nine

September 1939

With war underway, it is time for all Germans to unite and sacrifice and pull together to ensure complete triumph. This means all Germans. Except, of course, Jews, criminals, cripples, communists, and homosexuals. They have to be eliminated.

The children, too, must do their share, girls as well as boys. Silke Hartenstein and her brother Georg and their friends are all enrolled in the Nazi Youth movement and the Bund Deutsch Madel. For the boys, it means preparing for the battlefront. They will be the last line of defense if it comes to it. For the girls, it means doing everything else. Everything.

A proper German girl will make a proper German mother and hausfrau. She will know how to care for and raise children. Change their diapers, fix their meals, sew their torn clothes. It means that they will treat their husbands with respect, attend to their daily needs, kiss them, hug them and fuck them whenever the men so desire. But the demands on the BDM girl don't end with home economics. Not only are they expected to bear and raise a pure Aryan bloodline, they must prepare to fill in for the men who come home wounded. They must know how to cleanse and cauterize a wound, how to staunch the bleeding from a torn artery, how to function around the dead and dying. They must be able to cut and haul wood. They must learn how to bear the load that any German man might have to carry. They must know how to repair a car engine, how to install plumbing, how to pave a road, how to put together a radio transmitter. Oh, and one other thing. They must learn how to kill.

On this morning, as the German army continues to lay waste to Poland, Silke and her squad of BDM girls are learning how to fire Karabiner 98K assault rifles and Mauser C96 pistols being used this very day by the Wehrmacht as they race for Warsaw. Ernst Haefner has graciously turned one of his pastures over to a rifle range, and the girls, six in line, each are firing at targets pinned to posts. The targets are shaped in the form of the enemy. Each girl gets ten shots. Silke has hit her 'enemy' in the head ten times. Her friend Dora hasn't hit the target once. Even Frau Zoeller and Frau Goedeler are impressed.

"You must teach the others," Frau Zoeller insists. "How do you do it, Hartenstein?"

Silke envisions herself saying, 'I pretend it's you.' Instead, she tells the truth. "My brother Georg and I have been hunting squirrels around here since we were kids. He's even better than I am."

"Interesting. What do you think, Feliks?"

"What do I think?" The World War I veteran who is teaching them has an idea. And the next day while the girls are practicing, three cars pull onto the dirt road leading to the firing range.

"Hartenstein!" Frau Zoeller calls. "To me."

Silke has been waiting in line for her turn, helping to tutor some of the smaller, younger girls for whom holding a rifle and maintaining a steady grip is proving difficult. She notices the three cars churning dirt. The first two cars have their tops down so that she can see the passengers. There is a camera crew in the second car undoubtedly here to film more propaganda footage. Okay. No problem. Silke knows how to perform before a camera. It is the other two cars that cause her stomach to grieve. Both fly the insignia of the SS.

'Why are they here?' she wonders.

Frau Zoeller and Frau Goedeler yell at the girls to line up in formation presenting their weapons as they have been shown when being inspected by a superior. Who that particular superior is, does not become clear to anyone until a man in the full black uniform of a high-ranking SS official exits the back seat of the third car. Whoever recognizes him utters an astonished gasp in awe. That would be Fraus Zoeller and Goedeler, Dora, and a few of the other girls. Silke's heart pounds mightily. She also recognizes the short man with the glasses and thin moustache. Reichsfuhrer Heinrich Himmler.

Himmler is all smiles as he greets his excited fans, warm, gracious. He could be any man, father to any one of these girls. At least, he treats them that way without the slightest hint that he is the most important man in Germany behind der Fuhrer. When he comes to Silke, standing in the second row directly behind Dora, he stops, waggles his finger.

"Come, come," he says. "Step forward, my dear. I don't bite."

A couple of the younger girls in the front row titter. Himmler doesn't mind. They're only children, and he has amused them with his little joke. The camera is rolling, and the image he will make is a good one. Silke doesn't laugh. She is very nervous.

"So," he says to her, "you're the one who laughed in Goebbels' face, are you?"

Silke's face turns the color of Himmler's SS armband.

"Well…"

"Everyone at the Chancellery is talking about it. No fear, my dear. No one likes Goebbels. Serves him right, I might say. I will tell him I've met you and find you to be quite what we are looking for. You're a pretty girl. The pictures do you justice. The future of Germany rests between your legs."

It is at this point in the past that Silke might have burst out laughing. She is not tempted to do so today. Something in Reichsfuhrer Himmler's eyes tells her that he is daring her to do the same to him. Giggle. Titter. Laugh. Instead, he takes the rifle from her, hands it back after a short examination of the weapon, then tells her, "Let's see a demonstration. Your instructor tells me you are a superb marksman. Beauty and a deadly shot in one so young, well…"

Himmler glances behind him at his SS escort generating laughter.

"Go on, go on," he says. "We have to be at Dachau in a half hour. Just a few shots will do."

Everyone moves aside as Silke makes her way toward the rifle range. Her instructor and Frau Zoeller accompany her.

"Don't be nervous," the World War I vet says. "Be yourself. Pretend you're hunting squirrels."

"This could be very significant, very significant," says Frau Zoeller. "But if you laugh, so help me…"

Silke takes in a breath of air before raising and aiming her Karabiner. The camera is rolling. She can feel all eyes on her, Himmler's in particular. 'Go ahead. Miss the target. Make a fool of yourself,' he is saying to her. 'Laugh and, unlike Goebbels, I will not let you off the hook.'

Silke fires. Once. Twice. Three times. Four. The first shot takes out an eye. The second, an ear. The third strikes the enemy in the mouth. The fourth scalps it. When she lowers her rifle, though, she is in tears. Himmler doesn't even notice or praise her. By the time she turns around, he has returned to his car for his appointment at the death camp.

"Dry your eyes. You did good," Frau Zoeller congratulates her. "I could see it in his face. He has marked you for something, Hartenstein. You just better hope it's a good thing."

* * *

When she tells her mother and father and brother Georg that night around the dinner table, they are all thrilled.

"Himmler himself," Vitor Hartenstein says. "My God. What a blessing."

"You didn't laugh, did you?" His wife Gertrud prays not. "He'll kill us all."

"Relax, Ma," says Georg. "What can they do to Silke? Marry her to a Jew?"

"Shut up, Georg."

"Marry her to a Jewess?"

"I said, shut up, you little runt."

Silke is playing with her food, a dinner of rabbit and potatoes that she would normally wolf down. The first thing she did after her experience at the rifle range was hide behind one of Herr Haefner's barns and throw up all over herself. Frau Zoeller had been unusually kind and let her go home to change. Now her mind is adrift with worry but not about what her family thinks.

"You've been to the house, Ma," she says. "You've seen the girl?"

"What girl?"

"The new one. You know. The one Herr Haefner brought home from the asylum."

"The crazy one."

"Georg, if you open your mouth again, I swear..."

Silke threatens him with her fork. Georg shrugs and dips into his stew. "I saw her when we visited the institute. They treated her very unfairly, I thought. Very roughly. That is a bad place. Do you know, they kill children there?"

"We don't talk about such things," Gertrud Hartenstein says. "Do you want to end up at Dachau?"

"Family's send their own children there," says Vitor. "No one's forcing them. Imagine if we had a child like that, how could we take care of him on my income?"

"We do have one like that, Pa," says Georg and can't leave the table fast enough with Silke on his tail.

"Children, please!"

"The times are upsetting enough without you two fighting all the time."

Silke obeys her parents, though her dander is up and she is about to slug her younger brother in the nose. She sits back down, grabs a fork, but only pokes at her food with it.

"Killing children can't be right," she says, "no matter why they do it. And of all the nerve of Himmler. The future of our country is in between my legs. Fuck him."

"Silke!" Gertrud is appalled. Vitor is a bit amused but horrified at the same time.

"Silke," he says. "Seriously. Remember. Your brother is a member of the *Hitlerjugend*. Do you understand that it is his responsibility to report any such utterings to the officials? You could be sent away. We all could. As enemies of the State."

"I would never do that, Silke," Georg says. "I'm just fooling with you."

"Even so," says the family patriarch. "Watch what you say, where you say it, and who you say it to. I don't want to hear any more about Himmler, that girl, or anything else. Whatever they do at the institute is none of our affair. Right, Silke? Right?"

Rather than give her father an answer he won't like, Silke fills her mouth with a piece of the rabbit she shot two days ago.

After dinner, she goes immediately to her bedroom, closes the door, sneaks out a window, and heads for the large estate where Herr Haefner lives with his new bride, his elderly father, and now the black-haired girl rescued from the Hollenschloss Institute. The Hartensteins live in a cottage on the estate halfway between the main house and Haefner's barn and stables, about a mile distance. Herr Haefner has also built two additional structures that abut his home. This is where he does his scientific work. Silke has no interest in these. She wants to see the girl.

Silke is nothing if not brazen. She doesn't sidle up to the house, which is more aptly a country estate three floors in height with a circular gated drive fronted by gardens. She raps on the front door and waits, tapping her toe and twiddling her fingers. Eventually, her loud knocking gets the attention of a maid who answers the door.

"Silke," she says. She is an elderly woman, a distant relative, warm and kind, who has known Silke since she was a baby. "It is so late. Why are you here?"

"I don't want to bother anyone," Silke whispers. "I was wondering about the girl. You know, the one Herr Haefner brought home from the Institute. Is she all right? Can I see her?"

"I'm not sure if he would want you to." The elderly woman is hesitant, looks around. "It's been a rough few days. Getting accustomed. You understand. These transitions can be difficult."

"No. By all means."

From inside the house comes a deep male voice. In a moment, Herr Haefner himself appears. He is carrying a heavy textbook. There is music playing in the background. Silke thinks it's Beethoven. She has only been in the kitchen and cellars of the house even though her mother works here full time. As for Herr Haefner himself, except for her engagement with him on Hana's behalf, she has only met him in passing. She gives him a cute smile and a polite curtsy before cutting to the chase.

"Thank you, sir, for saving that girl. I wanted to express my deepest gratitude. It was a wonderful thing you did, saving her from…"

"From?"

"Whatever happens there, sir. I would like to see her if I might be invited inside." Silke's glance bounces from the old woman to Haefner, thence to his bride who makes an appearance from behind pushing an old man in a wheelchair. That would be Herr Haefner's ancient father August.

"Who is it?" Gretchen asks.

"The girl we met when riding the other day," Haefner replies. At first, he seems reluctant to honor Silke's request. Then, upon hearing a shout coming from deeper inside the house, he has second thoughts. "You know," he tells Silke, "that might not be such a bad idea. Hana is having trouble accommodating herself to her new surroundings. It's a complicated situation as you can imagine. Perhaps making a friend, another girl about her age, would do her good. Come in. Come in. Alfrieda will show you where she is."

"Are you sure that's wise?" asks Gretchen who only sees the face of a lovely younger girl entering her house.

"Since when has wisdom ever mattered around here? You can always divorce him, Gretchen. You're on the books for a healthy inheritance." This from August who, had he been a resident of Hollenschloss, would have been among the first to be gassed. As if his son hasn't considered it.

Alfrieda escorts Silke up a staircase that halfway to the next floor splits, one side going toward the right wing of the estate, the other side turning toward the left. As Alfrieda takes Silke to the right, they can hear more yelling, female, and now a second voice, male, trying to calm down the first.

"That would be Otto," says Alfrieda. "The son of Herr Haefner's attorney, Herr Froeling. He's a real sweet dear. But that girl. Honestly, Silke, I don't know why Herr Haefner brought her into this house. She is mad. There is no doubt of it."

"She's just scared," says Silke. "That's all. You would be, too, if you saw what I saw."

They have to travel down a long, carpeted hall with centuries of Counts Haefner portraits staring down at them. Near the end, at a distance where her screaming can't be heard in Ernst and Gretchen's bedroom at the opposite end, Silke barges past Alfrieda to enter Hana's room.

A young man is standing helplessly by the side of Hana's bed trying futilely to get her to stop ripping up wads of paper and tossing them all about the room. He is dressed for court. Hana is completely naked. It is a scene from Dante's Inferno. But when Hana beans Otto on the nose with a crumpled ball of writing paper, Silke lets go with a laugh that startles everyone.

Scene changes. Hell disappears. Otto rubs his nose. Hana stops mid-hurl and gawks at Silke. Abruptly, she lets down her guard, leaps from the bed, and throws herself into Silke's arms.

"You came," Hana cries. "I hoped you would."

"I'm here," Silke says. "Put something on, will you? This is embarrassing."

"For all of us," says Otto who, finding a chair, drops into it, exhausted. "I've been trying my best for two hours."

"I'm ashamed of myself," says Hana, who has in an instant quieted down, though tears are streaming down her cheeks. "I'm lost, so lost here. Aren't I, Otto? Esh-vie-esh-vie. No, stop, stop."

Hana smacks herself in the face. The self-assault doesn't help. It only brings on further misery, which causes her body to tremble such that it looks like she has just emerged out of a frigid shower and can't get warm.

"Hey, let me help," Silke says. She throws a blanket around Hana. "Come on, Otto. Pitch in. Hana. Look at what Herr Haefner has bought you."

The boxes of clothes that Haefner has purchased for Hana are lying unopened on the floor. The only old clothes that Silke can see is the drab gray patient uniform from Hollenschloss that Hana has obviously discarded at the entry to her private bathroom.

While Otto sinks into his chair, the girls go through the myriad of boxes from expensive Munich clothing stores.

"I'm not much for clothes," Hana says.

"Me neither," says Silke. "But between us, I bet we can find something you'll like. How old are you?"

"Fourteen."

"I'm sixteen. My name is Silke. You?"

"Hana."

"That's lovely. Let's find something to match."

"Only if you stay with me."

"Of course. Why do you think I came?"

Their find comes in box number four, one of the more modest dresses, one that reminds Hana of her expedition to Copenhagen two years before. A green dress with a flower pattern. Either Gretchen had done the buying or Herr Haefner has experience buying for women, for he has been spot on with underwear and socks and shoes that are both stylish and fit.

"He must have spent a fortune," Silke says.

"Three thousand, seven hundred and forty-six Reichsmarks," Otto says from his chair. "My father does all of Herr Haefner's accounting, too. I saw the ledgers. I could buy a house with that. A horse and a pig."

Silke laughs. "You have a sense of humor."

"One has to these days, don't you think?"

Hana tries on the green dress in front of a mirror. "I don't want to stay here, you know," she says. "You know what they do at the institute, don't you?"

"Yes."

"They killed my friend Sigrid. They murdered her. They were going to starve her to death. Then they just gassed her. I was going to die. I was going to be killed."

Hana crumples in tears again, leans against the door-height mirror until Silke wraps her up in her arms.

"But you weren't," she says. "You're here. You're alive. And you have friends. Right..."

"Otto," says the fatigued young man in the chair. "Yes, of course. Herr Otto. Take away the 'herr,' you've got Otto at your service day and night.

And you, I've seen your face."

"Unfortunately," says Silke. "Goebbels wants my backside. Himmler wants my front. The whole German nation likes my blue eyes, apparently. I'm just a collection of female parts to everyone."

This gets a laugh not only out of Otto but from Hana, too. She giggles through her tears and gives Silke a tight embrace.

"Don't go," she says. "Either of you. I won't be able to stand it here without you. I don't even know why Herr Haefner wants me."

"I suppose he'll let you know soon enough."

"Just cut out the hysteria, will you?" Otto begs. "Get along with him. Find out what he's after. Then plan."

"You sound like a lawyer," Hana says.

"I am a lawyer. Or a student. Trust me. You have something he wants. Your drawings. He was quite fascinated by them. What is it you do, when you're not ranting like a lunatic?"

"Nothing," Hana says. She looks about the room at the reams of paper she has wasted, years of research and drawings, and her personal diaries that Haefner has solicitously gathered on her behalf, shredded and discarded. "I do what I do to keep from going crazy."

"Message to Hana," Otto says. "It didn't work."

* * *

Haefner allots an hour of privacy to the two girls before he dares appear at Hana's bedroom. He is very wary about entering, pokes his head in first, and is relieved and pleased to see her, Silke, and Otto on the floor trying to undo the mess Hana has made.

"Has an armistice been signed?" he asks. "May I enter without fear of stepping on a mine?"

Hana still refuses to speak to him. Otto stands up, stretches. "Follow in my footsteps, Herr Haefner," he says. "You should be safe."

"For now? Or forever? Am I forgiven?"

Hana remains silent. Silke says, "You must give her time, Herr Haefner.

The strain, you know, of everything. She isn't crazy. She knows what happened."

"Yes. Well."

Haefner enters, stands just inside the doorway. He is thinking of something to add, something that will explain the world. It isn't easy.

At last, it is Hana who speaks, quite softly but like a knife to the heart of things. "Sigrid was your daughter," she says.

"Yes."

"You let her die. You killed her."

"She was going to die anyway. Slowly, painfully. This way..."

The three young people continue sifting through Hana's mess, sorting, arranging. They are content to let Haefner stew in his own steaming gravy.

Haefner says, "You should read Hoche's *Jahresringe*. It will explain everything. I just reread it myself. Once you have read it, you will understand why euthanasia is not a cruel thing. It is practiced everywhere in the world that is civilized. In the United States, they have sterilization laws. You are a brilliant young woman, Hana. In time, you will come to understand. Sigrid was very unhappy. I'm sure that if she could have spoken, she would have desired this."

The silence that follows unsettles Haefner. He tolerates it as long as he can before turning to leave.

"Tomorrow," he says, "Silke and Otto, you, too, can come with us. I want to show Hana my lab. It will be your lab from now on, Hana. I think I know what you are working on in that brilliant mind of yours. A twelve-year-old out-testing everyone in the university exams. Amazing. You will come to love it here, I know. No one will bother you. You will have all the time and space you need to conduct whatever experiments you choose to conduct. I will provide whatever you need. The finest equipment. University connections. This can benefit you. It can benefit the world, if you will only let the past go. Can you do that?"

Hana doesn't say. At least not directly. She gazes about the room, bare of anything pretty, anything girlish. She leaves Haefner with this final question.

"This was Sigrid's room, wasn't it?"

91

II

BOOK 2

Chapter Ten

May 1947

A vi Kreisler hates. You wouldn't think it to look at him. He is so gentle and quiet, almost dispirited, as if his soul has departed his body to scout ahead. He is a slight man. He lost over one hundred pounds in the camps and hasn't put a bit of it back on. His limp is due to the mauling he took from one of the SS guards who unleashed a ferocious German shepherd upon him at Dachau when he dared to sneeze one wintry morning during roll call. Surgery might restore full use, but he has declined it. He wears old clothes and has done everything he can to put away the man that he was. A German. A man who betrayed his own people.

The hatred he feels is mostly for himself. But he saves a little not only for the Germans but for the British who are arresting hundreds of displaced Jews who only want to find peace and resettlement in Palestine. This is why he is part of the Bericha Movement. Major Adams doesn't know this side of Avi. When he can, Avi forges documents, creates false identities, for fellow survivors who will brave the open seas to sneak into Palestine. At the moment, however, Avi has another axe to grind. Being a detective is still in his blood. Finding out who committed murder on the autobahn twenty kilometers from the Swiss border is his mission today.

He waits patiently outside a modest hotel in Nuremberg where Major Adams has been renting a room for his German lover. This is a fact that no one is supposed to know. Major Adams would certainly not want his wife of eight years or his children back in New Hampshire to find out. That is why the major is startled to find Kreisler on the sidewalk smoking a cigarette and reading a German newspaper.

"Ah, Major," Kreisler says with a guileless smile. "Good morning."

"Uh…" Major Adams isn't sure what to say. "How did you find me?"

Kreisler sniffs the air around the American officer. "German women love French perfume," he says. "French women love German men. Go figure. American men are very provincial. Even their officers. They are drawn to anything foreign. Women in particular, not that I find any woman particularly interesting anymore. But that's just me."

"You didn't answer my question."

"You wouldn't care for the answer. Shall we proceed?"

Major Adams doesn't know where Kreisler came from, where he stays, how he got here. That means Adams must surrender the use of his own vehicle. He will meet his subordinate at a pre-arranged location. He would tell Kreisler to go pound bricks except that now Avi has something on him.

"Where are we heading?" Kreisler asks once in the major's automobile. "This is a very intriguing case. Did you get the identity of either of the dead men?"

"The driver," Major Adams says. "Fellow named Sorensen. Works for the United Nations Resettlement agency. His family has been made aware."

"What did you tell them?"

"That his death was accidental."

"No open casket then. And the bodies? Where have you taken them?"

Adams takes a right turn onto Ernst-nathan-strasse. His attitude is not friendly. "You know," he says, "this is a military investigation. I am under no obligation to have you riding my coattails. Don't push it, Herr Kreisler. You may think you have me in an awkward situation, but that can be handled easily enough."

"You would kill me?"

"No, of course not."

"Then drive. Consider me an expert in forensics who can help you. I'm not interested in embarrassing you in any way. You'll end up doing that on your own."

"Thank you."

Their destination is the Klinicum Nurnberg. Adams tells Kreisler that it is the closest facility that has a fully operational morgue. They are met by the same lieutenant who had accompanied Adams to the original crime scene. They in turn meet with the American pathologist who conducted the post mortem exam.

The bodies are lying on consecutive tables each covered in sheets. The first body belongs to the American Sorensen. The pathologist lifts the sheet to expose the massively disfigured head.

"Skipping the obvious," he says, "we can say what sort of weapon was used. A Mauser C96 pistol. It's a favorite of the SS. One shot, right between the eyes. Either the shooter was lucky or damned good."

"Anything else?"

"I don't think the waffles he had for breakfast killed him, if that's what you mean."

Kreisler isn't interested in the American. While Adams and the pathologist have been inspecting the remains of the American Sorensen, Kreisler has wandered over to the second table and lifted the sheet.

"Herr Kreisler, must you?" Adams says.

"Avi, which is short for Aviel, which means 'God is my father.' I'm considering a name change."

Disobedient, like a magician revealing his startling trick, Kreisler suddenly draws the sheet off the second body, exposing it in its entirety. As if this is not enough, then, with a scream that shatters the silence of the morgue, he lunges at the corpse, wraps his hands around its neck, and begins to throttle it, cursing the dead man. It takes both Adams and the pathologist to drag him off.

"Jesus Christ, Kreisler! What the hell?"

Kreisler's panting persists for a few moments as he recovers, bent at the waist, hands on knees. "Sorry," he gasps. "Flashback. It happens occasionally. It won't again."

"It better not."

"Who the hell is **he**?" the pathologist asks of the rattled Jew.

"One of the unwanted. Can you tell us anything about this guy? Herr Kreisler…"

"Avi."

"Herr Kreisler says he's SS. There's a tattoo on his left arm under his armpit."

"I saw it." The pathologist replaces the sheet, keeping it just under the body's armpits. "We'll try to work up a clearer picture of what it says. Maybe it will help identify him, though the SS destroyed most of their records before we got to them."

"Fingerprints?" Kreisler asks.

"Taken. Again, with no corroborating records, what good will they do?"

"Then produce the best description you can. Post in all the papers. Offer a significant reward. Someone knows him. This is a poor country once again. Money will draw them out."

With effort then, Kreisler staggers out of the morgue. After a final word with the pathologist, Adams follows him. "Honestly, Kreisler," he says. "Why do you do it? Why do you stay? A Jew in Germany? Why?"

"Until my work is done," Kreisler says. Outside on the sidewalk, he pops a pill in his mouth. "Where to now? Have you visited this Sorensen's apartment?"

"Next stop."

"Good. He was a young man, and young men are stupid."

* * *

Bill Sorensen was young. But stupid? Hopefully. He lived in a high-class neighborhood of the city. And while this is post-war Germany, the rents are high. He could have chosen to live in more modest surroundings, but didn't. Money, therefore, was not a problem.

"Either he comes from it," Kreisler was saying as he, the major, and the lieutenant climb the stairs to the top floor. "Or he was raking it in. Or both. Capitalists are never satisfied."

Sorensen's landlord has given them a key. The apartment has two bedrooms, but the landlord assures Major Adams that Herr Sorensen lived here by himself. A guest once in a while, yes. Ladies, of course. Herr Sorensen enjoyed the ladies. But he was always quiet, always polite. His German was flawless and his rent was paid on time every month.

"Always nice to keep the locals happy," the lieutenant says.

"And apparently the locals kept Mr. Sorensen quite amused, as well," Kreisler says. He is exploring the bureau drawers in one of the bedrooms and has discovered not only enough condoms to satisfy a horde but photos of Sorensen alone with women or with American buddies and more women. He shows them to Adams.

"Oh," the major says.

"A party animal. You recognize someone? Or were you commenting on the blonde's exposed bottom?"

Adams doesn't say. Whatever evidence is collected, he takes, hands off to the lieutenant, who files everything away in a briefcase. In the second bedroom, he finds the most incriminating evidence of all. Wads of cash, neatly bound, stashed in a suitcase under the bed. In a side table, unfinished, newly minted passports, just waiting for a photograph and the accompanying false identification information. Adams locates a ledger book with dates, dollar amounts tendered and code names presumably for clients he has helped in the past. Since the dead man in the morgue was likely his most recent client, Adams focuses on the most recent code name 'Copenhagen.'

"Well, one can't accuse Herr Sorensen of being cautious," Kreisler says. "Copenhagen. I wonder what that means."

"He likes cheese Danish."

Kreisler grunts, laughs. "I hardly think so." Then he points to something else in the ledger book. His finger traces a direct line across the page from the name, the cash received, in this case, a scrawled note 'jewelry, value?', to a number that has been partially erased but which, on very meticulous and close examination by Kreisler bent over the ledger with a magnifying glass, is still readable.

"What is this, do you think, Major? A number. A phone number. Is it possible? Perhaps we should call it."

"I don't think so."

"Yes, yes. Why not? What harm can it do?"

"Later."

"Well, there's a telephone right over here by the bed. Should you call or me?"

Kreisler holds up the receiver. He has a finger in the dial when Adams grabs the phone away.

"All right, I'll call." But Adams isn't happy about it. "Herr Kreisler, you are the ants at the picnic, the fly in the ointment. I don't understand why you persist over some low-level SS functionary. The real issue is corruption among my people. Mine. It's our business, not yours."

Even so, Adams dials and is a bit put out when someone actually answers the phone.

"Yes? Hello?"

The voice on the far end is male. This being Germany and the number being a local Nuremberg number, Adams had expected, if there was to be a reply at all, that the answer would be in German. It wasn't. It was in English. And when Adams asks the most logical question, "Who am I speaking to?", he gets an answer he isn't expecting at all.

"Captain David McAuliffe. Why? Who is this?"

Adams doesn't answer. He hangs up the phone. To the curious Kreisler, he says, "Don't even ask." To himself, he is thinking 'This can't be good.'

Chapter Eleven

May 1941

Hana steels herself. She must do it. She has no choice. Her survival depends upon it, physically and mentally. They all must do it. All of the country's children.

War these days is not like it was when their fathers fought the Great War. Then, the greatest battles, the most deaths, were confined between trenches. Now it is everywhere. It is inescapable. You can't go to the market or the cinema without seeing truckloads of prisoners, mostly Russians and Poles, being hauled like cattle to the market that is called Dachau and its dozens of subcamps. Every once in a while even your own neighbors are plucked off the streets and sent somewhere. The Jews, of course, have no chance. But the wrong word from anyone can send anyone else away.

Hana stays as much as possible on the Haefner estate. She confines herself when she can in two specific places: Haefner's library, which is extensive, quiet, and unused by anyone but herself and Herr Haefner. Gretchen makes an appearance every once in a while, but if Hana is there buried in reading, Haefner's spouse will only groan, loudly enough to be heard, then back out. Gretchen and Haefner have arguments about this regularly, the girl. But Gretchen never wins and Hana is left alone to concentrate on her studies.

The second place Hana migrates to is Haefner's laboratory that connects directly from the house. Her 'benefactor' has no need for this exceptional facility for he has access to the labs at the university in Munich where he teaches. But, clearly, he prefers the privacy of his own expensive layout. He did before Hana arrived on the scene. He seems to prefer it even more now that she has joined his household. After all, Hana is a brilliant young woman even if she can be contentious, moody, and sometimes downright 'unavailable.' She is now sixteen, too, and that has changed the family dynamics a bit, as well.

She is sitting in a chair at a desk in the library when Haefner comes in. It is late afternoon, but the descending sun still shines through the window behind the desk putting Hana right in its warm path. There is an open textbook in front of her, and she is scribbling notes in a notepad when Haefner clears his throat to alert her to his presence. He shuts the door behind him. He has just returned from university and he is holding mail in his hands.

"You've been writing Caspersson, I see," he says, glancing at one of the envelopes in his possession.

"You're reading my mail?"

"Of course. Not all of it, but when you correspond with a Swedish expert on DNA, I would like to be alerted. He doesn't respond to my inquiries, but to you, for some reason, he can't help himself."

"I send him pictures of my cat."

Hana has taken in a stray kitten she calls Siggy. The kitten is curled up on the window sill behind her. As Haefner closes in, she picks up the kitten and cuddles with her.

Haefner pulls up a chair and pretends to browse through the mail. "You're reading Astbury and Bell's X-ray study, I see. Have you gleaned anything from it?"

Hana shrugs. Siggy purrs.

"You've been with us almost two years, Hana," Haefner says with a sigh. He lets go of the mail and eyes her not in an unkind way but in a frustrated one. "You still don't trust me. You still avert your eyes and pick up cats and do whatever you must to pretend I'm somewhere else."

"I can't forgive what you've done."

"I understand. But haven't I been good to you? If Sigrid had not died then, she would be dead now. It was only a matter of time." Haefner tries a smile. He leans forward in the hopes that she will raise her eyes to his. She won't. "That is an argument we have had a thousand times, Hana, and I won't keep bringing it up. Now look, see, I bought you a present. I thought it might induce you to tolerate me a bit more."

"A present?"

"From one scholar to another. An electron microscope made by Siemens. The latest. It cost a fortune, but in my view, you deserve the best."

Haefner is pleased to see that he has finally forced a happy look from Hana.

"Can I see it? Where is it?" she asks.

"It will arrive in a day or two. We'll make space for it, I think, don't you?"

Hana is delighted. For a moment, she has been transported out of her lonely dark world and can almost see what her future may hold.

"I must tell Silke and Otto," she says. She puts Siggy back on her warm window sill seat. Her mind is reeling with possibilities. Haefner has no idea what she is planning. They have this game, these two. She keeps stringing him along with hopes of some scientific breakthrough. He keeps reminding her that she is lucky to be alive.

"It's the structure of the DNA molecule that holds the key to everything," Haefner says. "I don't know if your friends would appreciate that, much as I admire Otto's academic efforts and your blonde friend's loyalty. What does a nurse at Dachau need with an electron microscope? But you and I...that structure I keep seeing in your work. That spiral with a ladder-like structure. What are you thinking, Hana? Is that it? Is that your idea? Is that what our DNA looks like? How does it work? You know, don't you, or at least you think you do."

Hana won't admit that what she has believed for some time is likely fact. She can't prove it. The vision of a double helix came to her in such a bizarre and troubling way, her concept would be laughed at from university to university across the globe. A double helix, with attaching bonds, like a spiral staircase, only the steps in between aren't made of wood or marble, but by chemical proteins. How odd it is that she should have Uncle Walter to thank for this vision. He, the rapist, she, his victim, locked in a tortuous embrace that resembles a spiral, their warring arms the chemical bonds that break apart leaving two strands to separate and go their own way carrying their distinct, now, perhaps, mutated codes for replication elsewhere.

A crazy idea. The product of a fourteen-year-old girl's desperate mind. But one she not only intuitively believes in but one, she prays, will lead her to her father. Proving this, however, is a long way off. Unless...

"You have to keep Gretchen out of my way," Hana says. "She doesn't like me and never will. And I won't let her work with me."

"Don't worry about Gretchen. Gretchen will do whatever I tell her."

Haefner rises. He is beaming. He has taken an important step. He may be a man in his forties, but he is still young. Gretchen hasn't borne him a child, an heir. Two miscarriages is all she can show for their marriage. But Hana is young. In two years, three years, when the war is over, who can say what their relationship will be like? Her attitude will change toward him. He will see to that.

"Tomorrow I want to take you on a little trip, my dear," he says.

"A trip?"

"Not long."

"Where to?"

"That will be a surprise. Tonight, another surprise. We're having guests to dinner. Fellow scientists. It's time for you to enroll at the university. It's hard enough to get such men to listen to a woman let alone a girl who hasn't got a college degree. I'll cover the expenses, don't worry. So long as they know you're my protégé, you're all set."

* * *

Hana can't contain her excitement. But she is also nervous and calls Silke to invite her friend for dinner.

"I'm really tired tonight," Silke says over the phone. This is no excuse. She would normally be more than happy to dine at the Haefner's expense in their high-class digs. But after what she has experienced today...

104

Silke is eighteen now, in her Aryan prime. But she isn't an American teenager. She's a member of the Bund Deutsche Madel and this is wartime. She's beginning to regret now her ebullience at being photographed and made into a German cover girl at such an early age. A role model. A polestar for all German girls her age. She's beginning to regret that she has blonde hair and blue eyes and features the men apparently desire. She has had to fend off numerous requests, proposals of sexual intercourse for the Fatherland. Her parents don't appreciate the stress she feels under. Boyfriends she can handle. But when the SS comes along and asks why she hasn't fulfilled her Lebensborn duty, it is harder to say 'no.' Harder to look her mother and father in the eye. They love her, yes, but they're also afraid that too many 'nos' will get them all into trouble.

Besides, Silke has had to forego any dream she has of acting or singing. She has been volunteered for duty at Dachau. While the men are fighting on the front lines, it is up to the women to take over. She has refused to become a guard. She has witnessed some of the things these women do, worse even than the male guards. She comes home with mementos of the camp every night and can't speak of them in front of her parents. Nightmares have hounded her for six months now. They never go away. Sometimes she thinks about killing herself, but then she recalls how she saved Hana from being gassed and she realizes that suicide is a coward's way out.

Even so, this afternoon, when Hana invites her over for a dinner, which is no doubt a hundred times more filling and delicious than what her mother can afford to serve, she wants to beg off.

"Maybe Otto," she says. "Call him. He has no social life."

"I like him."

"I know you do."

"But he's not you. I love you so, Silke. I miss you so."

"I know."

"Herr Haefner is hitting on me again," Hana says. It is a different tact. A more desperate one. Will it work?

"He is? That pig. One slap will put him in his place."

"I'm afraid I can't hold him off forever. Then what will I do?"

Silke is caving. Hana can tell by the way her friend hesitates on the phone. "He wouldn't dare touch you. Would he? He's married."

"He's been married four times," Hana says. "The last one before Gretchen, Sigrid's mother, jumped from a window."

Over the telephone, Hana can hear Silke utter a weary sigh. "Rumors. Who told you that?"

"I just know. Can you come? Just for an hour. I won't keep you. I know you're tired."

More than tired. But is that supposed to be an excuse for a BDM girl? In her own house, Silke glances at a clock perched beneath a framed portrait of Hitler. "Oh, all right. What time?"

Silke can never refuse Hana. In the two years that they have known each other, their relationship has blossomed in many unexpected ways. Hana has learned how to shoot rabbits and squirrels. Silke has learned the difference between meiosis and mitosis in cell division. Hana has grown into a young woman. Silke hasn't failed to notice the intense looks she gets from her friend. Hana intentionally isolates herself from the world. Silke can't. But when they can, they spend alone time together, sometimes in the surrounding woods, picking flowers, other times, finding space anywhere they can to unload the burdens of the world upon each other.

"Any day they could come for me," Hana has told her. "Herr Haefner tells me all the time of Jewish teachers at his school who have been terminated and sent away. Jewish farmers. Jewish children. Maybe if we bleached my hair blonde like yours..."

"You'd look like a dandelion."

The notion was cause for much giggling. But they actually experimented with it, turning Hana into a full-fledged Aryan blonde. Herr Haefner was appalled. "Your appeal," he told Hana, "is your difference."

Gretchen threatened to shave her head bald. "Then you'll look Jewish, all right."

Silke wasn't thrilled by the change and, frankly, neither was Hana. "I don't look like my mother now," Hana said.

"How do you know? She died so long ago, when you were a kid. You have a picture of her?"

"No. Just a memory. But she used to wear wigs a lot, I think. For the stage, so I'm really not sure what she looked like. Except for her eyes. I'll never forget those."

It has crossed her mind on many occasions that, if she does indeed resemble her mother, then she herself is the only remaining photograph of Ursula Ziegler. As for her father, how else to find him? If they look at all alike, how will she know him unless she remains true to herself? So, she has no right to alter her appearance come what may.

Silke arrives at the Haefner estate dressed in her BDM uniform. Her mother had warned her, "Take no chances. If there are any SS men among them, they'll be pleased. If you go like you just climbed off a horse, they'll wonder why. The whole country knows about the Goebbels incident."

"Oh, the whole country. They can go rot," Silke had said, but she obeyed her mother.

She arrives early, accompanied by Gertrud, who is helping with the dinner preparations. Alfrieda, who is a distant cousin of Gertrud, greets them at the door to the kitchen.

"You look lovely," she says to Silke. "Hana invited you, I take it."

"Will Herr Haefner be mad?"

"Not him."

It is Frau Haefner Silke wants to avoid, but Gretchen has a nose for the competition and catches her sneaking up the staircase.

"Oh, it's just you," she says. "You smell of the camps. Couldn't you at least have bathed before you came?"

"I did, Frau Haefner. Some smells you just can't wash away. Sorry."

Silke smiles, makes a quick curtsey, then hurries down the long hallway to Hana's room. She doesn't even have to knock.

"You came!" As if she might not. Hana closes the door behind them. "I'm so happy." Then hugs her friend. Her embrace pulls Silke in so that Hana can rest her head against the taller girl's shoulder.

"Maybe you should back off a little. Frau Haefner says I smell like the camps." Sniffing her underarm, Silke checks herself then shrugs. "Do I? I did wash."

"You do a bit. I think. I've never been there. To me, you smell like Hollenschloss. I'm sorry to say, it's creepy." She lets Silke go but takes her by the hand and sits her down on her bed beside the kitten Siggy who is curled up at Hana's pillow.

"It's the infirmary," Silke says. "That's where I work. Oh, Hana, it's really awful there. It's full of sick people. People die there every day. They reach out to me. They call my name, but they speak in Russian or Polish and I don't understand them. You're just beginning to get close to them, then they die."

"I'm sorry you have to be there," Hana says.

"Then their bodies are carted off and burned in the crematoriums. It does smell. The wind carries the odor beyond the camps and you can't get it off you no matter how hard you scrub."

Silke didn't intend to share her feelings or cry, but she does. Hana is the one person she trusts with the scale and depth of her unhappiness.

"I hate it," she admits, "but if I ask for a transfer, I could end up on the Eastern front banging away at those dirty Ivans who really aren't so bad once you get to know them. I definitely wouldn't like that."

"Me neither. I want you here." Hana lifts Silke's hand and kisses it. Wrapping an arm about her friend's waist, she cuddles. "We have to figure something out. We have to get out of this somehow."

"How? What can we do? We're just two girls. The war could go on forever. Sometimes I don't think anyone will survive."

"We will. We have to," Hana says. She wants to comfort her friend, her savior. She wants to kiss her. Not on the hand, either. Instead, she whispers to Silke as if someone, Gretchen, can hear her through the closed door. "I might need your help tomorrow."

"Again? Tomorrow night? I'm so tired, Hana."

"No. Tomorrow during the day. You'll be in the infirmary, won't you?"

"Unfortunately."

"Herr Haefner thinks he is pulling a surprise on me, but I know he plans on taking me to Dachau."

"Dachau? Tomorrow? You?" Silke is shocked. "That's cruel. Why would he do such a thing? That's no place for you."

"No, no," Hana insists. "I want to go. My father. He might be there."

"And if he is? What do you expect to accomplish? How would you even know what he looks like?"

"He'd look like me."

Silke gapes, wide-eyed at her friend, clasps her by the shoulders as if to steady her. "No, no, no, you don't understand," she says, horrified at the thought of Hana entering the gates marked 'Arbeit macht frei', work makes you free. "You wouldn't recognize yourself if you stayed in that camp two weeks. They work people to death there. That's the whole point of the camps. Like Hollenschloss. To kill people. Why would Herr Haefner want to bring you there?"

"I think he's doing a study of some kind using the people there. The least I can do is look."

"No, no, you can't. And if you think I'm afraid to tell Herr Haefner this, you don't know me."

Hana tries to appease her friend, gripping her by the arms. "Listen to me, listen, Silke," she says. She is no longer whispering. Neither of them is. "I have a plan. Not just to find my father. To help us. But you will need to be as brave as I know you are."

"Bravery has nothing to do with it."

Silke stands, angry. She is shaking, she is so angry. Why do men think they can treat us this way, she steams? She heads for the door, unfazed by Hana's attempts at calming her. She doesn't get very far, though. As soon as she opens the bedroom door to the hallway, her path is blocked by someone who has either just arrived or who has been listening in. If it had been just Gretchen Haefner, Silke might have walked over her. But it isn't. It's a man. In a uniform. Of the SS. It is Uncle Walter.

* * *

"Well, well," he says. He is garbed in the military gray uniform of a civilian

SS functionary. It is not meant to be stylish. It is meant to be intimidating. "May I come in? You're surprised to see me, I can tell. In fact, I told Ernst this morning, 'Don't tell Hana. Let it be a surprise. I want to see her face when she sees her mother's brother. So?" Walter doffs his cap. "What do you think?"

Hana can't speak. She hasn't told Silke about what her uncle did to her. She hasn't told anyone, even her psychiatrist Herr Doctor Koerner, how often he would come to her bedroom and have his way with her. He didn't care how young she was. He didn't care if she cried out. He would put his hand over her mouth and just proceed. What lifelong trauma she may face, he couldn't care less. She was available. He was randy. She was a virgin. That made it all the more fun. But Silke doesn't have to be an astrologer or a Freudian analyst to see the fear in Hana's eyes and to grasp the probable source.

"You're her uncle?" Silke says. She stands between Hana and Ziegler.

"Indeed. Her mother's younger brother. She met an unfortunate end, Hana's mother. It made Hana very sick. May I sit?"

Without waiting for approval, Walter takes a seat on the bed and begins to pat Siggy. This so upsets Hana, that she grabs her kitten away and thrusts it outside her open window. "Why are you here, Walter?" she says.

"To congratulate you on your good fortune. Nothing more. Like Daniel, you've escaped the lion's den. You can imagine your grandfather's apoplexy when he found out, but we convinced him that all was for the best. You haven't been by in two years."

"I wonder why," Silke says. "Come on, Hana, I think it's time for supper. Are you staying…?"

"SS-*Hauptscharfuhrer* Ziegler. I wasn't planning to, but now, with Graf von Haefner's permission, I think I might. I've been completely busy. The Fatherland calls, you understand. How can we reminisce in such a short time?"

Silke has to pull Hana out of the bedroom. Hana is dressed in a pricy blue outfit meant to show off her slender physique, but she is so hunched over with dread, Silke thinks she might just slide right out of it. Walter walks behind, cap in hand, eyes not on Hana but on her friend.

The evening, of course, is ruined. Haefner has invited several colleagues from the biology department of the university with their wives. He has bragged to them about his prodigy to the extent that they are prepared to meet Darwin or, at the very least, Einstein. Instead, they are confronted by a girl-child who can barely speak, who on occasion sounds like she is muttering some sort of incantation to herself, and who never lifts her eyes from her dinner plate let alone eats off it.

Gretchen tells the guests, "Such a disappointment. Who can understand children these days? She is not ours, you know. A *Juden*. They say her father was a *Juden*."

"Stop it, Gretchen," Haefner warns. "She's anxious, that's all. High strung. She's been anxious all day."

Of all people, it is Walter who saves the day. Before Silke can stop him, he scoops Hana up in his arms right at the dinner table and carries her upstairs. "My half-sister, she's no Jew, I can assure you. Just a little touched in the head. You know what they say about genius. Half brilliant, half mad. Tonight, you saw the latter half." He laughs her illness off as he laughs off most unpleasant things.

Hana has passed out. She is unconscious in her uncle's arms, head drooping, flaccid limbs bobbing up and down with each step Walter takes upstairs. Silke is right behind him. Instinct tells her not to leave him alone with Hana for even one second.

"You don't need to follow," he says sounding somewhat irritated. "She has a pet cat, not a cocker spaniel."

"I'll stay with her after you've left," Silke says. "It wouldn't be appropriate for an SS officer such as yourself to be left alone with a minor. You know how people talk."

"I do."

Walter's face gives away nothing. He is still a young man, not even thirty yet, making his way up the party echelons, growing in importance. But he is wise enough to know that other young SS men are trying to do the same. One slip-up, one false accusation, and down he would go to the bottom rungs. And this girl Silke Hartenstein, oh, he knows of her. Not only has he seen her magazine clippings, he's been aware of her for quite some time. Her tag is 'troublemaker', 'spoiled', 'just asking for it.' Which brings a broad smile to his face.

He deposits Hana on her bed, even pulls up the covers. But he doesn't leave. He closes the door behind Silke.

"And now," he says, "here is the deal."

"You're leaving."

"No. No, I am not. Not, at least, without an agreement in place."

He leans against the door, nonchalant, playing with his cap. Hana doesn't move under her blanket. She could be dead for all Walter cares. But Silke, she's another thing. Beautiful in a way that is Germany. All of it. Eighteen and brimming with vitality, strength, ambition. She is German womanhood. She is the future, she is what Hitler and Goebbels rave about, and to have her would be to have all of them, to lord it over all of them.

"You and I," he tells Silke, "are going to have a child. Maybe more than one. We'll see how things go."

Silke can't speak, she is so appalled.

"The Lebensborn Program in Bavaria has been turned over to me. We have a file on every girl who's a member of the BDM. And you are well aware, I know, of what your duty is. You don't have to love me. You don't have to have any feelings for me at all, although that would be a benefit in raising our son or daughter. You can hate me. It doesn't matter. You will have my child."

"I will kill myself first."

"No, you won't." Walter leaves his place by the door and comes to stand over Hana. "You'll do it for her if not for yourself. You see, I know everything about you. You might be lesbians, I don't care. My sister, you see, is half *Juden*."

"You don't know that."

Walter places his cap back on his head. He is nearly done. "It doesn't matter what I know or don't know. If I say she's an orangutan, she is. You know what will happen to her if she ends up at Dachau on the wrong side of the fence."

Silke says nothing. She does know.

"I will make the arrangements," Walter says. "I won't be a beast. I won't rape you. But when I tell you to come to me, you will. And you will give yourself to me freely as a loyal German woman. You will have my child, and you will raise it properly. Do we have an agreement on this, Fraulein?"

Silke lowers her head, sinks onto the bed at Hana's feet.

"Good." Walter is satisfied. He will give her a day or two. He might even shop and buy her something nice to wear, take her to see a film or to a nice restaurant. He would like her to be as cooperative as possible. After all, to be linked to this German teenage icon would be quite a coup. Who knows? Maybe he would be able to laugh in Goebbels' face one day.

With a bow and a polite good evening, Walter closes the door behind him.

Chapter Twelve

May 1941

How to describe Dachau? There are several ways. If you are a German citizen living within a twenty-square- kilometer range of the main camp or one of its many sub-camps, you would be forgiven if all you think of it is as a busy beehive. Vehicles are constantly coming and going. Trucks, vans, cars. Trains pull up day and night. If you live too close to the camp, you may be awakened by the engineer's blaring alert. Very unsettling.

There are many local citizens who work at the camps. As secretaries, cooks, nurses, electricians, and plumbers. They see things. They report back to their families. But to them, it isn't so bad. They aren't witness to the worst of it. Or, if they are, they won't talk. The one thing that is commonly known about the camps is the smell. Smoke from the crematoriums. The wind picks it up and circulates it across the neighboring countryside. What is it? Don't ask.

For the Germans who work and reside at the camps, Dachau is a logically organized business facility, albeit one that is also a prison surrounded by an electrified barbed-wire fence. It has been in operation since Hitler's rise to prominence. At first, it housed only political inmates. Then homosexuals, Jehovah's Witnesses, and other racially problematic individuals. Now, with the war in full swing, Polish and Russian prisoners of war are filling the camp, along with other inmates from Eastern Europe necessitating an expansion.

The entire site encompasses about twenty-five acres, most of which is taken up by administrative buildings, factories, an SS training center, and barracks for the soldiers who guard the prisoners. There are approximately thirteen thousand of those.

The prisoners themselves have a different perspective of the camp, as, naturally, they would. Those who are physically able, serve as forced labor at the munitions factory and to work on construction projects meant to increase the capacity of the camp. Most of the prisoners at the main camp are men, but there are women and children, too. Food is minimal. Nutrition unimportant. Health not a concern. The conditions are crowded, filthy, meant to promote disease, starvation, and death. If the workforce is thereby reduced each day, what of it? New trainloads of prisoners come in daily to replace the dead and dying.

On their trip to Dachau the next morning, Haefner is edgy. He has had little time to deal with Hana's issues but he isn't going to leave her at the house. Work must go on. Her brilliance must be allowed to shine through everything.

Sitting in the back seat of his car beside him, she is quiet, hardly speaks, but that is hardly surprising or unusual. Yet Haefner senses something different in his ward, a hardness that has somehow settled in. Her back is straight. She has a notebook on her lap, but she isn't writing in it. Her hands are folded over it. Only her head moves, her eyes taking in everything outside the moving car, like a landscape painter studying her intended subject before setting brush to paper.

"I appreciate your driving us, Otto," he says. "I don't think I would have been able to today."

"My pleasure, sir," says Otto from behind the steering wheel. His eyes flick off Haefner to Hana. "Anything to get out of classes."

"Don't tell your old man that." Haefner chuckles. He thinks he is a very modern parent with a liberal attitude towards the younger generation. Then he eyes Hana, and he's not so sure.

"War changes the world in ways most people don't appreciate," he says, trying to make conversation that will interest her. "It jumpstarts economies and puts pressure on science to experiment. What was a useful weapon in war a generation ago is today of no use. I remember when our pilots flew in machines little better than bicycles with wings. Now look. We can wake up, fly across the English Channel, bomb London and get home in time to scrape off the last of the shaving cream."

"Perhaps someday we'll be able to do that without war, Herr Haefner."

"I hope so, Otto. I hope so."

Haefner gazes at the stoic girl beside him. Still as a sulking child. Silent as a spoiled one. But she has changed in these two years since he saved her life. For much of the first year in his home, Hana kept to her bedroom or the lab, demanding privacy.

Gretchen complained, "What's the point? She stays in her room all day doing nothing but reading textbooks. No one I know does that. None of our colleagues. No one at the university. No one in the world. Einstein doesn't do that."

Haefner's wheelchair-bound father August, whether he knew it or not, was more succinct. "You picked a real winner this time, Ernst."

Yet beauty did find its way through the madness and despair. Hana doesn't know it. She doesn't realize she's become a woman. The fact that she reads so much research material and mathematical data, that she gulps down such quantities of scientific information, only makes her more enticing to Haefner. He can't keep his heart from racing every time he sees her. Who would have thought?

"Someday the progress we make in flight now will take us to the moon, eh, Hana?" he says. "For us, you and I, the future lies within. Not out there among the stars but within our own selves. Medical breakthroughs achieved as we try to succor our wounded soldiers. It is the age of Freud, psychoanalysis. Soldiers come home from war as mentally crippled as much as they do physically. Such an age discovers mental illnesses that didn't exist even five years ago. Those illnesses will require medication, which is what my company is working on, why we are heading to Dachau. For cures."

The mention of the prison camp's name is what finally draws Hana out of her reverie. She actually shifts her attention in his direction.

"Is that really why?" she asks.

"Yes, of course. That, and your own work in genetics. Everything in science goes hand in glove. How much of these illnesses I speak of are the result of things we experience in the world around us, such as war? And how much has been planted within us from birth? Genetics. Your field."

"Mine?"

"You have a gift, my dear. Forgive me if I tell you I occasionally take a peek at the work you are doing, the books you are reading."

"My mail."

"I only regret that you won't open up more to me. The people at Dachau, the prisoners, they'll be your sample grouping, your test cases. Russians, Poles, peasants, I give them to you as a gift. To poke, prod, collect whatever samples you need. The commandant of the camp has assured me that you can come and go as you please. Nothing will be off-limits. The only proviso is: you will share all of your data with me."

"You know, Herr Haefner," Otto says from the front seat, "you're talking to a sixteen-year-old girl. Wouldn't she be better off at university?"

"Like you, Otto? I'll send her, you can be sure."

Haefner doesn't appreciate the interference. Reinhardt's son will make a poor attorney if he doesn't learn to kowtow to his clients.

"You don't know Hana the way I do," he claims. "Some people with extraordinary intellects are better off outside of the strictures of academia. They flourish when left to their own wiles, when free to follow their hearts and minds wherever they lead. Hana is such a unique intellect. It is my duty, no, my honor, to give her this freedom."

Hana has been listening to all this attentively without the slightest hint of what she is thinking. She may appear stoic or resigned, but this isn't the case. Her future is unfixed, uncertain. She has ideas, hopes that she clings to. Nothing else. Haefner doesn't know that in the depths of her fear, curled up on her bed beside Silke the night before, she swore she would change.

"I won't let him do that to me again," she promised. "I'm going to be tough, like you."

"I'm not so tough."

"You are. And brave. We were going to be the Three Musketeers, you, me, and Sigrid. Now maybe it will be you, me and my friend Peggy. Somehow."

Somehow. But Hana, steeling herself to be brave, runs many risks. Who in this terrible world of war and sterilization and euthanasia can she trust? Silke only. And maybe Otto. She sees him eying her through the rearview mirror and she lets her gaze stay on his as some sort of mutual understanding not meant for Haefner's recognition. She is thinking. She is planning. She is wondering, too, if the answers lie, in of all places, Dachau.

* * *

Dachau, from Hana's perspective, is a forbidding, gloomy, dispiriting place. If Pablo Picasso were to portray the camp in one of his surrealist paintings, there would be no humans in it, nothing alive, only wire and brick, guard towers, and trucks. Here, there are only two ways of getting from one place to another on foot, marching or trudging. Dragging or limping only leads to getting shot.

Hana senses this even before the SS guards let Otto drive beneath the gate with the words '*Arbeit macht frei.*' It is as if the prisoners within, as yet unseen, are calling to her. Whether or not she is part Jewish, she doesn't know. But the instant she enters Dachau, she feels she might as well be. *L'chaim?* Not here.

Otto opens the door for her outside the infirmary. He has to hold on to his hat to keep the wind from blowing it away. The building is a lengthy single-story white structure, very plain, fronted by a spacious parking area.

"Don't do this," he whispers to Hana before Haefner can intercept and abduct her. "It will kill you."

Hana doesn't have time to respond, Haefner is so nimble around the car. He grabs her by the arm in a brusque, excited manner, causing her to nearly drop her notebook, which she needs as a sort of shield in her arms.

"Ignore the smells," Haefner tells her. "You'll get used to them. Your friend works here."

"In here?"

"Yes. That should help accustom you to everything. I can even insist that she be assigned to help you if that will make things easier."

"I think I will need samples."

"Good. Good. Fine. I'm not so good with blood myself."

"Not blood. I don't like needles."

Acclimating will not be easy. The moment Hana steps through the door into the infirmary, she begins to shiver. Goosebumps spread across her arms, and her face goes pale. Otto notices and hauls her back outside where, at least, the spring wind is warm.

"I told you," he says. "You almost fainted."

"What's the matter?" Haefner hurries out, giving Otto a sharp look. Is the young man trying to upstage him? Undermine him?

"Couldn't you see?" Otto tells him. "This is too much for her. She looks a wreck."

Hana trembles but is able to raise a reassuring hand. "No, it's all right, Otto. Thank you. I need to try this."

"Are you sure?"

"That is none of your concern."

Haefner again takes Hana's arm and escorts her through the door into the infirmary. In the lobby, they are greeted by a nurse and a doctor. Haefner introduces the doctor, a seventy-year-old man with glasses and a beard. "Herr Doctor Schilling," Haefner says. "Doing work on, pardon me, Doctor Schilling…"

"Malaria." Schilling smiles and offers his hand for Hana to shake. In December of 1946, he will be executed for his experiments, but for now, he is more than willing to help Hana in any way he can with her own studies.

She is thoroughly embarrassed. She recognizes him as one of Haefner's colleagues who had been a spectator to her behavior at dinner the night before.

"I want to apologize, Herr Doctor."

"No, no, no."

"About last night."

"No. Absolutely not. We all have our moments. Herr Professor Haefner gives you quite the recommendation, and why should any of us dispute it? You will brighten an otherwise very dingy place."

"Thank you. Maybe." Hana now turns her attention to the nurse who is much younger than Schilling, perhaps a BDM girl like Silke. She is disappointed it is not Silke. She takes Otto's hand. "Can we take a brief look around, do you mind, Otto?"

"I think you should make it quick for your first day," he says. "Wouldn't want you to get malaria or something."

"Believe me," says Haefner, "she won't."

The facility is crowded with cots lining either side down an aisle that stretches for forty meters. There isn't an empty cot. They are all filled with men, each contributing their own bodily odors to the general stench of the place. Some of the men eye her dully as she passes. Others are so ill, they see nothing. None of them speak. Some of them moan. None of the staff seems too perturbed. They have all grown used to the conditions of their patients and their workspace.

Schilling lectures as they continue the tour. "Reichsfuhrer Himmler has wisely given his permission for us, the medical staffstaffs here and at the other camps, to perform studies on the prisoners. You shouldn't feel bad for them. Many of them are common criminals who would have been executed by now if they hadn't volunteered to help the Fatherland. Other prisoners are allowed special privileges by volunteering. People get sick, yes, but no one dies. They are well taken care of by our staff which includes, as I understand it, a friend of yours."

"Yes. Silke. Is she here? I would like to see her."

"Of course, my dear." Haefner takes no issue with Hana's relationship to Silke, who is only the daughter of one of his cooks and his groundskeeper. It is Otto whose persistent claim to Hana annoys him.

Silke appears moments later carrying a tray of empty vials and used syringes. Her uniform is that of the *Deutsche Rote Kreuz*, a white smock over a blue gown with a distinct red cross on her cap. At first, she pretends not to see either Hana or Otto, giving the two men a polite curtsey, before giving a wink Hana's way.

"You came?"

"I did." Hana looks around. "So, this is where you work."

"My posting for Germany."

"Because you laughed at Goebbels," grunts Haefner. "Next time, keep it to a smile. You might find yourself a cushier position." He allows the reunion to end at this point, stating that, "Nurse Hartenstein has to go back to her responsibilities."

Then it's a quick tour of the other facilities, the labs, the laundry, and dining halls where the healthy patients get to take their meals. The medical personnel and officers of Dachau eat in their own more elegant quarters. Haefner was hesitant to schedule another introductory dinner in the fear of setting off another round of uncontrollable emotion. But Hana reassures him that she is ready this morning.

"I won't embarrass you," she says.

"I'm most certain," Haefner replies, "you won't."

Chapter Thirteen

May 1947

'The Future is Now, Charles McAuliffe for Congress in '48'

There are enough signs for Charlie's run for Maine's First Congressional District that it appears to his mother Elizabeth 'Liz' McAuliffe that a new and alien life form has sprung up all along Cumberland and York County roads. What if the election isn't for another year? The campaign begins now. Not for Congress. For the presidency. Her neighbors' yards all carry a sign indicating their loyalty. Next year, the *Portland Press Herald*, notoriously Republican in orientation, will endorse Charlie. Rural and small-town Maine may vote Republican, but the people around the state's largest city Portland and around its capital Augusta are more cosmopolitan, more liberal. They'll go for Charlie big time. Especially the way the McAuliffe's dole out their own money. Who's his competition? A washed-up, out-of-touch hick from Dexter.

Liz loves all the foofaraw. Politics runs in her side of the family, too. Her family is from Boston. Irish Duffys from Donegal, they've been connected to Boston politics for a good century. Her father, who made his fortune on the Atlantic, at first disapproved of a marriage that would take his eldest daughter to backwoods Maine. But love conquered. Harold McAuliffe was a Boston College man, after all, just as Irish as the Duffys. And he had an eye on Washington just as Leonard Duffy did.

As Memorial Day approaches, the unofficial start of summer, the McAuliffes and the Duffys have a huge lobster bake fundraiser planned at their estate in Cape Elizabeth. While the mighty Atlantic pounds away on the rugged, rocky Maine coast, Harold McAuliffe intends to pound the last hammer in the coffin of the man from Dexter.

Then the mail is delivered.

Normally, the McAuliffe's youngest daughter, ten-year-old Lydia fetches the mail running the quarter-mile to the mailbox with their Golden Retriever Milt. But Lydia is at an overnight at a friend's house. This left it to Liz to saunter down the tree-lined private lane in her deck shoes. In the past, she might have sent one of her staff to sift through the mail, but she doesn't want to take the chance that her secretary or photographer is actually working for the Republican. She will sort through it herself first, protective mother that she is.

The flag on the box is down. The mailman has come and gone, and the mailbox is full. The McAuliffes try diverting business mail to the campaign headquarters address on Congress Street in Portland. But fans and well-wishers rank in the thousands, so it can't be helped. Standing at the mailbox, a pleasant ocean breeze rustling her silk kerchief, she lifts her sunglasses to the top of her head and sorts the mail into categories.

"Business. Bill. Personal for Harry. Postcard. Bill. Bill. Personal for Lydia. Misdirected campaign check. Personal..."

She stops when she sees a letter addressed to Charlie. Though he gets bushels of letters, most good, some that go directly to the shredder, this one is stamped from an address in Germany. David is still in the army, still posted somewhere in the vicinity of Nuremberg. Liz is quite proud of him because he is attached to the legal team prosecuting Nazi functionaries who have until recently eluded retribution. But the envelope is not in David's cryptic handwriting. The letters are small, printed rather than in cursive, neat, forming an almost perfect square. Obviously female. This automatically pricks a nerve. Liz can't help herself. She tears the envelope open with a fingernail. Then she reads. The letter is not in German but in rather excellent English.

"Hana Ziegler," she says. "Ziegler."

The solid granite of Maine beneath her feet almost gives way. She has to grab onto the mailbox to keep from losing her balance. Her heart rate accelerates and her thought processes can't keep up.

'Not again,' she fumes. 'Not again. Isn't there one man on this planet capable of keeping it in their pants?'

Once the shock goes away, the anger sets in. But she dares not let it overwhelm her. Her first inclination is to lash out. But what good is revenge when the backlash will be far worse? She must deal with this in a mature way. Or, rather, Harold must. If he wants to stay married. If he wants his darling son to be president of the United States.

It takes every ounce of will she possesses to refrain from saying a word to anyone. While she apportions the rest of the mail appropriately in the house, she retains the Hana Ziegler letter in a pocket of her blouse. Through all of the afternoon's activities, through a lovely boisterous family dinner and a volleyball game in the evening, she behaves like the mother of the next congressman from the First District. She would have passed any lie detector test. The FBI could have grilled her all night, and still, she would have shown everyone the face of a queen.

It is when she is alone that night in the bedroom she shares with her husband that her rage finally spills out.

"Read it!" she demands, thrusting the letter from Germany into his grasp.

"What is it?"

"Read it!"

"You're angry?"

"For Christ's sake, Harry, read the damned thing!"

Harold is reluctant to. He has seen his wife acting this way only once before. In Copenhagen. And that almost cost him his ambassadorship.

"I'm sure you're overreacting," he says and takes his time turning on a standing lamp and sitting in a chair, and casually unfolding the letter. "Hana Ziegler," he says, adjusting his glasses. "Sounds familiar."

"Fuck you, Harry! Read. Then first thing tomorrow morning, you and Charlie are driving to Logan Airport and taking the first flight to Berlin.

That is the only acceptable resolution, or do you want me to bring up Copenhagen?"

Harold blanches. "I'd rather you didn't. We produced Lydia on that assignment if you recall. It's not as if you've been Joan of Arc."

"Again, fuck you. Read."

Harold does, and what he reads has a similar effect upon him as it did on Liz at the mailbox. He is stunned at first, then furious, crumpling the letter and hurling it against a window.

"That idiot!" he shouts.

"Be careful, Harold. He's your son. The acorn not only fell from the same tree, it sprouted a dick just like yours."

"Must you be obscene about it, Liz? He's your son, too."

Harold grips the arms of his chair as if unable to decide whether to rise and give vent to his fury or to sit back down and surrender to adversity. "Perhaps money," he says.

"She's not asking for any."

"Money always works. The Germans are so fucking poor, of course they want money. How much is the issue. I'll contact her. I'll negotiate."

"Now who's the idiot?" Liz retrieves the letter from the floor, opens it, and gives it a more careful review. "There's a baby involved," she says.

"Which is why I said 'money.' We'll pay for the kid to go to college. In America, if that's what they want. That'll keep them quiet."

"No, it won't. Don't you remember this girl, this Hana from Copenhagen?"

Harold has to think back. It's been over a decade. Friedrich Ziegler's kid? No, grandkid.

"She was a little whacky, wasn't she? Hung around with Peggy. Two peas in a pod."

"Well, that may have been the case then. But this one doesn't appear to have had a lobotomy."

Liz is beginning to come to a boil like the lobsters they both love so much. Her face is appropriately shaded and her claws are definitely out. But Harold has no defense for this. Peggy is a mess of his own making, one Liz will never let him live down.

"It was for her own good," he says helplessly. "You know that. We've been over that a thousand times."

"Without an apology ever coming from your lips," Liz shouts. "You never told me. You did it behind my back."

"Can you lower your voice, please?" Harold says. "Yes, I did it behind your back. I did it so it wouldn't get out in the papers that one of my children, Charlie's twin sister, for God's sake, is mentally ill. Do you think for a minute that the press would let that story go? You think the public, the voters, wouldn't wonder, 'Gee, if she's a whack-job, maybe the brother is, too.' Genes. Genetics, it's all the rage these days. And you could kiss Washington goodbye, Liz, if that ever happened. Or if it happens now. This thing must be quashed. I agree with you there. Why couldn't he have just stayed in his barracks? Played cards with the boys. He didn't have to fuck the German bitch."

"Thousands of German bitches were fucked after the war. Boys being boys, you said. Well, now the chicken has come home to roost. With an egg in its basket."

"Yes. Well." Harold finally rises out of his chair with a long sigh of frustration. "I will go. Tomorrow, as you say. We'll tell the campaign, the press, that I am simply visiting David, watching him at trial in Nuremberg. They'll buy that. 'Congressional dad visits rising star attorney'. But Charlie stays here. He's got to keep campaigning. Foot to the floor. I don't even want him knowing about the letter."

"And his baby?"

"Rest assured," Harold says, stiffening his resolve, "that will be dealt with. David, I can rely on. One way or another, this dies fast."

Chapter Fourteen

Summary 1941

War never occurs by consensus. It is brought about by those few who will benefit from it. For financial profit. Acquisition of territory. Power. Religious fanaticism. Everyone else is dragged into the misery by being convinced that war is the only way to go. Brilliant propagandists like Adolf Hitler and Josef Goebbels can rouse a mob into doing their bidding with gigantic promises and glorified visions of the future. They succeed in getting their desires fulfilled by vainglorious boasting and by pointing the finger at the enemies of the Reich who are really to blame for the vile conditions that can only be ameliorated through the mass loss of life.

For the vast numbers of people, who would just as soon get up in the morning, have breakfast, earn a good day's wage, come home to the missus and the kids, and go to sleep in a comfortable bed in a warm house, the firm ground that they have taken for granted all their lives is suddenly gone. Even a difficult life, if it is at least consistently difficult, can become routine, something to depend upon. With war, no one can wake up in the morning and know with absolute certainty what their lives will be like that night before they go to bed.

Silke feels this way. She feels that her entire life has been stolen from her. It may come back. It may return, the horseback riding, the treks into the woods, the singing, and laughing. Then again, it might not. As a nurse, she finds herself crying over German boys who die in her care fighting for the Fatherland. Yet, she despises the Fatherland and wants it to lose the war. Fast. Her life at eighteen has become nothing more than obeying the will of doctors who decide who lives and who dies. And now, they are performing experiments on prisoners. Gruesome experiments that she has no choice but to be complicit in.

They're volunteers, she is told. They're criminals, murderers, she is told. This one raped a child. That one murdered his family. The rest are just Russians, and God knows what they've done. And now, they've dragged Hana into their world. Clinical research. Industrial testing. Data collection. All with an eye to that glorious future, which will look like, what?

Silke waits for Hana outside the infirmary on days when Hana is brought to Dachau with or sometimes without Ernst Haefner. Time and duties permitting, they eat lunch together outside in the parking area. Silke doesn't like eating with the doctors or other nurses. They talk business. They recite injuries and death in statistical terms. Everyone is very serious about the research they do.

"You're getting used to Dachau," Silke says to Hana one afternoon. They sit beneath the shade of a tree beside a parked car, as the day is hot and the breeze minimal. Hana brought lunch from home, pea soup in a Thermos, and bread with butter. Silke has grabbed a tray from the canteen. Soup and crackers with mixed vegetables.

Hana says, "They pretty much leave me alone to do what I need to do."

"Does it bother you?"

"Being here?"

"I'm beginning to wish I had given Herr Goebbels a blow job."

Hana spits out her pea soup on her lap, bursting out in giggles, then blushes. "A blow job?"

"You know what that is, don't you?"

Hana's embarrassed silence gives her away.

"Oh, Hana. Really? You're too nice. If you don't know, I'm not going to be the one to tell you. Not here anyway. I don't see how you can stand this place. There are Jews here, you know. New arrivals."

Hana sets her soup aside, avoids her friend's direct stare. "Does it matter if they're Jews?" she says.

"Doesn't it?"

"I don't know. Yes, I suppose it does."

"You know it does. You're still looking for your father, aren't you? I don't know how you can do it. From what I've heard, there aren't any Jews left in Germany except in the camps. There are children here, too."

"Children?"

Silke sets her tray aside, wipes her mouth clean. She has upset Hana. "You didn't know? You eat with the doctors. Schilling, Rascher, Brachti. This new doctor, Mengele, he's looking specifically for twins. He and Herr Haefner's frau."

"Twins? I wasn't told." As warm as it is in the shade of the tree, Hana begins to shiver. "Gretchen?" she says. She still wakes up at night crying for Sigrid. "Of course, anything's possible with her. We never speak."

"I just found out myself. Mengele's doing his experiments in secret at one of the sub-camps. I only found out because my friend Dora works with him. I don't ask what he does with them. She doesn't tell me."

"I can find out," Hana says. "Children."

"You're just a kid yourself, honey," Silke says. "Be careful. These doctors don't know you might be part..."

"Jew?"

Silke has noticed a change in her friend. Sometimes she forgets that Hana is only sixteen because around the scientist doctors, she is in her milieu. Hana can talk to them on their academic level. It can be worrisome to Silke, especially when she has been assigned to work with Hana who will walk among the patients as if she is a full-fledged doctor herself taking a variety of bodily samples and meticulously jotting down all the information. In the time since she has begun working at Dachau under Haefner's aegis, Hana has come to know most of the patients by name, age, place of birth, height and weight, race. If Silke throws out a name, Hana can spew all of that patient's relevant information. The patients themselves have come to be amused by the young girl barely five feet tall, swabbing their mouths and clipping their fingernails. 'Little Daughter' some of them call her. But they don't know why she is doing what she does and neither does Silke. Cataloguing. Always cataloguing. That's Hana.

In the evening, if they are both leaving work at the same time, Haefner will pick them up and drive them home or have them picked up. Silke's father Vitor often volunteers for this chore. Tonight, another car rolls into the lot while they are awaiting Haefner or Vitor. The rear window rolls down, an arm sticks out, and a finger suggests that the girls should approach. Neither moves. SS flags fly from the hood.

"Come. Come. You. Yes, that's right, you."

Hauptscharfuhrer Walter Ziegler leans out the window. His black hair is slicked back. He is wearing his SS uniform.

"The little Jewess can stay," he says. "Don't be shy, Hartenstein. You must be tired after such a long day. Let me treat you to dinner. I've selected a very fancy restaurant in Munich."

Silke's shoulder's sag. Fatigue has nothing to do with it. Hana whispers, "Why are you going with him? Don't go."

"I promised I would."

"What promise?"

"One I should have made to Goebbels."

It suddenly dawns on Hana just exactly what Silke's promise entails. She grabs Silke by the arm. "It isn't funny. He raped me, Silke. Don't go!"

"But…"

"He's a monster. There's nothing he can tell you that should make you think otherwise."

"Schnell. Schnell, I'm growing impatient," Walter calls.

"What did he say to you? What is making you do this?" Hana practically shrieks.

"Nothing. Duty. The Lebensborn Program. Don't worry, Hana. Calm down. I can take care of myself."

Hana doesn't believe her. "What did he threaten you with? Tell me, Silke. I won't let him hurt you. I'll kill him if he does."

"Hartenstein!"

Silke puts on a smile, her best, and kisses Hana on the cheek. "You continue to underestimate me, Little Daughter. What's the worst that can happen? You become my baby's godmother."

Walter is just getting out of the car to get her when Silke hurries in his direction. She gives him an impish smile, which he likes, and, being a gentleman, he allows her into the back seat first before telling his driver to go. For Hana, he gives one last look back.

"Don't worry, my dear. She's in good hands."

* * *

Walter is as good as his word. Money is not an issue. He has booked a suite at the Kempinski Hotel and purchased a sexy expensive wardrobe for Silke to wear. The latest from France, he claims.

She bathes in the privacy of their hotel suite removing the Dachau grime. Alone, she prepares herself for what she is about to undertake. Her mother has always said that Silke has a mind of her own. But tonight, that mind is confused. She cries softly, not for herself so much as for the child she is going to provide, if not to Walter then to the Fatherland. Will she keep it? Does she even have any idea of what it takes to be a child's mother? Or will she consign it to the Reich to be adopted by a family better suited to raise it? Will it be happy? For the love of God, Hana's uncle, her rapist, couldn't possibly want to raise it, could he? Marry her? Could it possibly be happy in a world like that?

"How are you doing?" Walter calls from beyond the bathroom door. "You haven't drowned yourself, have you? I've paid a lot of money for this room."

"I'm just shampooing my hair."

"Good. Good. Lavender, I hope. I love the smell of lavender in a woman's hair."

"If that's what you like."

For dinner in the hotel, he orders meat for both of them. Big portions. Due to food shortages and rationing, Silke hasn't had protein of this magnitude in years. She defers on the wine, but willingly orders dessert. She's always had a weakness for ice cream with cold chocolate syrup and strawberries.

"Is it true what Hana says?" she comes out at one point, an unexpected question delivered with ravishing innocence while licking syrup off her spoon.

"About what?'

"What do you think?"

"I would consider anything to do with my sister's child an inappropriate topic of conversation. We are having such an exemplary time."

The restaurant has a dimly lit romantic ambiance, and Walter decked out in his gray SS uniform, is actually a companionable handsome partner.

"You know what she claims."

"I can well imagine," Walter says. "Your friend, my niece, has never been right in the head, sorry to say. Like my own sister."

The thought crosses Silke's mind to ask him if he raped her, Hana's mother, too. She resists the temptation. "What was she like?"

"Who? Hana?"

"Your sister. Ursula."

"A tart. A flirt. A whore. Roll all that up into one dame and you have my sister, the actress. She should never have kept Hana. Hana was nothing but a prop. For that, I feel sorry for her. But you mustn't. You have your whole life ahead of you. The Fatherland's golden girl."

Silke snorts. Ice cream sprays from her nose. Walter chuckles. He finds himself liking this girl more than he expected to. Silke is not oblivious.

"What about her father?"

"Why do you care?"

She prods. "Did you ever meet him?"

"I met many 'hims.' Which one was Hana's father? Who knows? Who cares?"

Walter offers his cloth napkin to wipe off Silke's chocolate-smeared face. Silke glimpses herself in a small hand-held mirror, puckers, and before she knows it, Walter has moved his chair to sit beside her and wrap an arm about her waist.

"It's time to go," he says.

"I'm not finished eating."

"You licked your plate clean."

"I thought we had theatre tickets."

"Forget them. We'll go another time."

He practically hauls her up out of her chair and, with a pleasant nod to the maître d', escorts her to the lobby and the bank of elevators.

"You are incredibly beautiful," he whispers in her ear. She smells the wine on his breath.

"Her father, though. You insist he was a Jew. Why? This belief is driving her mad."

"And you are driving me mad with this annoying habit of talking about Hana."

The elevator doors open. Walter bows to a higher-ranking SS official out with his matronly wife. Once the doors have shut again, leaving him alone with Silke, he says, "If I tell you what I know, will you leave it there? The man is dead anyway."

"How do you know?"

"He's a Jew. They're all dead, or will be soon enough."

The elevator climbs to the fourth floor. Walter is impatient. The doors open on another couple just heading out for a night on the town. The man nods at Walter. The woman eyes Silke with distaste. At their suite, Walter unlocks the door and opens it for Silke, but she strategically hesitates to enter.

"All right. All right," he says. "I have my suspicions. I confronted one of her lovers once in Berlin. Don't ask me how I knew he was a Jew. Some things are obvious. It's the way they wear their clothes, the way they cut their hair, the way they talk. You can tell Hana, if it pleases you so much, that the man she is looking for will have a scar on his cheek where I took a knife to it."

After that, there is no escaping the SS Lebensborn official. Walter takes her to bed. He is surprised to discover she is a virgin. Silke takes it all in stride, wondering, as he is panting above her, if this one time will make her pregnant or if he will insist on having his way with her as many times as it takes. And then some. When he is done and flops beside her satisfied and pleased with himself, she merely rolls over to try to sleep.

"Aren't you going to wash?" Walter wonders. "Or will we lie together in a pool of your blood?"

Silke doesn't particularly care. "I'm exhausted. You wore me out."

"I should say, but you should still get clean. I am not done with you yet. I expect you to keep me informed."

"If I'm pregnant."

"Of course. What else? But I do like you, Silke. And we do have a play to see. So, I will check my calendar. Yes?"

Walter doesn't get the answer he expects. He waits a moment before turning his head to repeat the question and is met with disappointment. Silke is snoring. She has fallen asleep.

Chapter Fifteen

June 1933

On the first day of summer, eight-year-old Hana Ziegler has her first appointment with Doctor Lorenz Koerner at his office in Munich. Her grandmother Ilse accompanies her. Ilse never learned to drive, so it is up to her youngest son Walter to chauffeur them in the family Daimler-Benz. Hana sits quietly in the back seat holding a pink rose from her grandmother's greenhouse and a figure of the Lord Jesus on a cross given to her by her maid Hilda.

"Talk, that's all you have to do," Ilse tells her granddaughter. She is aggravated by Hana's morose attitude. "Just don't sit there like a little dummy. It will only make the doctor think the worst. Do you want to get sent away? Because that's what will happen. You don't know how I defend you against your grandfather. His patience isn't infinite, I can assure you."

Hana is also cradling a book on her lap. Jesus and the rose are resting on the cover, blocking the title from Ilse's view.

"You know I love you," Ilse says. "I don't mean to sound harsh, but things have to change and I don't know what else to do. Doctor Koerner comes highly recommended."

"He'll have to be more than highly recommended," Walter says.

"Be quiet, Walter, and keep your eyes on the road. I don't want us all being killed before we get there. Honestly, I don't know why you boys like to speed so much."

In 1933, the world is changing. Hitler has come to power only a few short months ago and already villainy is abroad. Munich in particular is a hotbed for Nazi propaganda. Storefronts promote his likeness ahead of their own wares. Nazi flags fly from upper floors and on street signs. The *Braunhenden*, Rohm's Brownshirts, are on every street corner passing out fliers.

As Walter maneuvers against congested traffic, Ilse is startled out of her dark thoughts by the sudden hammering on Walter's window. Hana jumps, too, and lets out a cry, gaping at the face of the young man who had banged to get their attention.

"Don't roll down your window," Ilse orders.

But Walter doesn't listen. He lowers the window and takes a flier from the young man.

"Tonight, on the main square," the boy yells at them. "This is a list of writers and books. If you have any, you must bring them. We're going to burn them."

"Books now, is it?" Ilse says, eying what Hana is hiding in her lap. "Give me the list, Walter. God help us if your brother's name is on it."

Hana doesn't surrender her book, her flower, or Hilda's cross when they park and leave the car behind. She carries them up three flights of stairs to Doctor Koerner's office. This far up, the noise on the street is somewhat muffled, but Hana can still hear the occasional honk of an irritated driver stuck in traffic.

"So, this is the young lady," Koerner says holding out his hand to shake Hana's. Since hers is full, he says, "May I take some of that? What do you have? Oh, a flower. May I smell it?"

"It's one of mine," Ilse says. "I grow them. Hana helps. She's really quite efficient when she wants to be. I might make a horticulturalist out of her yet. That would be nice, wouldn't it, Hana?"

"*Ja, Grossmutter.*"

"What?"

"*Ja, Grossmutter!*"

"You might have to bend to hear her, Doctor," Ilse recommends. "The way she talks and the way her grandfather listens, it is quite comical sometimes."

Koerner escorts Hana into his private office and closes the door behind him. Because he specializes in child psychiatry, his office is lined with children's toys, games, and books.

"Let me see yours," he says. Hana willingly gives it up. Erich Kastner's popular sequel in the Emil detective series, *Emil und die Drei Zwillinge*, Emil and the Three Twins. "A favorite of mine and my daughter Marta, who is your age. Eight, right."

"Yes."

"Your grandmother is right. You do speak softly. Like a little mouse. Do you mind talking so I can hear? No one else is listening, and I promise to keep whatever you say a secret between us. Okay?"

"Yes."

"A little louder, Liebchen."

"Yes!"

Koerner sits down cross-legged on a woven Persian carpet and invites Hana to do the same. The sunlight falls on them both from a window, as Koerner now focuses on the third item in Hana's possession, Hilda Schoenweis's Jesus pendant.

"Do your grandparents take you to church, Hana?"

"No. Sometimes."

"Do you like church? The psalms. The candles."

"They're okay."

"You can expound, Hana. I mean, you can speak freely here. Your grandmother is very worried about you. She says you keep to yourself all the time, that you have no friends, that you sometimes stick sharp things in your arms. Is that so? Why do you think you do that?"

Hana shrugs. She gazes about the office. "You have a lot of books," she says.

"You can take any of them home that you choose when we're done. But I want you to earn that reward by talking to me. Is that so difficult?"

"*Nein.*"

"Louder, please."

"*Nein!*"

Koerner leans forward and peers up into Hana's downturned face. "When a child does something like that, when she sticks sharp things in her arms, it tells someone like me that they're unhappy. Is that so, Hana? Are you unhappy?"

Hana nods.

"About your mother? Your grandmother has told me about her. I bet you miss her very much."

Hana repeats her disinterested gesture. Still, without looking directly at Koerner, she says, "Are you a *Juden*, Herr Doctor Koerner?'

The innocent question not only startles Koerner, it makes him visibly quiver.

"*Ein Juden?*"

Taken thoroughly aback, he scans his office, every inch of it, taking a survey of all of its contents. "Why do you say that?" he whispers. "What would make you think that?"

Only now does she turn her eyes up at him. "There are certain traits that can't be hidden," she says.

Koerner blanches. The truth is his family did convert to Catholicism many decades ago, in the last century, for the love of God. No one knows. No one. How did this girl, this child, guess?

"Are you a geneticist now?" he tries to laugh off her response. "What traits? I am as Catholic as you."

"Okay."

"I am. It is important that you never say that sort of thing about anyone, Hana. Do you understand? It could get them in a lot of trouble, and you don't want that, do you?"

"No."

"People may look like one sort of thing when they are actually very different. What would you say if I said you were a *Juden*? What would your grandparents think?"

"That's what they do think," Hana says. "I hear them talking. What is a Jew?"

Koerner settles back. He is breathing easier now. "Someone who is not

138

pure German, like you and I," he says. "The term is used in a derogatory way, do you understand? It's like calling someone fat or stupid. It isn't a nice thing to do, and it isn't something you should do, all right?"

"All right."

"Good. We must focus instead on you and why you are unhappy. Why you hurt yourself. Why do you think that is, Hana? Tell me honestly like a good girl."

Hana doesn't even pause for a moment. She knows full well why no one loves her. "Because I'm a Jew," she says.

* * *

"We have a lot of work to do with her," Koerner says to Ilse when the session is over.

"Tell me about it," Walter remarks, bored, leaning onto the window sill and looking out onto the street below.

"She's beginning to open up, though, so I'm optimistic. We should see each other every two weeks at the beginning. Then as we progress, we can space the sessions out farther apart." Koerner writes out a prescription and hands the paper to Ilse. "Invite friends over to play. She needs lots of companionship beyond, if you don't mind my saying so, yourself. She's an extremely intelligent young lady, aren't you, Hana? I would also encourage you to enroll her in a private school that specializes in the sciences. She definitely has an aptitude for it. She might thrive."

At that point, Koerner pulls Ilse aside and whispers to her while Hana opens her *Emil and the Three Twins* book. Although she isn't intentionally listening to the two adults, she can hear a word or two of what is being said, the word *Juden* most audibly. When her grandmother and her psychiatrist are finished confiding in one another, Ilse takes Hana in her arms and gives her a hug.

"I think we've earned a reward, my dear," she says. "Lunch? A new outfit? A music box?"

"A book?"

"Just a book?" Ilse reacts with disappointment. "Well, I suppose, if that's all you want."

"About the brain. I want to find out why I'm so sad."

"Hah!"

Walter chokes back laughter. Ilse isn't so predisposed to find Hana's remark funny. Thanking Herr Doctor Koerner, she takes Hana by the hand and leads her downstairs. Outside in the fresh air and bright sunlight, Hana still cradling her items, they are jostled by a gathering crowd of people who are listening to a sidewalk propagandist. His harangue is sharp, angry but greeted with cheers.

Hana drops her book, but before she can pick it up, a young student grabs it off the ground.

"Ah! Kastner! A Jew!" he cries. "Is this your book, little girl?"

"She found it," Ilse interrupts, not giving Hana the chance to reply. "On the ground. Back there. Someone else must have dropped it. She was bringing it to you."

"Good girl. Do you like fires? Stay and watch us burn it."

Chapter Sixteen

May 1947

T he Pan American flight out of Logan Airport arrives in Munich at ten in the evening. David McAuliffe is there to greet his father. Harold wants no fanfare. He wants complete anonymity for the first time in his life. There was Copenhagen, of course, when Liz discovered his affair with Ilse Ziegler. That could have turned into a real publicity fiasco. Luckily, Liz didn't know how far back the affair went. Off and on, almost twenty years. Though she ripped into him plenty, she was a good sport about the whole thing, in the end, eliciting from him only a promise that he would never embarrass her that way again.

"Have your miserable liaisons," she told him. "But you'll regret it deeply if I catch you at it."

This time, at least, it was Charlie who fucked up.

David grabs his father's suitcases, one in each hand, and steers them toward his rented car. He is wearing casual summer clothes per his father's orders. A uniform would attract too much attention. Harold will sleep on a couch in his son's apartment rather than register at a hotel.

"Did you have any idea about any of this?" Harold asks, the first words out of his mouth to David.

"None. Do you know who the mother is?"

"The letter was written by a woman named Hana Ziegler, but it isn't clear if she's the mother or not. You can imagine your mother's reaction when she read it. Nearly took my head off."

"And Charlie? Does he even know?"

David drops the two suitcases in the trunk of the car. It's a drizzly night, which his father wasn't prepared for. They both are wet to the skin when they get into the vehicle.

"Oh, Charlie knows, all right," Harold says. "Now. But it came as a complete shock to him. The child is almost three years old."

"What's her name?"

"Does it matter? David, for Christ's sake, your brother's political future is at risk here. Who the hell cares what the damned kid's name is?"

David steers the car out into traffic. Windshield wipers clear the glass. His father has a way of making him feel like he's still a child, a second-rate one to Charlie's numero uno. What makes him special in his father's eyes is his Harvard law degree, his involvement with the war crimes trials which will set him up nicely for a future as America's attorney-general. So, now it is important from this point on in their relationship to proceed, not as Harold McAuliffe's son but as Charlie McAuliffe's defense attorney.

"I remember Hana," he says. "She and Peg got along pretty good while we were in Copenhagen. If I'm not mistaken, they maintained a pen pal relationship until the war. I'd like to read that letter, if you don't mind."

"Of course. Yes. I have it in one of the suitcases. When we get to your place."

As David drives, he tries to bring back memories of those long-ago days in Copenhagen. Yes, he remembers Hana quite well. She and Peg got along fabulously. As a matter of fact, Peg was at her most serene and manageable when she accompanied Hana for walks about the city. This relationship was encouraged by both families who wanted both girls out of their hair.

David enjoyed those excursions himself. He, Peg, Hana, and Hana's nanny, a name he can't bring forth, were a constant quartet. The weather was generally decent and Copenhagen had many fine parks. And, of course, there were the botanical gardens in which Hana thrived lecturing the others about the various genus and species of plant life and how she and her grandmother cross-bred different strains to see what they could get.

He remembers, too, how their conversations, particularly between himself and Hana, diverged into the cross-breeding of humans, genetics, how traits are passed along good ones and bad.

Hana had told him, "If Darwin is right and evolution makes us stronger with every generation, why are there people like me and Peg?"

"What's wrong with you and Peg?"

"Why, we're crazy, hasn't anyone told you that?"

At the time, David laughed. It was hard, even then, to imagine that Hana was only twelve years old. She talked like a college professor. Maybe that was the problem. Lesser people didn't appreciate her genius. They were threatened by it, so they labeled her crazy to be done with her. Which brings to mind something, someone, else.

"How's Peg?" he asks his father who appears about ready to fall asleep in the car.

"Peggy? What does she have to do with this?"

"Nothing. But I haven't seen her since she went upstate and I went to law school. Just a few letters, that's all. It's been years. I mean, is she doing better?"

Harold yawns with fatigue, removes his glasses, and rubs his eyes. He is skilled at devising ways to consider the correct answer before speaking.

"She's happy," he says. "No more of that craziness. Your mother and I are considering bringing her home after the campaign."

"Really?"

No, but David doesn't have to know that yet. Not now. There are more important matters to deal with.

It is almost midnight before Harold can settle onto his son's couch for a much-needed sleep. He is awoken in the morning by a knock at the apartment door. Once he puts on his glasses and glances at the alarm clock on the neighboring coffee table, he realizes he has overslept.

"Jesus, David, you let me sleep."

David has been up for several hours. One of the last things his father did before falling to sleep the night before was to show him Hana Ziegler's letter. He has been reading and rereading it since breakfast. It is five typed pages long. As an attorney, he studies it as potential evidence. As a brother and son, he gets to see his family in a different light. As someone who, if only briefly, had known Hana Ziegler and had felt the stirrings of romantic interest, even for one as young as she was, he is sensing unfathomable mysteries in her that trouble him.

"Are you going to answer the door?" Harold asks.

"Are you going to get dressed?"

David is upset basically because he's not sure why he's upset. Charlie fools around. Nothing new there. Charlie gets a girl in trouble. Oh, if only Harold and Liz realized how often David had bailed his brother out on that end. No, there's more to this than meets the eye. Then there was that strange phone call he got the other night. The hang-up. That was no accident. He recognized Tom Adams's voice.

"David."

"Tom?"

And now, here was the mystery caller in the flesh. Having opened the door to his one-bedroom apartment, David is surprised to see Adams accompanied by a junior officer. They've known each other for many years. Tom and Charlie roomed at college, played varsity football together, enjoyed the women of Wellesley together.

"You called me last night," David says.

"You recognized my voice?"

"I thought you were pranking me like the old days. Come in. What's up?"

"Who is it, David?" Harold pulls up his pants, takes a moment before recognizing the man in the uniform as an old friend of his son's. "Oh, it's you. Tom. Tom Adams."

"Is Charlie with you?" Adams asks as he steps in.

"No. We left him behind," Harold explains. "The campaign, as I'm sure you're aware, is in full swing. I know it's a year away, but I view it as a healthy preparation. And a good thing, too, all things considered. What brings you around? How did you know I was here?"

"I didn't, sir. It comes as a surprise. Not an unpleasant one."

Adams glances at the room. It might be considered a bachelor pad except he knows David is not the type to fool around. He is all business, and the war crimes trials take up so much of his time.

"Breakfast?" David asks. "Have you eaten yet? My treat."

"Do you know what time it is? It's almost noon."

"Then lunch. On me."

It's a Saturday. Generally, a day off to relax, though David uses it to prepare for the ongoing trials. Dachau is on the menu now. While most of the major Nazi criminals have already been brought to justice, tried, found guilty, and either hung or sentenced to prison time, there are still many smaller figures to go after. The lesser officers. The prison guards. The doctors who experimented on the prisoners. The nurses who assisted them. David is preparing briefs on a man named Haefner. Hana Ziegler's name has come up in the interrogations, a fact that dismays him beyond mollification. Especially now that her name has popped up again in these more intimate familial ways.

"If you're paying," Adams says. He's not one to pass up such an offer. "You know a Bill Sorensen?"

David emerges from his bedroom, having changed into his own uniform. "Bill? Yes. You know him, too, don't you? He and Charlie used to pal around. Why?"

"Well, for one thing," Adams says, "he's dead."

The declaration is intended to pull the legs out from under anyone who has something they are hoping no one will discover. David is caught open-mouthed trying to fasten the last button of his shirt. Harold is trying to remember someone named Sorensen. Sorensen. No, no, unfamiliar.

"What does this Sorensen have to do with us?" the elder McAuliffe asks.

"He was killed, murdered, shot on the highway driving a former SS official toward the Swiss border. Our best guess is Sorensen has been helping Nazis escape to South America, forging documents, getting paid to resettle them, you might say."

David has to take a seat. "But what does that have to do with us? Yes, we knew him. But whatever he was doing, we have no involvement."

"We found your phone number, I assume the phone number to this address, in one of his ledger books, where he kept records of clients and payments. That's why I called you. Must say, when you answered, it came as quite the shock. Why your phone number?"

David is at a loss for an explanation. So is his father. It is now only beginning to dawn on Harold the possible devastating links to his son the congressional candidate.

"You're not suggesting...?" Harold says.

"Charlie and Bill were friends," David says. "Stress on 'were.' This used to be Charlie's apartment. I took it over when I came to Germany. That's why I answered when you called."

"Okay." Adams seems relieved to have at least one thing cleared up. He looks around. His lieutenant is jotting everything down behind him. "The thing is," he goes on, "there was a second man killed, shot right between the eyes. We haven't been able to tag him with a name yet, but we believe he was SS. Problem is, it seems he also had Charlie's phone number on his things."

"Oh, good Lord." Harold throws up his arms in disgust and futility. "What next? We poisoned Roosevelt to get his dog?"

Adams's lieutenant can't help uttering a laugh. Adams, too, is amused. "Well, perhaps we'll get into that, sir, after we clear up this mess. Basically, we don't think either of your boys has anything to do with whatever Sorensen was involved in. I don't recall him from my Harvard days. But Charlie might know who this SS fella was. I mean, before the war, perhaps. You were ambassador to Denmark, sir. You did affiliate with Germans."

"Industrialists. Men of money. Not scallywags like Hitler."

"Of course. But such men, like Thyssen and Frick, are on trial. So, it isn't much of a stretch..."

"No, it isn't." David rises. He has his feet solidly planted beneath him now. There is no question in his mind of his brother's innocence regarding Sorensen. That leaves only the paternity issue which Hana Ziegler could easily have wrong. How could she possibly be able to prove that Charlie was the father of the baby in the letter?

"Well," he says smiling, "this can all be straightened out fairly easily, I should think. We'll call my brother and ask him what he knows, who he knows. Maybe there was someone back in Copenhagen, Dad."

"Maybe."

"After lunch. Then Dad and I have other business to attend to."

Adams is open to being fed. He is comfortable that his investigation is on track. Less official now, he shares stories of the days when he and David's brother were known as the Two Horseman of the Apocalypse around Harvard Square. His anecdotes come to a halt, however, as soon as they hit the pavement. A man is waiting for them outside, sitting on the stoop, smoking a cigarette and reading a newspaper, which he folds and places under his arm upon seeing Major Adams and his companions.

"Why am I not surprised?" Adams says. "If Sherlock Holmes were Jewish and irritating, he would be Herr Kreisler."

Kreisler gives a nod of deference, tosses his cigarette away. "Pardon my intrusion," he says.

"On the Sabbath, no less," Adams remarks.

Kreisler lifts his hands in a gesture of 'whatever.' "God has to eat, too, doesn't He? Not that I take pleasure in disrupting one's dinner plans, but I think I know the identity of your SS man, Major Adams. Do you wish to know who I think it is?"

Adams releases a sigh that, whatever his desire is, yea or nay, Herr Kreisler will nevertheless say whatever is on his mind.

"All right, Kreisler, Avi, we're all waiting for the Titanic to sink. Who is it?"

"Walter Ziegler. A name, I should think, your American friends here know quite well."

Chapter Seventeen

Winter 1942-43

America is fully committed to the war now. The Nazis have begun to implement the Final Solution. All the prison camps in Germany and Poland are filling up with Jews and Gypsies and prisoners of war. Those who aren't slaughtered in their backyards are transported to the burgeoning camp system either to work as slave labor or to be immediately gassed. Ernst Rudolf Graf von Haefner's company manufactures the Zyklon-B that has become the favorite killing agent of the Nazis. But the gas, profitable as its manufacture is, is not the primary focus of Haefner's research and development. Neurological science is his interest, the development of drugs to counter the various psychoses that existed before the war but which will proliferate now because of the war.

His wife Gretchen specializes in neurology. She is one of the first women in Germany to get her doctorate in the science. That was how she had met Haefner. Her mind is fascinating. It is complicated, contradictory. Brilliant on the one hand, decaying from the inside on the other. Haefner wasn't particularly interested in her background, which is dull, bourgeoisie. Her mind is useful and her body pleasurable. In bed, she can be quite extraordinarily unrestrained, demanding, commanding, a sexual partner who is hard to resist. In this, she is the polar opposite of someone like Hana Ziegler who resists all of Haefner's efforts to seduce her, which are not infrequent. In Hana, he sees someone more his equal, perhaps someone even intellectually superior. Gretchen, on the other hand, sees her as a rival. Someone who must be dealt with before it is too late.

"Killing her would be the easiest thing in the world," Walter tells Gretchen on a morning when they are alone at a laboratory Haefner has provided for her studies on the brain development of children.

"I don't need her dead," Gretchen replies. "I just need her gone. You're SS. Can't you do something about her?"

"My own niece?"

"So, now she's your niece? A minute ago, she was just a Jew."

Walter lifts his shoulders. He has a passing interest in Gretchen's studies as they entail working with twins. He had a twin sister Luisa who died of the mumps when they were three years old. In the one surviving photograph he has subsequently destroyed of his departed twin, she looks a great deal like a young Hana. At the moment, twin girls, heads shaved, are sitting in dental chairs facing one another. Electrodes are attached to their skulls, and Gretchen is turning up the juice as she speaks to Walter. She is noting their responses on a chart as first one then the other, jerks and hollers.

"Alas," Walter says, "I made a promise to someone that I would leave her alone. At least, for the next nine months."

"Oh. I see." After all, Gretchen is a scientist. Not specifically a mathematician, but she gets Walter's drift. "Who's the lucky woman?"

A boost in the electricity, and one of the female test cases passes out.

"You know her," Walter says, being coy. "She's very beautiful. I find that I actually enjoy her company."

"Well, if she isn't permanently damaged, that must mean something." Gretchen takes medical readings of the still conscious twin, with a stethoscope and blood pressure monitor.

"I find, as well, that I like the idea of being a father. Maybe we'll have more than one."

"Good lord."

Gretchen jots data onto her chart then pats the conscious twin on the cheek. "Better than yesterday, Klara," she says. "Maybe tomorrow, even better, *ja?*"

"You do know that you're a bitch, Frau Haefner," Walter says, eying the dazed twin with dispassion.

"Am I?"

"All women are in the end. But my Silke, she's different. Worth exploring. That means Hana stays around a while longer. If she is that insufferable, you'll just have to manage."

"Then you'll kill her?"

"Then we'll see."

* * *

Over dinner that evening, the Haefners have a guest. His name is Josef Mengele. He's a doctor known for his studies in eugenics. He has a fascination for twins and the work that Gretchen has been doing. His wife Irene is with him. They are eating their dinner alone with Haefner, his father August, and Gretchen chatting up their mutual interests when Haefner happens to see a car drive by a window. Minutes pass in continued conversation. There is an empty chair at the table reserved for Hana. Suspicious, Haefner begs the Mengeles' pardon and leaves the table. He is just in time to see a figure sweep beyond the stairs to the second-floor hallway.

"Hana!" he calls. "We have guests."

She ignores him. Moments later he hears her bedroom door slam shut. Unperturbed, he follows and knocks on her door, finds it locked when he tries to open it.

"Hana, don't be rude." He raps again and gets more silence. "We received three boxes from the Siemens Company. Chemicals for processing your tissue samples. I can throw them out if they're of no use."

That gets the door open.

"Don't, please." Hana peers out. "Tell them I'm very tired, that's all."

"You tried to sneak by us. Shame on you, Hana. We have guests. Doctor Mengele would like to hear about your research."

"I detest the man."

"You don't know him."

"I don't have to know him. Can't you just tell him I'm sick?"

Haefner has no intention of letting her beg off that easily. He hears movement behind her. "There's someone in there with you, isn't there?" A secret lover? Is it possible? His Hana whose every movement he monitors? He pushes by her.

"Otto."

Otto doffs his hat and offers Haefner a polite bow. "Herr Haefner. If you think we are having sex behind your back, Hana is too genteel for that. I am merely here as an escort."

"Up to her bedroom?"

"We Froelings offer door-to-door service."

Haefner scowls. He is growing to dislike his attorney's son. Not so much a law clerk as a spy. "Nevertheless," he says, "if Hana is going to be able to pursue her studies, she is going to need friends, other than myself, of course, in positions of importance. Doctor Mengele is a rising star. All you have to do is introduce yourself. Then you can claim fatigue."

In hesitating, Hana makes the mistake of turning her gaze to Otto, which only increases Haefner's anger. He is being displaced in her heart even before he can gain access to it.

"All right," he says at last, relenting. "Have it your way. Sometimes I forget how young you are, how fragile. I'll bring your packages up to you later. Get some sleep. Otto, your mission is complete. Your father's firm charges by the hour. It's time to leave. Tomorrow, Hana, you and Gretchen will show Mengele your work at the camp. All I ask is that you be gracious."

Haefner steps aside and makes it clear he has no intention of leaving before Otto does.

Outside, with the door closed behind them, both can hear Hana break down into tears. Putting his hand firmly on Otto's arm, Haefner steers the younger man away. "Be careful with love," he says, as advice or as a warning is hard to say. "It can get you into a lot of trouble."

* * *

151

Awkward is a politic way of putting the trip that Hana shares with Gretchen the next morning. It has begun to snow with the forecast for several inches. Both are dressed for warmth with fur hats and mittens. Neither speaks until they reach the outskirts of Dachau. It is only then that Gretchen opens her mouth though whether she is speaking to Hana or to their driver is unclear.

"A train has arrived."

Hana sits up. Her attention has been on a book on cells that she has been reading, underlining an occasional phrase or paragraph.

"How can you tell?"

"The traffic up ahead is blocked. That'll mean more prisoners have arrived. We should head right over to the station. I want first pick."

Hana has an interest in new prisoners, as well. But not for the same reason. "I wonder where they come from?" she asks.

"I hope there are fresh twins. My pool of subjects is too small. I put in a request for more weeks ago."

"What do you do with them, Gretchen?"

Gretchen sits back in her seat as the driver turns off the main road. "Do I ask what you do with your prisoners?" she says. "Don't ask what I do with mine."

"I don't hurt mine."

"It isn't a matter of hurting. It's a matter of investigative science. Christ, Hana, you're wasting Ernst's time and money. I've told him that a hundred times. Once he realizes that, you'd better hope he stills likes you."

The station at Dachau is frequently busy with trains delivering prisoners from the east. Hitler's eastern front is collapsing. Thousands of wounded Wehrmacht soldiers are flooding German hospitals. Room must be made for them. Polish, Russian, and Ukrainian civilian slave labor arrives replacing German workers in munitions factories to bolster the war effort. Other camps closer to the Russian advance have to be abandoned. Useless prisoners are gunned down and tossed into makeshift mass graves. The reasonably healthy and useful are transported to the west to stuff already over-crowded facilities. The work goes on. The number of the dead increase. But German science will out. No one is saying 'surrender' yet.

The prisoners are still crammed inside the boxcars when Hana and Gretchen pull into the station. SS guards in boots and winter gear patrol the platform, guns at the ready in case anyone foolishly thinks to try to escape into the surrounding woods. Officers are shouting orders tramping through the already fallen snow, six inches deep. It is cold and blustery. But, so what? This isn't the Riviera in summer.

Being longer-legged and better suited, like a bear, to the turbulent conditions, Gretchen plows ahead of Hana, first shopper through the doors on market day.

"I see Doctor Mengele." She points ahead, then waves to him, calling out, "No pulling the fish off my line."

"I wouldn't think of it, my dear."

Mengele is huddled in an officer's greatcoat, standing with two SS officials. One of them is Walter Ziegler.

"My niece," Walter says to him, indicating Hana.

"The one who was ill last evening. I hope she's feeling better this morning. A rough day to be out if you're sick." Mengele comes forward and offers his hand to Hana. He seems a pleasant enough fellow, handsome, dashing even. Certainly polite, probably erudite, and, in his chosen field, accomplished. But the presence of Walter on top of Mengele forces Hana to dig deep inside herself to bear the worst. She is the proverbial lamb, but she is learning how to keep the slaughterhouse at a distance.

"I am well enough," she says and allows him to clasp her mittened hand.

"Herr Haefner tells me you are his most brilliant student," Mengele pays her a compliment. "You have insights into the structure of the gene that are far ahead of our time. For one so young, no less. Remarkable."

"And your studies, Doctor?" Hana wonders.

"Just beginning, my dear. Just beginning."

The doors to the boxcars begin to slide open now revealing their human contents, men, women, and children stuffed into unheated containers like meat carcasses strung up on hooks in a butcher's freezer. As soon as the doors open, bodies topple out into the snow, prisoners who have frozen to death or otherwise died during the trip to Dachau. Occupant labor of

153

Dachau, dressed only in vertically striped prison garb, rush over to clear away the corpses, haul them on stretchers to the crematoria. The other passengers, one at a time, slowly drop onto the ground, ragged, tattered shoes all that keep them from feeling the snow directly on the soles of their feet. Some have no shoes at all. None have coats. All of them tremble from the cold. There are children among them. The adults try to shield them from the wind but are thrust aside by yelling armed guards so that the culling can begin.

"Ladies first," Mengele says.

"Are there any twins among them?" Gretchen asks the SS officer in charge of the train.

He's not sure, and has to ask a subordinate who checks through the inventory. "Only a single pair, so far as I see," the junior officer says.

"Just one?"

"I'll take them!"

Hana steps in front of Gretchen and grabs the inventory from the SS man. "Where?"

The man shows her. "The Radichevski twins, boy and girl, Anatoly and Xenia, ages nine, Ukrainian, parents deceased."

"Healthy?" says Gretchen.

"If they didn't die on the train."

"Perfect. Not identical, but a boy and a girl."

"Mine," insists Hana.

"Your research has nothing to do with twins!" Gretchen shouts. "You're doing this just to get in my way."

"I'm doing this to further my research on inheritance." Oh, Hana is learning, all right. She is only seventeen, a wisp of a thing, but has come to recognize the need to appear bigger, stronger, louder, smarter, less likely to tolerate the idiocy of lesser mortals. "What car are they in?"

"Number six, at the end."

But before Hana and the SS officer can move, Gretchen acts, shoving Hana to the ground, to the snow. Her angry shout captures the attention not only of the SS guards but of some of the prisoners lining up for roll call.

"Doctor Mengele," Gretchen pleads her case, "surely you won't give those children to another child? One who is so sickly herself. My work is far more advanced."

"I'm just a visitor here, Frau Haefner," he says raising his hands in a gesture of helplessness. "I have been assigned to another camp at Auschwitz. Can't you decide this between you?"

Hana starts to rise but is driven back to the snow by Gretchen's booted foot.

"Stay down, Jewess!" Gretchen screams. "That's who she is, though no one says it. A Jewess. Look at her, Mengele. Look at her."

Mengele refuses to. Herr Haefner's frau is not making a good case for herself by acting like a starving German shepherd unchained. Jealous bitch, is what is going through his mind. He is about to say, "Give the twins to Fraulein Ziegler," when he is prevented from doing so by an unexpected act of kindness.

To his and everyone else's astonishment, one of the prisoners from the train breaks ranks and at risk of being shot, comes to Hana's aid. Helping her to her feet, he wipes her bloodied mouth with his icy cold fingers.

"There, there," he says when he is immediately struck down by the butt of a rifle. Then it is Hana's turn to prevent a violent act, inserting her body between the SS guard and the injured prisoner. But the moment she locks eyes with him and the daring prisoner locks eyes with her, it is as if the world has gone off its orbit.

"Hana?" whispers the man with the scar on his cheek.

Hana freezes then faints, dropping like one of the dead onto the station platform.

"There," Gretchen says triumphantly. "You see? A Jew. Now the twins are mine."

* * *

Hana comes to the infirmary, dazed, lost. Thankfully, lovely friendly eyes smile down at her. Silke bathes her friend's face with a warm cloth. The

155

white cotton is smeared with Hana's blood.

"Brave girl," Silke says. "Foolish girl. You're lucky Walter was there."

"Walter?"

"Odd, isn't it? Of all people."

Hana is still having trouble collecting all of the data she needs to figure out how she ended up here. "I saw this face," she says. "Where is he?"

"Who?"

"The man who helped me. With the beard. The scar. On his face. He spoke my name."

"A scar?"

Hana tries sitting up, desperate to rise. Two things prevent her. First, a wave of dizziness. Then the gentle press of Silke's hands. Silke doesn't want to alarm Hana. Walter prevented any further investigation into Gretchen Haefner's ridiculous charges, but he didn't stop the man with the scar, among many other prisoners, from being designated unfit for work. Unfit meant, rather than being selected to labor at Dachau, they have been chosen instead to be transferred to one of the death camps for immediate disposal. Hana's father might well be dead already.

"You're reading too much into it," Silke says. "I need you here and now."

"But he might be my father, Silke. You told me he would have a scar on his face, and he did."

"Many men have scars. It's war. Think of the coincidence. How many prisoners are there? How many camps? How many trains? For him to appear today just when you happen to be in the camp is beyond coincidence. You're the mathematician. You tell me the odds."

"But he knew me. He called me Hana."

Hana weeps. Silke consoles. She says, "Here. Feel my belly. I want you to feel something."

It is meant as a distraction, the life growing inside her, Walter's baby. Hana can feel it move within.

"That's amazing," Hana says. She sniffles.

"Yes. Due in two months. You'll be her godmother, of course."

"Her?"

"I don't know. Walter wants a boy. The last thing I need is another Walter."
Hana smiles, keeps her hand on Silke's protruding belly.

"Walter will let you keep her?"

"Walter doesn't care one way or the other."

"You're very young. You have no experience as a mother."

"I have a mother. She has experience. My brat isn't going to be raised by anyone but me."

Hana is glad. She believes Silke will make a wonderful mother. "Is he still having sex with you? My uncle is so stupid. Does he believe he can get you pregnant while you're still pregnant?"

"Walter is the only man I know who can rape a woman without laying a finger on her."

The girls laugh. It is an improbable thing to do in a place like this when death is everywhere. But that is the magic of Silke. To the point where Hana suddenly leans forward and kisses her friend on the lips and whispers, "You deserve to be happy. I love you."

Silke's response is a deep blush. She's at a loss for words. A rare occasion. "Well," she says, "I hope nobody saw that, or we'll both be shot." She stands, perplexed as to whether she should turn left or right, right or left, up or down.

"Don't worry," she says. "We'll get through this."

A voice calls for Silke just then. She and Hana stare into each other's eyes making a firm commitment to one another. As Silke is about to go, to return to her nurse's duties, though, Hana calls her back.

"The twins. The Radichevski twins," she says. "They were on the train, too. Find out what happened to them, will you?"

Chapter Eighteen

May 1947

The drive out into the German countryside is beautiful. If David didn't know any better, he'd swear he was driving up Route One in Maine. Farmland. Forests. The occasional pond or stream. Rural tranquility, punctuated by horses and cows and slow-moving tractors. Even in post-war Bavaria life goes on.

If you had money before the war, you still had a good deal of it now. Leading industrialists are on trial for their collaboration with the Nazis to enhance the Third Reich's war machine's efforts. But their punishments will be light, and money will continue to flow. The rich never seem to suffer the way the poor and working people do. David does not come from a poor family. Yet he has immersed himself in the lives of the downtrodden and has had many second thoughts about the plans his father has drawn up for him.

"Let the attorneys do the talking, if you please," Major Adams says. He is doing the driving now. David sits beside him. In the back seat, Avi Kreisler and Harold McAuliffe, as mismatched a pair as matzo balls and lobster bisque, listen. Adams doubts they'll obey.

"Our case right now as it stands," says David, a heavy briefcase resting on the floor at his feet, "is with Herr Haefner. It's not a great case, to be honest. There is some interest, rather, in the work of the young woman commonly thought of as his research collaborator, Hana Ziegler. Some say they are lovers. Testimony from some prisoners has her doing research on prisoners at Dachau, particularly children. Mengele-type stuff. But proof is sketchy. We've lost Mengele."

"Maybe thanks to your old friend Sorensen," Kreisler suggests.

"I hope not. In any case, much as I regret having to do so, I have to consider Fraulein Ziegler a potential criminal, as well, someone we are considering prosecuting for inhumane acts against prisoners at the Dachau Concentration Camp."

"But today we're focusing on the murders of Bill Sorensen and Walter Ziegler," Adams reminds everyone. "We suspect a man and a woman were involved. Haefner and his gal pal? Why not? It's as good a theory as any."

Someday movies will be filmed at the Haefner estate. Period pieces. PBS miniseries. No one suffered under the Nazis here. Even Harold is impressed by the wide-open spaces and the nineteenth-century extravagance. "I never got to meet Haefner while I was ambassador," he says. "I wonder if he'd sell?"

"Dad."

"Just pondering. Why Miami, when we could buy here? For a song."

Adams drives through the linden tree-lined private road and into the circular drive. He parks beside tennis courts and a structure that appears to be a converted barn. He thinks in a rural setting like this there should be a dog hanging around, barking at them, and chasing after their car, but instead, he catches the tiny form of a cat lazily watching from a box on the front steps into the house. Someone has thoughtfully furnished the box with a blanket and pillow.

The other three men stand back as Adams lifts the bronze door knocker in the shape of a spiral and bangs out four loud raps. When the large door swings open, they are all somewhat surprised to be greeted by a little girl about five years old.

"*Guten morgan, mein Herren. Wer sind dir?*"

"We're friends of the family," responds David in German. "I must say, we didn't expect such a lovely young lady to answer the door. What's your name?"

"Ursula."

"That's a very pretty name." In his head, he does the math and thinks, 'Well, she can't be Charlie's.'

From behind the girl, who has blonde hair and blue eyes, comes a female voice not so sweet. "Ursula, how many times do you have to be reminded not to open the door to strangers?"

A matronly woman, as impressive a figure as any of the men, takes Ursula by the shoulder and moves her behind.

David introduces himself. "I'm Major McAuliffe, Madam, with the International Military Tribunal. I understand Herr Haefner is present."

"With his attorney."

"Of course."

"And these others?"

"My father."

"Your father? Why is he here?"

A reasonable enough question. David would just as soon have left Harold back at his apartment. The senior McAuliffe is already irritated. "What is she saying?" he asks. "Why is she not letting us in? Who the hell is she?"

David puts up a restraining hand before completing the introductions of Major Adams and Avi Kreisler. "And you?" he asks the daunting matron. "You do look somewhat familiar to me. Have we met before?"

"Copenhagen," Hilda Schoenweis says. "I suppose I have a rather forgettable face. Copenhagen."

"Oh. Yes. Fraulein Hana's nanny. It's been so long. I apologize for not remembering. My attentions were elsewhere, I suppose. May we come in?"

Hilda steps aside and lets the men in. The war has aged Haefner. He is sitting in the parlor, rises when the four others enter. In his early fifties, he appears older, his face lined, his hair gone mostly to gray. He is tall, heavyset, but stooped as if the war effort has been too much for him personally to bear. With him is a much younger man who also rises.

"Otto Froeling," he says. "I'll be representing Herr Haefner if the matter comes to trial. We are hoping to avoid that."

David shakes his hand. "I was expecting someone older," he says.

"My father had a heart attack two weeks ago. We buried him last week."

"I'm sorry to hear that. My regards to your family."

"If the need arises, I will also be representing Hana Ziegler," Otto says. "I can speak from personal knowledge that any evidence you have of crimes against prisoners at Dachau is false and malicious. Hana would no more hurt a butterfly than another human."

"At the moment I can't dispute that," David says. He finds a seat as do the others around a mahogany table set with cheese, fruit, and pitchers of tea and orange juice.

Kreisler alone decides to sit apart in a chair by the fireplace, content, it would seem, to just listen. Haefner glances at him with suspicion.

"My own father August passed away a month ago," he says. "It's been a bad year for fathers. Would you say that yourself, Mr. McAuliffe?"

"I wouldn't know."

"Or, in your case, perhaps it's a bad year for sons."

If Haefner's throw-away comment is meant to get a rise out of the elder McAuliffe, it is successful. Harold pounds the table and points a menacing finger at the German industrialist. But before he can utter a word in his defense, another woman makes a timely entrance into the parlor. She's not alone. Toddling along beside her is a girl even younger than Ursula, maybe two years of age.

"Well," says David.

"Yes. Well," says the woman, refined, aristocratic, elderly. "Say hello to Charlotte."

Harold McAuliffe is speechless. The family resemblance is unquestionable. The little girl, dark of hair and eye reminds him of Peg before anyone knew there was something wrong with her.

No one says a word. The parlor has become a hall of statues. From his chair, Kreisler takes in everything, all the faces, all the reactions.

"May I ask where the lady of the house is?" Kreisler asks.

"There is no lady of the house," Haefner replies.

"Then the young lady of the house. You know who I mean, Herr Haefner. The one they called Little Daughter at Dachau. Is she hiding on us?"

"Kreisler, I'm warning you." Adams has to speak up now and take control. He stands to do this. "Your perception, all of you, is that I am here to discuss the trials. I am not. What Herr Haefner may or may not have done, what Hana Ziegler may or may not have done, during the war years, is of no interest to me. What is of interest is the murder of an American named William Sorensen and a German, a former SS officer, named Walter Ziegler. I'm thinking that some of you or even all of you know something relevant to this case. Walter Ziegler is, was, Hana Ziegler's uncle. You might even be guilty of this crime yourself. To begin with, Madam," he says to the older woman, "who are you?"

"Ilse Ziegler," she replies. The disdain in her voice is strategic. It sends a message. No matter who you may think you are, Herr Major, I am better.

"The grandmother?" Kreisler wonders.

"Of whom? Hana or Walter?"

"Of Hana."

"*Ja*, I am her *grossmutter*."

"And Walter Ziegler's mother."

"*Ja*. I am his mother."

"Was," says Kreisler. "Not a good year for mothers either. But congratulations are in order, Frau Ziegler. Your line of descent is marked by SS murderers and torturers of children. You didn't know he was dead? You don't appear particularly distraught."

"Kreisler!" Adams at this point has to tell the Jewish survivor to keep quiet. "You're here to listen, not to interrogate, do you hear me?" he says. "Keep your vendetta to yourself. Another word, and I'll resettle you in the middle of the Pacific."

"Unless they were involved, none of them knew Walter Ziegler was dead," David says. "You didn't know until the other day, Tom."

"And yet no response from the mother."

"Kreisler!"

Adams's anger finally causes Kreisler to back off. The major senses that more is at play here than he is aware of. Why else the presence of Harold McAuliffe? But he must remain focused. "Your son," he says, "if such is true, was shot on the highway not far from the border with Switzerland. He was trying to avoid criminal prosecution with the help of Mr. Sorensen.

Apparently, someone didn't want him to enjoy the sunny climes of South America. Perhaps your granddaughter. So, if you know where she is, I would advise you not to hold out."

"No one is holding out on you, Herr Major." Otto shifts in his seat, reaches for a slice of Emmentaler cheese. His great big yawn is a testament to his lack of concern. "As I have said, Fraulein Ziegler has retained me for counsel. I can assure you she is innocent of everything. From the Lindberg baby to Hiroshima and Nagasaki, she is free of all guilt."

"And Ursula's mother," David wonders. "Where is she? I assume it isn't Hana. Is it?"

"Silke Hartenstein." Otto says this while chewing on the cheese and pouring himself a cup of orange juice. "This information is yours for free, Herr McAuliffe. The oldest child is Walter Ziegler's. You've heard of the Lebensborn Program, no doubt. It was a purely political relationship, the desire of the Nazis to produce a pure Aryan stock. Fraulein Hartenstein, as a member of the Bund Deutsche Madel, had little choice but to comply with Herr Ziegler's wishes to procreate with her."

"Delightful," Harold mutters. "Then it's the other child who interests us. What did you say her name was?"

David, leaning over, puts a restraining hand on his father's shoulder. Harold knows fully well what the girl's name is. "Not now, Dad," he says. "As Major Adams says, our focus is on the Sorensen-Ziegler murders. Committed, we believe, by two people. A man and a woman."

"The woman was the shooter," Kreisler says from his chair. "The suspect list is, in my view, quite short."

"Thousands of men and women survived the camps, Herr Kreisler," David replies. "So, the list may not be as short as you think. But it would help if we could speak to both Hana and Silke. Where are they now?"

The answer doesn't come from Ilse Ziegler, nor from the silent Ernst Graf von Haefner, nor from Otto, picking at his teeth.

It is the little girl Charlotte, who, like a student at school blurting out an answer to get the praise of her teacher, cries, *"Mit dem blumen! Mit dem blumen!"* With the flowers.

Chapter Nineteen

Winter 1943

Ⅰt is a Garden of Eden, Ilse Ziegler's greenhouse. In the midst of the worst of winter weather, Hana can seek retreat in the warmth and spring-like beauty of geraniums and daffodils and roses. It was this way when she was a child and is still so now that her grandfather Friedrich is dead. An apoplectic fit following an argument with his son Walter. That's what Hana has been told, though, frankly, she doesn't care. She's glad he's dead. This allows her to return to the place of her childhood. It is particularly nice now that Walter is also away.

Hilda will accompany her at times. While Hana is botanizing, Hilda is sewing or reading from her Bible. Silke also comes, bursting at the seams to have her baby already. The three women wile away the time away from the war, away from Dachau. Hana has not fully recovered from the beating Gretchen gave her, nor the possible loss a second time of her father. An idea is brewing in her head. This is the thing that keeps her going, keeps her sane.

"I've talked this over with Ernst, Herr Haefner," she says to her companions. "Thanks to you, Silke."

"What did I do?"

Silke sits on a stool, her great weight causing her to look like an unsteady bowling pin.

"You found Anatoly and Xenia."

164

"The twins?"

"Yes. Gretchen hasn't begun to abuse them yet. She wants them to gain weight first, so she's feeding them like little pigs for the slaughter. She wants them healthy before she begins to dice them up."

"Bitch," Silke says.

"*Nein*, Silke," Hilda says, eyes peering over the top of her bible. "It is bad luck to speak unkindly of others while you're pregnant. Your daughter will grow up to be just that."

"My daughter is going to be loved."

"I'm sure. Even so. If you must call Frau Haefner anything, call her a cow. At least then your daughter will be assured of having enough milk for her own daughter."

Silke might be tempted to laugh at Hana's nanny, but she knows Hilda to be quite serious, so she refrains.

Hana says, "Ernst is going to convert the barn into a shelter. Whenever the trains roll into Dachau from now on, I'm going to take the children. If I can't get them all, I'll at least take the ones who are sickly. I will claim, with some honesty, that I need them for my research. I may poke or prod them once in a while, take blood samples and such, but I'll really be keeping them alive until the war ends."

"Good luck with Gretchen," Silke says. "Herr Haefner looks at you like a boy on a first date. She hates you. Walter hates you. Those two are close. Any excuse they can use to be rid of you, they'll use. Gretchen won't give up her twins."

"Oh, she will," Hana says. "Oh, she will. Or she'll find I can be as brutal as she."

The three women look up then as the door to the greenhouse opens. Standing framed in the doorway, clothed in winter wear, Ilse Ziegler waits. Though the greenhouse belongs to her...everything on the estate belongs to her now that her husband is gone...she hesitates as if not sure she is welcome.

"May I?" she asks. "Am I disturbing anything?"

"We're just gabbing, Grandmother," Hana says, clipping leaves from a plant.

"Please come in."

"It's good to see that I can now hear you without having to ask you to speak up," Ilse says. Just inside the door is a rack. She hangs up her coat and removes her hat, scarf, and gloves. "I think it means you're finally coming into your own as a woman. Now that your grandfather is gone…"

Ilse is such an aristocratic presence that she brings with her into the greenhouse a change in atmosphere. It's as if the last holdover of the nineteenth century is refusing to give up its hold on the modern world. As if she must step down off a pedestal of some kind to interact with women with whom she has little connectivity. As if she is a woman who never had a childhood and finds making friends a profound struggle.

Hilda bows out, claiming it's late and she must begin to prepare dinner. Waddling, Silke follows needing to use the bathroom. Hana is uncomfortable alone in her grandmother's presence. In the old days, when she was a child and Ilse invited her to work in the greenhouse together, at least then they had the work of botany to bring them together. Hana appreciates her grandmother, but that's it. There is no love.

"Hilda and Silke don't like me," she says.

"Well, it is dinner time and Silke is pregnant."

"I suppose. It's lonely out here now," Ilse admits coming in to admire her floral arrangements. She is still managing to make a profit on the sales of her roses. "Your grandfather and I never spent a lot of time together. And Walter and Edward are away all the time. I have no friends. Just these."

"How's Edward doing?"

"He's in France, did you know that? In Paris, writing. He's happy, it seems. He's taken up with a man of all things. A Frenchman. Well, the times are what they are, aren't they? He'll survive. No matter how the war turns out. Who can say about the rest of us?"

Hana lays down her clippers. Her apron is soiled. She wipes her hands on it, unsure how to proceed with her grandmother.

"If he's happy," she says, "you should be happy. Are you?"

"Do I look it, my dear? I hate this war. I hate everything to do with it."

"It's not a woman's war," Hana says.

"Name one that was."

Ilse dons an apron, but no sooner has she tied the ends and rested her hands on the long table than she starts to weep. Her tremors rattle the table and shake her flowers. Her tears water nothing but the ground at her feet.

Hana watches, never moving to comfort her grandmother. This is a woman she has never seen before. Even when Hana was being driven to Hollenschloss, even when her grandmother knew full well what was going to happen, did she try to intervene? Did she put up a fight? Did she curse and holler and try to drag her granddaughter to safety?

"Did you ever love me?" Hana asks.

It is the most vulnerable of moments. It is as if she is asking, 'Why should I care about your sorrow when you never cared about mine?'

Ilse shudders. Her hands cover her eyes. Moments pass. Minutes, before she can wipe her eyes with the palms of her hands. "Would you believe me if I said 'yes'?"

"No."

"Well, I hardly blame you. Not only was I a terrible grandmother, I was a horrible mother, as well. I drove your mother away. Friedrich blamed you for her death, but he was wrong. It was my fault."

Ilse's crying resumes, even intensifies. Hana still can't bring herself to comfort her. She returns to her labors, now using a trowel to dig around the roots of an orange tree. One of Hana's fondest memories is of the orange juice that she could drink even in the middle of winter. Hana's grandmother raises other fruit, as well, which she sells at market in Munich. Pears. Peaches. Crossbred. An unappreciated talent.

"I'll need your help," she says.

"Help?"

"With Ernst Haefner and his wife. Gretchen has it out for me. So does Walter, which really shouldn't surprise you. I'm going to ask Ernst for something. I'd like your support."

"For what?" Ilse dries her eyes.

"My own greenhouse as it were. For children. There is some risk to it. You must keep Walter off my back. And Gretchen, if you can."

"Gretchen," Ilse says. She doesn't call the other woman 'bitch' but the emphasis is there. "Just tell me, dear, what you need me to do."

"Be there for me. When I need you most. Can you do that, do you think?"

Of course, Hana is remembering when Ilse wasn't there for her, when the gas valves were about to be turned on, when the needle was poised over her arm, when the crematorium was primed for the remains, and still Ilse Ziegler, her grandmother, did nothing to stop it.

Shamefacedly, Ilse does remember. "You are of my blood," she says. "And from this day forward, I will be there for you always."

No more words need to be spoken. In fact, whether or not either of them realizes it, an entente has been forged. For the next hour, they work side-by-side collecting baskets of fruit that Ilse, with Hilda's help, will bring to market in the morning.

"We'll grow some for the children," Ilse says. She's happy when she exits the greenhouse to bathe and prepare for dinner, leaving Hana to clear away the remaining debris beneath the trees.

Hana is just about to take off her filthy apron and hang it up, when she spots something under one of the trees, pressed up against the edge of the wide porcelain pot. Just a corner is sticking out from the soil but enough such that the light overhead gleams off it. Curious, Hana grabs her trowel and begins to dig around the object, which is metal and turns out to be a box about four inches by ten. While there is a silver hasp and an accompanying lock, Hana has no trouble prying it open. It is rusted and the sides of the box are dented. It has been handled many times, though, perhaps, not recently.

Hana lays the box on the table to reveal the contents. Letters. Dozens of them. Still in their original envelopes. Some lovingly bound with ribbon, they are all addressed to Frau Ilse Ziegler. Hana doesn't know what to do with them. They aren't her property. They belong to her grandmother. Letters dating back decades. But when she recognizes the return address of one of the missives, she can't help herself. From Berlin. The Wintergarten. From her mother to her grandmother.

'Oh, my,' she thinks and drops onto a stool.

There is even a crayoned envelope addressed from Hana in big green letters to her *grossmutter*. She doesn't dare open it. It will only bring fresh tears. Those from her mother she handles with an intense desire to read. She refrains from tearing them open only with the greatest effort. After all, she can always rebury the box and find it later. If she wants. Why delve into a past that is only an unhappy one? Then again, why not?

Hana has no idea what Ilse's responses were to her daughter's letters, but it is obvious to her that Hana's mother never stopped looking for love and acceptance and Ilse never quite got around to surrendering it.

'His name is Louis, Louis Marksohn, and he's really a decent guy, Mother. If you could just meet him, just once, you'd fall in love with him the way I did. But you won't ever let that happen, will you? Are you so afraid of Papa?'

Hana holds this letter in her hands until they are shaking. She stares at the name on the page, Louis Marksohn, as if by rearranging the letters and using the ink with which they are written, she can create something wholly different, she can gaze into the face of her father.

It is a third group of letters that catches her eye before she closes the lid. These are also banded as a unit and laid beneath the rest as if intentionally hidden. Doubly hidden. In the ground, in a box, at the bottom covered up by much more innocuous mail. These letters have a return address from the United States. From a place called Cape Elizabeth. From a man named Harold McAuliffe. At the moment, these letters have no interest for Hana. But they will.

* * *

Hana now feels more in a position to make demands that in the past she wouldn't have dared insist upon. Ernst Haefner is a married man in love with a much younger woman to whom he is not married to. He can't have both.

These days she and Gretchen live apart, about as far apart as possible. Hana takes her meals, when she is 'home' in her lab. Since the death of her grandfather, she has been spending more and more time at the Ziegler estate. In the evening, she goes right to her room, reads for a while before turning out the light. In the morning, she is up before dawn and rides with Silke to Dachau.

Vitor Hartenstein is the willing chauffeur in his beat-up 1934 Volkswagen. It is Hana's intention on this early spring day to finally confront Haefner. He has agreed to modify his barn on her behalf, but she hasn't explained to him in very pertinent detail what she wants him to do and why she wants him to do it. She needs to do it tonight because in the morning, tomorrow, another trainload of prisoners is due in and there will be children on it.

Fate intervenes when Silke goes into labor in the Volkswagen.

"Oops," she says. "Water."

"Water?" Hana has no idea what that means.

Vitor, the owner of two cows, knows exactly what his daughter's shorthand indicates. "Hang on," he shouts and spins the car about. "You aren't having my granddaughter at Dachau."

The nearest hospital is in Munich. It takes an hour to drive to the city, but before they even reach the outskirts, Ursula Hartenstein is suckling at her young mother's breast. Vitor, the handyman, turns out to be very handy on the side of the road while cars, trucks, and military vehicles are speeding by.

Hana assists in the delivery. She briefly holds the child before Silke is able to take over.

"Oh, she's beautiful," Hana gushes. "I'm so glad you're not giving her up. Now I want to have a baby."

"You're too young," Silke tells her. "They don't all come squirting out like mustard from a tube."

"Walter did something good. Thank you for naming her…"

"Well, it's a good name, after all."

Silke doesn't start hemorrhaging until they reach the hospital. Hana notices the blood when Silke stands, dripping down both legs. Silke doesn't pass out, but her father has to carry her into the hospital, Hana following with Ursula cradled in her arms. Dachau, the prison train, and any confrontation with Gretchen are now the last thing on Hana's mind.

"I'll stay with her tonight, Herr Hartenstein," Hana tells the worried parent. "Go home. Bring Frau Hartenstein in the morning."

"What? Are you going to breastfeed her while I sleep?" Silke jokes. "Not with those little things, you won't."

"You don't know how big my breasts are," Hana says. "And what does it matter if they are small. Most mammals just have nipples."

"Nipples, yes. Let's see yours."

Now that Silke is recovered, Hana feels much more relaxed. When Silke isn't nurturing the baby, Hana enjoys snuggling with her. She wonders if her mother ever did the same with her. Or if Ilse ever breastfed her daughter. Or how often Hana's father, Louis Marksohn, got to hold his baby daughter. 'If you don't show your children love,' she thinks, 'your children will ultimately turn on you. Then their children will turn on them. It's a terrible cycle that can begin in the most mundane of ways. But if you show them love unending...'

After a few hours of bonding, Ursula is brought to the nursery allowing both Hana and Silke to sleep. Silke is still buried in a dream when the father makes an unexpected appearance. SS Hauptscharfuhrer Walter Ziegler has been shown his daughter and is impressed. He wants to express his sincere gratitude to Silke, but finds her unwilling to wake up.

Hana stirs when Walter accidentally bumps into the chair she has been sleeping in.

"A girl," he says, standing beside the bed, hat in hand, rigid in his SS uniform. Hana wonders how such a man can father a child. A healthy one at any rate.

"Yes. Are you pleased?"

"Very much so. It's too soon to tell who she looks like. But that she is pure Aryan is obvious."

Hana doesn't move from her chair. Even now, Walter's presence frightens her. He began molesting her when she was eight. He didn't have any concerns about her heritage then. He even called her pretty. He always found ways of getting her alone, which in the Ziegler household wasn't difficult. In the bedroom, in the cellar, in the fields, even in her grandmother's greenhouse. Any time alone with him is a dangerous time.

"I understand she's been named Ursula," Walter says. "I assume that was your idea."

"Is that a problem?"

"Not at all. Not at all. If she grows up looking like your mother, she's fortunate. So long as she doesn't become so dramatic."

Hana has no response to that. She can't help wondering if her mother was ever one of Walter's victims. The thought makes her want to scream, to leap out of her chair and beat her uncle to death. But her arms and legs are weighted down by too much fear.

"Tell her I was here, will you?" he says. "If I have the chance, I'll drop by tomorrow. I'd like to purchase a gift for the baby. If you have any thoughts on the matter, let me know." Walter heads for the door, turns just before leaving. "By the way, there's a train coming into Dachau in the morning, you know. Gretchen will be there. You're looking good, Hana."

Walter departs the way a nightmare does, leaving a palpable measure of apprehension behind. Apprehension, anxiety, and disgust. Hana doesn't even tell Silke Walter paid her a visit. So far as she is concerned, Ursula is not his child. She belongs to Silke and God.

"You're a good friend," Silke tells her in the morning. "If anything happens to me..."

"Don't even say it, Silke."

"But I have to. I don't want Walter to have any say in the matter. I want Otto to draw up something legal that names you as Ursula's godmother and the sole care provider of Ursula, well, with my parents of course, if I should die. I don't know if Walter will even care, but I don't want to take any chances."

Hana won't hear of it. What a terrible thought.

When Vitor and Gertrud Hartenstein arrive to give Hana the chance to go home, she still can't get the concept of Silke dying out of her head. As a child who barely escaped death herself, Hana obsesses about the fragility and uncertainties of life. She wasn't born with this worry. She was gifted it by her family. What God wants or doesn't want is irrelevant.

Walter has had Silke once. What's to stop him from wanting her again and again? Even Hana isn't certain of what Walter is capable of beyond what he has already exhibited. Killing is something the SS is good at. When they are done with you, you are just trash to them.

Hana frets about her friend's safety the entire ride back to the Haefner estate. It is a bone-crushing feeling that in a world such as this nothing ever turns out right.

Haefner himself has driven to Munich to get Hana. He says all the right things. How is the mother? How is the child? What gifts do they need? Was Hana able to get any rest?

"I don't care about me," Hana tells him. "Did that train arrive from Dachau?"

"Yes."

"Did you go?"

"I have no interest in prisoners."

"Gretchen does. Did she go?"

"It's part of her research, Hana, you know that."

Hana seethes. Gretchen is another one who, like Walter, exudes nothing but treachery and selfishness. "I suppose she selected some of the prisoners."

"I never ask her what she does in that regard. But you're probably right."

Haefner drives. His attention is on the road. He doesn't see the rage in Hana's eyes. "I want them, Ernst," she says. "Whoever she took, she can't have them. Anymore!"

"Well, I don't see what I can do about that."

"You can make a choice."

"Gretchen has a mind of her own."

Hana feels like throttling Haefner even if it means them both flying off the road into the surrounding trees. He is acting so mild, so distant. Either Haefner truly doesn't understand the depth of Hana's feelings or he is far more ignorant than Hana believes.

"I'll kill her, if it comes to it!" she yells at him.

"Hana, you don't mean that."

The children! The children! That's all she can think of. Sigrid. The boy she witnessed at Hollenschloss being put down like a scared unwanted pet.

Hana is weeping when she grabs Haefner's arm and threatens his ability to control the car.

"Pull over!" she yells at him. "Pull over!"

"Hana!"

"Now!"

Haefner has no choice. She'll kill them both if he doesn't. But the moment he has parked at the side of the road, Hana leaps from the car. Rage has wound her up. She mutters. She paces, her feet crunching on dirt and pine needles. Back and forth. Back and forth. Her green dress is rumpled from a night sleeping in an uncomfortable chair, and her long hair has fallen loose to flow down her back. The muscles of her arms are taut, her fingers curling and uncurling into fists and claws.

She doesn't see Haefner get out of the car to join her. She doesn't notice the look in his eyes. The desire. He's fifty. She's eighteen. She is slender, lithe, more vibrant, and powerful than he has ever seen her. She is a wild animal. Small though she may be, she is not to be impeded. She is in charge. She could own him with a word. Haefner has never been so aroused.

"Do you love me, Ernst?" she hollers at him.

He stutters. The sun is beating down on him. Sweat pours off his brow.

"Do you?"

"Yes!"

"Do you want to fuck me?"

Haefner has absolutely no clue how to answer this, though the answer is obvious. He would take her now, on the road, if he could.

"Do you, I said?"

"Yes. Yes."

"Then listen to me."

Hana confronts him between the car and a railing, right as men are heading to work and women are going shopping and prisoners are being gassed at the camps. She grabs the lapels of his coat.

"The DNA molecule consists of two spiraling strands, a double helix. You've seen my drawings. The strands are connected by a latticework of proteins. These strands break apart and reunite to form a different entity, to identify who we are, who our ancestors were, who our descendants will

174

be. The proteins themselves form a code, Ernst, like a secret message that has to be unencrypted, a massive incredibly long code, a unique code of life for every living thing on this planet, which, if deciphered, could open the world to us."

"You don't know this. You can't possibly know all this."

"I'm telling you."

"You're bluffing."

"All I need is time." Hana backs away, releases Haefner from her grip, attempts to compose herself. Once she has, she stares him square in the eye. "I want my work, unimpeded. No one bothers me. Not Gretchen. Not Hitler. I want a baby. Give me both and I am yours. Do you have a backbone, Ernst? Can you promise me these things? I need to know now."

Hana folds her arms across her chest and waits. Not long.

Haefner, breathing heavily but totally under her sway, tries to compose himself. Who knows which promises can be kept and which ones, no matter how well-intentioned, will ultimately die?

But for the moment, Haefner can say only one thing. "How should we do it?"

Chapter Twenty

May 1947

Major Adams has decided that, for the benefit of his investigation, he should descend upon the Ziegler estate minus two of his passengers, Avi Kreisler and Harold McAuliffe. They can share a beer in Nuremberg, for all he gives a damn, while he and Captain David McAuliffe seek out Hana Ziegler and Silke Hartenstein.

"You knew her?" Adams asks his fellow officer on the way.

"In Copenhagen. Briefly. While my father was ambassador. She was just a kid, a harmless kid with an IQ off the charts. The way she bonded with my sister..."

"Margaret."

"Peggy. Peg. That's what we call her," David explains. "They were both outcasts, I think. Hana's parents, no, they were her grandparents, I thought were extremely cold to her. And her uncle Walter..."

David pauses remembering.

"Her uncle Walter? You mean, the dead guy?" Adams considers the implications. "You knew him back then? He knew Charlie?"

"Yuh. They palled around a bit. I had to keep him away from Peggy. He was a little older than us but I'm sure he would have..."

"What?"

"If the opportunity had presented itself. I'm sure you know what I mean."

"Fucked her? Jeez." Adams doesn't need the full version. "A real dog, huh?

176

I always thought your sister was…you know. How is she?"

"She's a full-time resident at an institute in upstate New York. Dad put her there before the war. It specializes in adults with neurological problems. I feel guilty for not having been able to visit her to see how she's doing. I used to be her protector, you know. Sort of."

"From Walter. The dead guy. What the hell. The war fucked us all up in a lot of ways. What are you gonna do?"

They are driving through pristine countryside. David can understand why Hana prefers to stay out here rather than live in the city. He remembers their visits to the Copenhagen botanical gardens and how at peace they all felt. Even Peg.

"In any case," David says, "I find it hard to fathom that the Hana I knew is the same Hana people claim tortured prisoners at Dachau."

"There are plenty enough affidavits from witnesses."

"Affidavits which I have read and which, if I must act as the defense for the moment, are quite vague. No one actually saw her do anything. They witnessed her selecting children off the trains. There is no confirmed record of what she did with them."

"She took thousands of tissue samples from adult men and women while she was in the camp," Adams argues. "There are plenty of witnesses to that."

"For what purpose? Did she harm any of them? For everyone else, there is a clear, documented evidentiary record of gross mistreatment, torture, murder. But not her."

"Because," Adams says, steering the car now onto the property of Ilse Ziegler, "she did everything at Haefner's place. She even had him convert his farm into a laboratory where she could conduct her experiments on children without anyone else knowing what she was up to. It's called corporate secrecy. Face it, David, what you see as genius, is very likely depravity."

"I don't believe it."

"Don't. You're the one who brought up neurological problems. Bonding."

Adams points to a greenhouse and slowly brings the car to a stop.

"Besides," he says, "once we found out Walter Ziegler's identity, I had my lieutenant round up everything we could find on him. He was SS, a very efficient, good record keeper."

"So?"

The men start walking toward the greenhouse. Two shapes move inside.

"So," Adams says, "not only did he document the experiments that your Hana conducted on twins, he suspected that your old friend murdered Haefner's wife to get her way with him. It's like her uncle was obsessed with her. Had a dossier this thick. Nice, huh? Motive to kill?"

David walks, eyes down, noting the flowers planted along the walkway to the greenhouse. Beautiful colors. Clipped shrubbery. A lawn recently mowed. The smell of the grass is strong.

It's late May, after all. The sun is high in the sky. An Alpine breeze is a welcoming, modifying sensation. How could anything as bad as Adams is suggesting have happened in a place such as this? At the hands of a teenage girl?

David isn't buying it. Not yet anyway. He looks up at the sound of a motor. A man wearing a straw hat is operating a tractor. He calls to them in German.

"You gentlemen looking for someone?"

"Hana Ziegler," David says. "That her in the greenhouse?"

"She and my daughter."

"You are?"

"Vitor Hartenstein. You leave them alone now, you hear? Haven't you Americans done enough? I know what you done to my Silke."

"Not us," says Adams, hands raised, palms open.

But David turns a guilt-ridden face away from the man, a gesture his fellow American doesn't miss.

"Should I ask?" Adams wonders.

"No."

"Anything to do with your dad being here?"

"A complication, that's all. Nothing to do with your investigation."

"I hope the fuck not."

David's first inclination is to knock on the greenhouse door. A foolish thought, he decides, born of years of being told always to be polite. Six years of war, millions dead, should have cut that habit out of him. It hasn't, but he opens the door anyway without announcing himself causing the two young women inside to stiffen with a natural reflex borne on two million rapes.

"*Alles gut,*" Adams says. "*Macht nichts.*" Don't worry.

David recognizes Hana right away. The other girl is more Germanic. Sturdy, taller, blonde, quite stunning even in a filthy apron and boots. Hana, he thinks, has blossomed, as well. Not so shy. Not so bent in on herself. There is a more confident manner to the way she confronts a stranger, shoulders straight, eyes unwavering. Startlement gone, she stands erect. Pregnant.

"Well," he says smiling and taking off his cap. "Sorry for busting in on you like this. Do you remember me, Hana? From Copenhagen? David McAuliffe."

"Yes. Of course. David." Her stepping forward to take David's hand allows Silke to relax, as well. Even so, Silke stands firm with trowel in hand like a soldier guarding her leader, ready to use that weapon in her defense.

"This is Tom Adams," David says.

"Major Thomas Adams. At your pleasure, ladies."

"We speak English here, gentlemen," Hana says. "Are you thirsty? It gets hot in here. We have orange juice."

Hana offers a pitcher of juice that she and Silke have just squeezed out of the fruit from one of her grandmother's trees.

"Maybe we could speak outside where it's cooler," Adams says. "You are aware, or perhaps you aren't, of your uncle's murder? Yes? No? On the way to Switzerland. Sorry if this comes as a shock to you. It doesn't seem to. Tried for the border, didn't make it. Nor, unfortunately, did the American who was driving him."

There is, of course, a good reason for broaching the matter in the way Adams does. It is meant to elicit a response.

David notices that Hana's is one of surprise but not shock. Walter Ziegler's abrupt and violent end doesn't cause any kind of strong emotional upset, but it does disturb her. He can see it in her eyes. Her mind is actively working. An alibi? Silke, on the other hand, he notes, shows nothing at all. Adams could have told her it was going to be sunny and warm tomorrow, for all the response she gave.

"Can we?" Adams gestures toward the door. "Outside? Unless you don't mind the heat."

Hana lowers her gardening tool and unfastens her apron. Silke does the same and they precede the two men outside. Beneath a lime tree, Ilse has set up a pleasant place to take lunch, an umbrellaed table with four chairs. David pulls a chair out for Hana then follows suit with Silke who lets him have an unsettling flirtatious smile before sitting.

The married Army officer Adams wants to get right to the point. "You're pregnant," he says. "May I ask who the father is?"

"Is it relevant?"

"In a police matter, everything is relevant. Your uncle was killed. A man was involved. And a woman. Is it intended to be a secret? The father's name, I mean. Or is it, you know..."

David intervenes. "He means, he doesn't see a wedding ring on your finger. It really isn't his business. What you do..."

At that serious, potentially incriminating moment, the two women do something that takes the course of the conversation on an unexpected detour. They break up into hilarity. Silke's old habit conferred upon Hana. The men's consternation only heightens the gales of laughter, until Hana and Silke can barely breathe and collapse into each other's arms.

"Otto," Hana manages to splutter at last. "Otto, my lawyer, he's the baby's father."

"That is advocacy these days in Germany," Silke says, hiccoughing, eying David, still with that twinkle in her eye.

Adams sits in stone-faced embarrassed silence. David, at least, is somewhat amused. You see, he wants to tell his colleague, how can this beautiful, happy young woman be a Nazi torturer, a killer? As for her friend...

"Seriously?" David says "Otto? I wouldn't have pegged him as your type."

"A little too starchy, too German, for my tastes," says Adams. "Stiff."

"Oh, then, you don't know our Otto," says Silke. Her laughter has mutated into something far less frivolous as she turns her gaze on David. "He's our

Cary Grant. But now your brother, that's another matter."

"My brother."

The conversation has shifted. Adams, annoyed, persists on his own course, tunnel-visioned. "So, you're saying, Otto killed your uncle because…Walter was a threat to you. He had direct evidence against you, and Otto was trying to protect you."

"Otto hasn't the instinct to commit such a crime," Hana says. Now she is utterly serious, as well. "None of us do. You're questioning the wrong people, Major."

"Gretchen Haefner?"

"Why do you bring her up?"

"Your uncle Walter did. He thinks you killed her."

"The German police declared her death an accident."

"The German police," Adams says. He feels he has Hana on the ropes. Young. Inexperienced. Guilty as shit of something. "Your uncle left behind documents, letters. His opinion of you is short of eulogistic."

"My uncle…"

"Her uncle…" Silke raises her voice. She leans forward and thrusts a warning finger in Adams's face. "…was an SS official who fucked me so he could have a pure Aryan baby. Then he kept on fucking me because he wanted more. Did you read any of that in his files? Did he ask? Did he care what I thought? How I felt? Did he care when they drove Hana to the Hollenschloss Institute when she was fourteen years old…fourteen…to have her euthanized? That's what they tried to do to her. Euthanized!"

Silke has to take a breath. She is hyperventilating from rage. But she's not done yet, and the men are wise enough to let her go on.

"Walter never knew, never realized, how many abortions I had. Was it two, Hana? Or three?"

"Two."

"I could have had a third, you see, Herr McAuliffe. But I didn't. Have you met my little girl, my little Charlotte? Should we tell your friend here who **her** father is?"

Adams has no riposte for this. He can guess, doesn't really want to. Sinking back into his chair and turning his gaze on his friend, he knows he is losing this round.

"David," he says, "it's Charlie, isn't it?"

After all, if Hana has a motive, and Otto has a motive, and Silke has a motive, so now do the McAuliffes.

"Palling around with Walter, you said, David."

"That's the buzz. In Copenhagen. Years ago. I rather doubt they maintained any kind of relationship once the war began."

This is not the way David meant for the subject to be broached, though he supposes no time would have been a good time. His burst of laughter isn't because he finds the whole situation comical, but because there is no better way, that he can think of, to confront the absurdity of it all.

"President Charles 'Sir Lanceslot' McAuliffe," he says through his subsiding fit of merriment. "Would I be making a complete ass of myself if I told you, Fraulein Hartenstein, that at least he has excellent taste?"

"You would," she says. "Rape is rape whether by an SS officer or by an American liberator. You don't want to know the things I saw in those last days while we were being liberated."

David nods. "I think I **will** take some of that orange juice now," he says. "Don't get up. I'll get it. For all of us? I do apologize, Fraulein Hartenstein."

Once he is gone, Adams takes measure of the two young German women sitting across the table from him. Both in their twenties. Yet, somehow, together, they are formidable.

"Are you sweating them?" he inquires. "You know what I mean. Hitting the McAuliffes up for cash? Bribing them? How do you even know Charlie McAuliffe is the father? Are you trying to tell me he's the only man you had sex with in forty-five'45? You just said..."

It is Hana who, rising from her chair, slaps Adams across the face.

"Didn't you just hear **what** she said? Old women were raped by your soldiers. By the French and the English, too. Little girls. Whoever had a vagina and was available. How dare you?"

When Hana retains her chair, she is trembling. Silke takes her hand. "I'm not stupid, Herr Major," she says. "Walter stopped coming to me when he saw the war was a lost cause. As bad a man as he was, he was careful, always planning ahead. He went into hiding. He covered his tracks. I don't know where he was. Neither of us did, so we can't be your killers."

"As for how we know David's brother is Charlotte's father," Hana adds, "it's really quite simple. He thanked Silke for the good time and left his number. Now **that's** stupid."

David returns then, carrying a full pitcher in one hand and managing to hold onto four glasses with the other. Everyone is silent as he pours, silent as he sits down and empties his glass.

"Isn't anyone else going to drink?" he asks.

"I will," says Silke. "*Danke*, Herr McAuliffe."

"As if that isn't proof enough," Hana says as if her conversation with Adams had never stopped, "David's brother left a sample of his manhood inside Silke."

"Yeah. So?"

"That sample contains genetic information that can only be traced to the person who deposited it. And that genetic information matches perfectly to Silke's daughter. Case closed, Herr Major."

Adams says nothing, fingering his glass nervously, glancing at David as if Charlie McAuliffe's brother can refute the German genius's claim.

"Is that true?" he says. "I think you're bluffing. Who's ever heard of such a thing? No one can do that."

Hana stares Adams down. If she is bluffing, if her science is really just science fiction, she isn't giving anything away.

"That will be easy enough to disprove," he says. "Even if you are right, no court would take your experiments on children as evidence in court. Which still begs the key question: who killed Walter Ziegler and William Sorensen? My money is on someone sitting at this table, and it sure as hell wasn't me."

Chapter Twenty-One

June 1944

Among the other construction projects that Hana has been able to finagle out of Haefner is a small play area for the children she manages to save from the gas chambers. In the very week the Allied troops are landing in France and beginning the long road to Berlin, Anatoly Radichevski and his sister Xenia, age nine, are playing on a seesaw. Silke is watching them carefully, for around Gretchen Haefner one has always to be on the alert. The children could be kidnapped and returned to the camps for extermination.

The Radichevskis are the first children to occupy the shelter space created out of Haefner's barn. The stalls have been turned into separate sleeping areas. There is a bathroom, classroom, dining area, and large closets for their personal items, which were very few to begin with. Anatoly and Xenia are excited because they've been told more children are coming to join them today.

"How many? How many?" they wonder. "How old will they be? Like us?"

"I don't know," says Silke who has been given time away from her nursing duties at Dachau to care for her newborn Ursula who she is breastfeeding on a bench while the twin Radichevskis play.

Anatoly and Xenia are certainly much healthier than when they arrived, Silke thinks. Hana takes good care of them. She's a good mother. An overprotective mother. She has to be around Gretchen whose work persists, now at Dachau, but who will bear an eternal grudge until one or both she and Hana are in the ground.

"Look!"

Xenia notices the bus first and leaves Anatoly not only high and dry but on the ground with a plunk as he was up in the air when Xenia deserted him.

"Walk, Xenia," Silke shouts, following with Ursula in her arms and an uninjured Anatoly giving chase after his sister.

The bus stops on the drive before the great Haefner estate house. Hana trips on the step coming down and nearly falls, she is so anxious to show off her pediatric inventory.

"Six of them," she shouts at Silke. "Six of them. I was only allowed to take six, but, oh, how wonderful they all are."

Hana is laughing. She is crying. She can't stop babbling.

"Six," she says, "but there were so many others. It was awful. A mother pushed her child into my arms. 'Take him! Take him!' she cried. And I did try, Silke, I did, but the SS officer wouldn't let me. 'He's too fit. He can still work.' Can you imagine, Silke? Such cruelty."

"Gretchen?"

"Yes, she was there. She took her share. What could I do? It's a miracle we got any of them. There'll be other trains. There'll be more."

The children descend. Six of them. Six saved from the gas chambers at least for the time being. Hana has a bill of lading, a list of the children, who are still in shock as they leave the bus and gaze at their new surroundings. Silke peruses the list.

Oleg Baranowski, age 10, Strabismus, Cross-eyed

Monica Baranowski, age 6, Disambiguation, Stutters

Renata Lembeck, age 7, Polio

Shmuel Ganz, age 9, Polio

Sara Lewinsohn, age 11, Orofacial cleft, Cleft palate

Zaidie Steinberg, age 4, Undiagnosed brain disorder

"Line up, children," Hana says, "so we can get a good look at you. No, no, don't. It reminds me too much of the trains. Just…"

185

"Calm down, Hana."

Silke hands her infant to Hana and heads toward the play area, gesturing for the children to follow her. "Let them have a chance to play," she says. "Let them see we mean them no harm."

Hana follows. She is lucky the Radichevski twins have been with her for a few weeks. They take the lead, showing the other children that it's okay to have fun. The only one who holds back is the six-year-old, Monica Baranowski, the stammerer, who sucks her thumb and stands off to the side.

"I don't know if I can do this," Hana admits, watching the children roust about. She has her own thumb stuck in the corner of her mouth, surveying the wild activity of the suddenly released children. "I may have taken on more than I can handle. I was never a child like this. How do I do it? How do I keep them alive?"

"Not by yourself," Silke says. "I'm here. Hilda will help, and I bet if you ask your grandmother, she will, too. My mother definitely will. We'll be a team."

Hana wraps an arm about Silke's waist and rests her head on her friend's arm. "This war can't last forever, can it?" she asks. "I hear planes going overhead almost every night. The stories about what the Russians are doing to our people in the East are terrifying. And I hear all the women talking. They say the Americans will burn everything to the ground. Ernst is worried they might bomb Dachau and kill all of us and the prisoners as well as the SS. How can we keep them safe when we can't even keep ourselves safe? Look at that one."

Hana leaves her bench. Children can adapt, and the others are climbing the slide, swinging, and digging in a sandbox. The six-year-old, Monica, just watches. Her clothes are the same clothes she has been wearing probably for weeks. Rags. Slippers on her feet. Her hair is filthy. They all need baths, which should be the first item on the agenda, Hana thinks.

"Don't you want to play?" she asks the girl.

A vigorous shake of the head is all Hana gets.

"We have swings, a seesaw, a slide. Doesn't any of that interest you?"

Again, the negative. But this time, the little girl adds a humming sound which only grows in intensity every time Hana tries to convince her to be happy. When she brushes the child's cheek with her fingers, Monica jerks away and utters a cry.

"I only want to help you," Hana insists. But each attempt Hana makes to corral Monica to comfort her only makes the disturbed child back farther away. She is mumbling to herself, a heartbreaking sound Hana is all too familiar with.

"You remind me of me when I was a little girl," she says. "I used to hum like that when I was afraid. Do you feel unloved, too? I can't imagine the things you've seen. We won't hurt you here. We'll love you."

For the moment, herself feeling overwhelmed by the task she has taken on, Hana merely tries a smile. Patience will serve this child more than anything, she thinks.

This one, I will take under my wing.

* * *

But it won't be easy. She was only given permission to extricate the children from the other prisoners bound for Dachau on the premise that she needed them for research purposes. The SS, in turn, will want to see proof that that research is bearing fruit.

Over the following weeks, Hana develops a routine. It's the scientist in her. Somewhat rigid, but at least the children know what to expect. She is studying them with an intensity demanded of a medical student. Haefner has provided her medical textbooks from the university. Each night before she goes to bed, after a ten-hour day spent with the children, drawing blood, taking tissue samples, weighing them, measuring them, giving them psychological tests, giving them personal therapeutic time, she spends at least two hours reading about their conditions.

The children don't speak the same languages. So, time is devoted to learning simple German. Hana adds reading, spelling, and math to her curriculum and makes sure several hours each day are spent in the classroom.

All Germans know how important exercise is. Silke helps there. As a BDM girl, she knows her calisthenics and leads the children through common drills to help make them healthy again. She can also teach them how to take care of their bodies. Somehow, she always gets them laughing, too. Even Monica.

Grandmother Ilse, when she deigns to look in, says Hana is spoiling them by not making them clean up after themselves. But she is happy to have them visit her greenhouse on occasion to learn about flowers and trees. She even buys them their own gardening tools and can be seen, when she is caught unaware, smiling, daydreaming, perhaps, how life would have been different with her own daughter had she the chance to redo things.

Silke's mother Gertrud does the communal cooking based upon her own old family recipes, and Hilda seems to enjoy coming over to bathe the children and dress them properly with clothes Herr Haefner has good-naturedly purchased. A team effort indeed.

Frau Haefner is still an issue to be dealt with. Gretchen. Haefner has said he will file for divorce. But Hana has her doubts. At heart, she knows he is a coward and prefers to deal with difficult matters through his attorney Reinhardt Froeling.

"Fine," Hana tells him. "But I won't let you touch me until she's gone."

The whole arrangement is beyond acceptable to Otto. He's been a very tolerant Uncle Otto for several months, even given to piggyback rides when pressed into duty. But he was never happy with the acknowledged quid pro quo.

"I won't stand for it," he rants one rainy Friday afternoon in August just after his father has shown him the Haefner divorce papers. He waves these about as he yells at Hana. "Screwing that old man. You can't be serious. What? Are you really planning to marry him? Have his children? Absurd!"

Hat in hand, he marches back and forth behind her, as she jots data into her ubiquitous notebooks in the office Haefner has created for her in the main house. Otto vents.

"It's just an arrangement," Hana insists.

"Not in Haefner's mind. He wants you, body and soul."

"So, do you."

"That's different. I'm young. He's old. He's a Nazi. I'm not."

"When the war's over..." Hana seems to promise.

"When the war's over, what?" Otto ceases his pacing and lays a gentle hand on Hana's shoulder. "I love you, Hana. You don't know how much. Sometimes I don't think you care. It's the children. It's the work. God help us, what if the Nazis win? Have you thought of that? Then what? You know what. All is lost."

"Otto, please..."

"You must be realistic. You of all people should know what the world can be like. I love you, Hana. I have since..."

"Yes. I know."

"Forever. But you won't marry me, will you?"

"Not now, Otto. You know, it's impossible."

"Yes. Well..."

Otto puts his hat back on and turns to leave, knowing full well that the girl he is desperately in love with will never change her mind. Once she is committed to something, she can't be torn away from it. And these children...he... He hears them outside playing, happy, laughing. Not dead, as they would otherwise be if not for her. He pauses at the door. She has managed to make him feel depressed and guilty as usual.

"You'll need a plan," he tells her. "An escape route. That's the only way. If I can think of one....If not...."

Some possibilities are inconceivable. Like the one reasonable Otto has said could very well come to fruition despite all the news from East and West. Hitler wins. Himmler wins. Goebbels wins. Walter and Gretchen win. What then?

It is that very night that Hana decides, without consulting Silke or anyone else, that the plan is obvious. Her plan, at least. Carrying it out will not be easy. She's not even sure at the moment how she will do it. Such a thing will damn her for life. But it is clear. She must kill both Gretchen and Haefner. Walter, too, if need be.

It rains that night. Is God warning her to back off? Or is He offering encouragement? 'Get a backbone, Hana,' He thunders. 'Look what they've done to you. Think of what they'll do to you, to the children.' Well, what of it? Isn't God a murderer? Hasn't He either drowned, burned, or brought plagues into the world or, at best, turned a blind eye when men do His dirty work for Him? Why should Hana feel any guilt?

As it so happens, the night is a Friday. Three of the children Hana has saved from Dachau are Jewish: Shmuel Ganz, an orphan from Poland; Zadie Stein, the youngest, whose mother died on the train and whose polio would have had her eliminated minutes after she entered Dachau; and Sara Lewinsohn with the cleft palate, at eleven, the oldest of the children.

Sara has been teaching Hana Hebrew. A little every night before the lights go out and the children go to sleep.

"I'm part Jewish," Hana has told them, quite openly.

"Part is plenty."

On Friday evenings, they have even been lighting a single Sabbath candle, though in secret. Gretchen still occupies the house and has spies among the Haefner staff. Sara says the prayer over the candle, Hana and the other Jewish children whispering along. But Hana is distracted tonight, her mind elsewhere, her senses tuned to things beyond the ken of the children.

"Do you think we'll really live?" Sara asks her, the light of the single candle flickering on her face.

Hana is startled. Her eyes were turned toward the window of the barn, her ears listening for the sound of an engine.

"Of course. Why not? Would God abandon you?"

"He has already, hasn't He?"

"Well, I won't. You can be sure of that. You know Uncle Otto."

"Yes."

"He has a plan."

Hana says this cradling Monica on her lap. The girl who hardly spoke upon arriving at the Haefner estate, has begun to open up though it's still sometimes hard to understand what she's saying.

"W-w-w-what p-p-p-plan?"

"Remember what I taught you," Hana encourages the girl. "Think about what you want to say. One word at a time. Plan it out in your head. Then say it like you're speaking to someone who is old and going deaf. What."

"W-what."

"Better, see?"

"What. P-plan. Plan!"

"Yes! Perfection! My grandmother Ilse always said the same thing about me," she tells the girl. "And my grandfather. You wouldn't have wanted to meet him, I can tell you. Speak up! Speak up! What are you? A mouse? Who can hear anything you say?" When Hana nibbles on Monica's ear lobe, the girl brays an equine snort that makes everyone else laugh.

For a moment, Hana is reflective. Yes, genetics is key, but so is environment. How different things might have been had her mother lived, had her grandparents cared about her. It is Hana's belief, the lynchpin of her research, that both genetics and environment can be overcome. 'What was' can be undone. Unfortunately, cradling Monica, gazing at all of her kids, she knows full well in a world such as this that the same thing can also be said of the 'what is.'

The children can't possibly know everything that is going through her mind at this moment. Past, present, and future. It all seems a blank right now. Uncertainty is the catchword for the night. What will happen if Hana dares to take the syringe filled with nothing but air and sticks it into the arm of the sleeping Gretchen Haefner? Will suspicions be aroused? Will Haefner, even if he suspects the truth, give her up? Will God?

"With all due respect for you boys, Anatoly, Shmuel, Oleg," Hana tells them when she returns to the present, "we girls can't afford to be quiet. People will take advantage of us, you see. They won't see everything that we can be."

"Like you," says Renata, the seven-year-old with polio.

"Well, maybe more like your aunt Silke."

Hana stays with the children until the wax has melted and the flame burns out. Then she kisses them all good night. Outside, she looks for the car Gretchen drives to and from Dachau. Some nights, she doesn't bother coming home. She stays in a hotel in Munich at Haefner's expense. Why she bothers to continue to occupy this house at all remains a mystery. Perhaps she is planning to do away with Hana so Haefner will give up his pursuit of divorce. Pure hate can act as motive, too. Racial hatred.

There is a BMW in the garage. Hana only recognizes Gretchen's vehicle when a bolt of lightning briefly brightens the grounds of the estate. Her heart rate quickens. Her belly aches with dread. Her head spins. Can she do this thing? Does she dare?

Dipping her head, which is uncovered, she braves the rain and doesn't realize she's been followed until she reaches the house. Then, just as she is opening the door into the kitchen, she feels a tug on her coat.

"Monica, honey," she says, "you're getting soaked. Why didn't you stay in bed?"

"It's my birthday."

"What?"

"My b-birthday!"

Hana swings the door open and hurries her ward inside. The kitchen still smells of the pancakes and sausages that Frau Hartenstein prepared for supper.

"Your birthday," Hana says, dripping rain on the floor. "Why didn't you tell us?"

"I did. You d-didn't hear."

"You see? Speak up."

Now Hana doesn't know what to do.

"Can I s-sleep with you t-tonight?" the now seven-year-old begs. "As a p-present? J-Just this once?"

How can Hana say 'no'? Her plans have been frustrated. On the other hand, what a blessing has been granted her. Monica may be her angel sent from God, after all, preventing her from committing a horrible crime.

"Check in the refrigerator," she says. "See if any of Frau Hartenstein's strudel is left. We can snack in bed. How's that?"

Strudel and two glasses of lemonade made from lemons grown in Ilse Ziegler's greenhouse. Hana is actually feeling lighthearted now, as if she, like the children of Dachau, has been saved from a terrible fate. Even running into Gretchen on the back staircase with Monica doesn't cause her to lurch

192

and drop the strudel.

"Frau Haefner," she says, "it would be a lot easier on both of us if you would simply accept me for who I am."

Gretchen pauses on the staircase going down. She is wearing pearls and an expensive gold bracelet and a new outfit as if she is going out on the town despite the rain.

"I can't," she says. "I respect your intelligence, Fraulein Ziegler. You're clever, one can't deny that. But you can never change who you are, no more than can these children of yours. And Germany will have an end to it. It's just a matter of time."

Gretchen resumes her descent. Hana offers a comforting smile to Monica who is too young to understand Gretchen's condescension. What Frau Haefner doesn't understand, Hana thinks, as she steers her child toward the bedroom, is just how lucky she is that she will not die tonight.

* * *

There is a box of syringes lying open on her desk. Hana closes it and hides it in a drawer before Monica can find it. She has begun writing a diary, and while Monica is allowed to bathe herself in lilac bath bubbles with a dozen bath toys, Hana jots down whatever emotions are most prevalent at the moment.

In some ways, her maintaining a personal log is an act of science, an impersonal recording of her emotions that would fit as well on a graph or chart. As a graph, her day today would appear like the Alps, sharp peaks and valleys. An analyst might say this signifies the neurological map of a person with a severe bipolar condition. Hana knows better. Rather, it is symbolic of what it is like to live in a world that constantly traumatizes its inhabitants. One moment, you're full of hope. The next, none. For adults, such a world is hard enough. For children, she thinks, the effects must be devastating, possibly permanent. She reminds herself that neurological testing on the children will have to commence soon.

Hana looks up from her writing. Can the outside world affect our genes?

Can mutations be caused by someone hating you so much, you incorporate that hate chemically. Your genetic structure is altered and you pass that hatred on to your children so that they come to hate for no reason other than that is how they were born?

Something is going on out in the yard. Hana hears shouting, yelling. She rises and gazes out her window into darkness and a downpour. Men are out on the driveway and in the yard, a lot of them. She can see them because they're all carrying flashlights.

"*Schnell Schnell*! Over there! Spread out!"

SS. All helmeted and armed. Their leader is yelling orders at them. They are searching for something. They are searching for someone. Hana's immediate thought is, 'The children!'

"Monica, come out of the tub now."

She whisks the girl out of the water and throws a towel around her. "Get into bed," she orders.

"What about m-my clothes?"

"Never mind. I'll get them."

"Can I have the l-lemonade?"

"Yes. Of course. But in bed. And turn off the light when you're done. Don't wait for me. I'll be right back."

Hana puts on her shoes and grabs a raincoat from her closet. Downstairs she is joined by Haefner and Gretchen who appear to have been in deep discussion in the parlor when they, too, were disrupted by the shouting.

"SS," Hana says.

"Yes, I know."

"What could they want? Why are they here?"

Hana's suspicious gaze turns on Gretchen. "Don't look at me," Frau Haefner says. "But if it's the children they want, so be it. I told you so."

Hana dashes out into the rain and runs toward the barn. "*Was ist los? Was ist los?*"

Pools of water have collected on the path. She splashes through them unmindful of the soaking she is getting until in the darkness she runs headlong into an SS officer who turns a pistol on her.

194

CHAPTER TWENTY-ONE

"What's going on? Why are you here?" Hana demands.

"Who are you?"

"I live here."

"Then go back inside. It's dangerous out here. Some prisoners escaped from Dachau. They stole a vehicle. We found it on the side of the road just a kilometer from here. They're armed."

Hana doesn't consider retreat for a moment. Rather, she disobeys the SS officer and runs to the barn, ignoring his order to stop. Throwing open the doors, she hurries down the aisle between the stalls-turned-sleeping quarters. As she goes, she counts each child. Anatoly, Xenia, Oleg, Renata, Shmuel, Sara and Zaidie. Not one of them has been wakened by the shouting.

"Thank God," she says. A blessing.

She intends to stay with them until the SS catch their men or just go away. Then she hears something. Movement in the back of the barn by the closets. Whimpering? Crying? Recounting the children, she knows it can't be one of them. Perhaps an animal, a badger, or a marten out on their own evening hunt.

"Hello? Hello? If there is someone there, I'm not going to hurt you."

Hana doesn't dare switch on an overhead light. She doesn't want the children to wake. She doesn't want them frightened by the very men who were prepared to send them to the gas chambers at Dachau. Instead, she creeps forward, her attention divided between the sound of the SS soldiers approaching the barn and the shape she can now see huddled between a closet and a trough-now-toy chest.

"You, there."

The shape groans, cowers.

"They'll find you sure enough if you stay where you are," she says to it. "You don't have much time."

"Hide me. For the love of God, hide me, or I'm a dead man."

'Then why did you come here?' Hana wants to shout at him. Of all places.

"You should have kept going into the forest." Instead, she is thinking, you have put my children at risk.

The SS men are now at the barn, the beams of their flashlights playing over the sleeping forms of the children who begin to stir and call out.

Hana says, "Quickly! Quickly! This way."

The man rises with difficulty. Perhaps he has been wounded. So much the worse for him. But there's no time to be sympathetic. He has to hurry. Now.

"In here," she tells him. It is another trough, this one filled with bedding for the children. She can hear them crying and wailing and calling her name. But that's a good thing, for they are causing a delay, forcing the SS men to look under their beds and question them.

"Are you sure?"

"Get in."

The escapee from Dachau no longer hesitates, and the moment he is curled up inside the small space, Hana closes the lid and sits down on it. What a funny thing fate is, she thinks, as the SS troops close in. Strange how the vagaries of life can twist things in such bizarre ways.

She is scared, for herself and for her children. And yet there is room in her mind for one other less frightening concept. Fascination for the odd way life brings some unpredictable elements around full circle.

How else to explain the arrival of the prisoner from Dachau? A man she knows as her former psychiatrist, Lorenz Koerner.

Chapter Twenty-Two

May 1947

"Do you really want to know how it was? I was a witness to it all. The day you Americans liberated Dachau."

Silke makes her testimonial offer in the Hartenstein parlor. She has been studying to return to school. Her days as a BDM girl deprived her of much of the true education she would have preferred. Auto mechanics? Really? Loading ammo onto a tank? Please. It was her nursing responsibilities at Dachau, with Hana's encouragement, that decided her that, if she ever got the chance, she would become a doctor.

The arrival of David McAuliffe and his father Harold has upset her lesson in organic chemistry. Hana has been wonderful in letting her have free rein in the Haefner labs to put into practice what she is learning from her textbooks. Hana has the kids today, Ursula and Charlotte, giving Silke the time to study. Unfortunately, her concentration was broken the moment she heard the car motor and, shortly after, the loud voice of the elder McAuliffe saying, "She better cooperate."

"Why must I better cooperate?" she asks them, allowing them in. She does so with a smile because, despite feelings of unease, she thinks she has in David a not-so-secret admirer.

Now she is sitting in the parlor with them by herself. The children are with Hana. Her parents are working. Her brother Georg is dead, May 1945, a seventeen-year-old Nazi youth soldier in Berlin defending the German capital from the Russian hordes. Oh, well, that worked, didn't it?

She has offered them no food or beverage. She dislikes Harold McAuliffe intensely. To her, McAuliffe is the American poster boy, brash, arrogant, thoughtless. He is rich, vain, expects to be handed anything he wants without the slightest impediment. The only thing he isn't is Texan.

"I've come a long way to hear the truth," he tells her from a rickety old chair that squeaks whenever he leans in her direction. "I brought a checkbook with me, and I'm a reasonable man. Charlotte is your daughter, apparently with my son. What do you want? That is to say, how much?"

Silke sits in a rocking chair, one formerly used by a grandmother who did all her knitting here in front of the fireplace. She is as calm as can be, hands folded in her lap. Dressed for the summer weather, she shows off the tops of her breasts though this is not to impress the younger McAuliffe. She knows he is already hooked.

"I thought Hana made it clear in her letter to you that money is of no interest to us," she says. "We simply want your son, your other son..." said with a smile at David, "...to own up to his responsibilities. To admit his paternity and to be a father to Charlotte. How hard is that?"

David, who is sitting in a more solid leather chair beside his father, can't help lowering his eyes. He doesn't want Harold to see how amused he is by the proceedings. *This girl Silke*, he is thinking. She can threaten in the sweetest way. She beguiles him and he can't help but be entertained by the way she is twisting his father around her fingers.

Harold isn't quite so enthralled. He has an angry vengeful wife to go home to and a son whose political career is hanging in the balance of these ridiculous negotiations.

"I'm afraid that isn't possible, Fraulein," he says. "It was an irresponsible act on the part of your friend to try to hit us up for money."

"Which, as I said, is not her intent."

"Nevertheless, it's all the same. You're studying, I see."

"Yes."

"Good. Good for you. You wish to be a nurse."

"I wish to be a doctor. Perhaps I'll go into research. I haven't decided yet.

It's a long road."

Harold is caught off guard by the unexpected. A woman? A doctor? Is she playing with me?

"Well, however long the road is," he says, "a good education has costs. Tuition. Books. There'll be college, then med school. We'll cover the entire thing. For you and for Charlotte who will have an even longer road. Fraulein Ziegler, too. She's pregnant. What does she need? I'm making a very fine offer here, Fraulein Hartenstein. Turning it down would be absurd."

"And yet, nevertheless," Silke says, "that is what we are doing."

Her smile has vanished. Now she is staring down the former ambassador to Denmark, daring him to make the same offer twice. That would be a sign of insanity, wouldn't it? Repeating the mistake over and over again?

"Can he not come here himself? He has to send his father and his brother, the lawyer?"

"My son is quite busy."

Harold looks to his youngest son for support. 'For God's sake,' he is trying to convey with his eyes, 'you're the lawyer. I paid all that money to put you through Harvard Law. Do something.'

"Politics," David says to Silke.

He feels compelled to help in some way. But not for the reasons his father thinks. He is fiddling with his hat on his lap, finds it hard to maintain eye contact with Silke. She has all the beauty and charm of a Hollywood actress, but life has hardened her in ways that only the most astute can perceive. He sees it. His father does not.

"I want to hear your story," he says. "Maybe that will clear things up. How it happened? How my brother and you, shall we say, met?"

* * *

"'Met' is a nice neutral way of putting it," Silke says. "Luckily, my English is a lot better than it was two years ago when your brother and I 'met'."

Sitting alone in her parlor with the two Americans from Cape Elizabeth, Maine, Silke has to be a real magician, or, better, a Hollywood make-up

199

artist. She has learned over the years of Nazi rule how to present one face to the public while hiding her true feelings. Mr. McAuliffe is no Himmler, but, in a way, he is of the same mold. A powerful man who thinks he can get anyone, particularly a weak woman, to do his bidding. She didn't show Himmler or Goebbels weakness then. She won't show McAuliffe weakness now. Yet, having to relive those last few days at Dachau is not easy.

Germany was in a panic that April of '45. The Russians were bearing down on Berlin from the East. The Allies were crossing the border into Germany from the West. In Dachau, the SS were frightened. All their crimes would be discovered once the camps were liberated. Payback would surely follow.

Hauptscharfuhrer Walter Ziegler was sent to the camp to help cover things up. Dachau is a mess. Evacuations of other camps have already begun. But in Dachau, the SS have waited too long.

Walter finds Silke in the infirmary, filled to the rafters with the sick and dying. Typhus hit the camp the past autumn, killing hundreds of prisoners, but there are still thousands to be disposed of.

"Round them up," he yells at Silke and the remaining nurses who haven't fled. "I don't care how sick they are. I don't care if they can't walk. Drag them out, or we'll shoot them where they lie."

Silke has always been the brave one to stand up to authority, but this is different. This is chaos. No one cares what she thinks. No one wants to hear her excuses. If she doesn't obey, they'll simply shoot her, too.

"But where? Where are we supposed to take them?" she cries. "Look at them. Children."

"Himmler has ordered us to march them south to the Alps, toward the border with Switzerland," Walter tells her. "We hold out there. We negotiate. Who knows? It's over, Silke. It's every man for himself."

Doctors and nurses, who days before were helping some patients to recover, are now yelling at them to get up, get out. SS guards, men, and women, are threatening the delinquents with pistols. Silke's friend Dora is among them.

"*Rouse! Rouse!*" Dora behaves in a frenzied way, as if she's been downing caffeine and nothing else for weeks. She has lost her humanity. "Don't just stand there, Silke!" she screams. "The Americans are coming. They'll fuck you to death!"

Cabinets are overturned. Drawers thrust open, contents, records, removed, burned. It's chaos. Silke spots Gretchen Haefner throwing herself at an SS officer.

"My research! All my research!" she is hollering.

"Burn it!" he shouts back at her. "Burn it or be prosecuted for it. Your choice if you want to hang."

There are over thirty -thousand prisoners at Dachau. How do you get rid of them all, Silke wonders? She can't hide. She can't run. Some prisoners have. In the madness, some have managed to escape and are heading toward the Allied lines. Others are stuffed into trains, onto trucks, and hauled away.

Who is giving orders? Is anyone? A fire has been lit at Dachau and everyone is running for the exits. A large portion of the prisoners, over seven thousand, are forced to hit the road, without food or water, with just the minimal clothes on their backs. They are being force-marched to the Swiss border. They will serve as a barricade or a bargaining chip. Those who hold up the evacuation because they are too weak to move are shot and tossed aside.

Silke stays behind with those sick people who couldn't move if threatened with a bayonet up their asses. In the insanity and racing around, some prisoners manage to hide. Silke doesn't give them away. Rather, she gathers what medicines have not been appropriated for the SS wounded and stows them in places where she can recover them once the camp is empty of all but the most sick.

It takes two days. Two days to empty as much of the camp as possible. And days such as these can never be erased from the memory. Silke sleeps all of an hour, or here and there, when she can. Hard to sleep when there is so much yelling and screaming, when gunfire is constant.

On her way out aboard one of the last trucks to abandon the camp, Dora tells her there's been an insurrection in the town of Dachau. Even their own fellow Germans are turning against them. But the SS, she says, took care of them.

"What are you going to do, Dora?" Silke shouts at her friend as she is climbing into the back of the army truck.

"Come with me, Silke. Don't be crazy. You think they'll know you laughed at Goebbels? You won't have a pussy left once they get through with you. Curse your looks, girl. I always knew they'd get you into trouble."

But Silke won't leave her patients. Men, women, children. The helpless. They need her. And she's not alone. A few other nurses stay. A doctor, or two. Some of the guards. The camp is now under the direction of a minor officer named Heinrich Wicker, a mere lieutenant, a family man with a wife and children, who lives in a small house in the nearby town.

He tells Silke, "All we can do is hope the Americans treat us better than we treated our prisoners."

"You're a good man, Heinrich," she says. "You should have left with the others, gone to your family. At least, take off your uniform."

It is April 29 when the Americans finally arrive, the 157th Infantry, the 45th, and the 222nd. Silke doesn't know it, but Captain Charles McAuliffe is part of the 42nd Rainbow Division.

As the Americans invest the camp, they are duly horrified by what they see. The dead are everywhere. Piles of them. Stacks of them. The camp still smells of smoke and decaying bodies. Gunfire can be heard in the distance. The war isn't over yet.

The numb SS guards who have been left behind are now unarmed and at the mercy of the prisoners. Lieutenant Wicker maintains the illusion that the German camp hierarchy still exists and that he has the duty, the responsibility, to turn over the camp to the Americans. He does so with the full expectation that he will be treated as a prisoner of war and will have the chance to say goodbye to his family before he is arrested and becomes a prisoner himself.

Silke sees all this from the distance of a mind that is unable to fathom what is happening. She is exhausted, starving, emotionally drained. She is only twenty-two years old. She goes through the motions of caring for people when she can't even take care of herself. She wants to sleep but finds herself at night wandering the camp looking for something to eat. The American

Red Cross has brought food but not enough, not for her and the prison personnel who are being purposefully targeted for neglect.

In her wanderings, she stumbles in the dark, trips over a body. Rising to her hands and scraped knees, she realizes that there are many bodies, bullet-riddled, clothes ripped off, faces beaten in, punished in gruesome ways which, perhaps, these former SS guards deserved. But she doesn't believe Lieutenant Wicker deserved to be gunned down. It is his body she has tripped over.

She staggers to her feet. There is light coming from the Dachau commandant's headquarters. Music is playing, gay and lively. She doesn't recognize it. Big band. American. Maybe Jimmy Dorsey or Glenn Miller. The men inside are having a grand time. Well, why not? The war for them is over. Their laughter is relieved, raucous, unrestrained. Undoubtedly, they are drunk and their commander is fine with it.

Unwittingly, thinking there might be food to be shared, Silke pushes the door open and enters a scene of utter pleasurable merriment that would be worth joining if not for the women who are being shared by the victorious soldiers. Silke recognizes them as women who have worked at the camp in various capacities. But Silke stands out. She is beautiful. The moment she steps through the door, she becomes the grand prize.

"Well, well," she hears someone say, "Christmas in April."

"Christmas, Thanksgiving, and Happy New Year."

Silke's lips are so dry from thirst, she can hardly get any words out to explain that she is just looking for something to eat. As it is, her English is poor, so all she can do is gesture feeding herself.

"I think she wants to eat, Captain," a soldier close to the door chuckles. "You haven't had any yet. Why don't you feed her something?"

Laughter fills the room. Charlie McAuliffe hesitates at first. He is the officer in charge, after all. But in the back of his head, always there, is the voice of his father telling him, 'For the love of God, Charlie, just don't do anything stupid.'

Problem is, he's had too much to drink and he's the type of officer who likes being liked by his men. What harm can come of it? And, dear God, the

German bitch is beautiful.

"You're hungry?" Charlie says to Silke, rising and bringing her a plate of chicken and sauerkraut, half-eaten. "You look like shit. Have you slept at all? Eaten anything?"

"*Nein*," says Silke, gazing at the contents of the plate. "*Bitte*. Something to drink?"

"Oh, you'd like something to drink, too? Fine. Beer, boys. We need some beer here."

Request made, offer fulfilled, Silke takes a long swig of beer followed by Captain McAuliffe. He smiles. She smiles, and it is as if some unspoken agreement has been reached. It hasn't.

* * *

"Then he took me upstairs to the first bedroom he came to and raped me."

"He was drunk. You were drunk. Shit happens."

Harold stares unmoved at the young woman who is threatening his son's political future.

She says, "Shit does happen. I know that better than anyone. But a brave man steps forward and accepts his responsibilities. Is your son a brave man?"

"Yes, he is." Harold is quick to answer. "He served his country on the front lines when, as a son of privilege, he could have been assigned a cushy desk job. Do not question either my son's bravery or his integrity, young lady. You who served at Dachau."

"Was forced to serve at Dachau."

"Someday my son will be President of the United States!" Harold exclaims.

"Not with my vote!"

The meeting has reached a point where punches might be thrown. Even Silke has lost a measure of composure. David would almost like to see what happens next. But he compels his father to sit back down and raises his hand palm up to try mitigating the damage Harold has done.

"Fraulein Hartenstein," he says, "let us for the moment let cooler heads prevail. My father is guilty of loving his son too much. You can understand his wanting to be protective. You would be, too, under similar circumstances. Our offer has not gone away. We'll be in touch. Perhaps in a few days, this will all sort itself out."

He doesn't really believe that. He believes his brother should come clean. What his father isn't taking into consideration is this other mess regarding Bill Sorensen and Walter Ziegler. That could be a far more odorous kettle of fish to have to resolve.

He bids Silke a pleasant farewell, hoping he can get to see her again under better circumstances. Outside, he admonishes his old man.

"That was some negotiating, Dad."

"You didn't help."

"Well, maybe Fraulein Hartenstein is right. Maybe it's time for Charlie to grow up."

They walk to their German-made car. Harold gets into the passenger side, but before David can sit behind the wheel, another automobile speeds into view and comes to a squealing stop spraying David with dirt. The driver rolls down his window. David recognizes the lieutenant who works under Tom Adams.

"Glad I caught you, Captain McAuliffe," the lieutenant says. "Major Adams wants you to follow me right away."

'With my father?' crosses David's mind. "Why? What's so important?"

"They found something at the Haefner estate. Up in the woods." The lieutenant is excited. He's even out of breath as if he's run the entire distance rather than driven it.

David can't imagine what the cause could be. "Why? I know he got a warrant to search the place. What did they find? Trees?"

"No, Sir," says the lieutenant. "A grave."

Chapter Twenty-Three

D octor Lorenz Koerner is very lucky to be alive. Not lucky entirely, else how would he have ended up in Dachau?

Hana sits atop his hiding place the entire time the SS soldiers search the barn. She even opens the other side of the trough to show the hunters the bedding that is stored there. Satisfied, they move on. Even then she remains seated, shaking uncontrollably, until the crying of the children forces her to leave Koerner where he is.

"Stay put until I fetch you," she orders him through the closed lid.

"I'm suffocating."

"Then suffocate. It's better than being shot."

Or gassed. Or injected with a needle, which is what would have happened to her six years ago had Doctor Koerner's recommendation been carried out.

She has to see to the welfare of the children first. By now, they're all awake and all crying for attention. Hushing them, telling them everything will be okay, is insufficient because they can still hear the SS men outside.

"They're not interested in you," she tells them. "Some men ran away, and they're looking for those men."

"Are they looking for any children?" Shmuel asks.

"No. No children. You're safe with me."

"Will they shoot them?" asks Renata.

"I don't know, *Liebchen*. Maybe. But you're safe. No one is going to hurt you."

It takes a great deal of patience and physical comforting to finally get the children to lie back under their covers. The only lullaby Hana knows is one her mother used to sing to her, but she can't remember all the words. Where the words fail her, she hums, accompanied by Sara who mimics Hana from her bed until, from the oldest to the youngest, all of the kids eventually drift off to sleep. Then all is quiet. Even outside.

Until Koerner stirs.

"Thank you, Hana," he says. His voice is hoarse, dry.

She jerks upright, having dozed off herself. "I told you to stay put."

Koerner is leaning against one of the stalls, gasping for air. The rain has stopped. High humidity has replaced it.

"I was suffocating. Asthma. I've had it all my life."

"That's not my concern. You put the children in jeopardy coming here."

"I didn't know they were here."

Hana whispers a curse. Then she relents. Partly. She hasn't forgotten what this man did to her. "You can't stay here," she says.

"I'm afraid to leave. They'll kill me. Where can I go?"

"I don't know. I'm tired. It's late."

It's a good thing the children haven't woken up again. She goes to the entrance of the barn to see what she can see.

"It looks like they're gone," she says with a weary sigh. "I can't think straight right now. Stay here tonight. In the back. And don't wake the children."

"I'm awfully hungry."

"But alive, yes? All right. I'll see if I can find anything in the kitchen. But in the morning, you've got to find somewhere else to go."

There are two slices of Frau Hartenstein's strudel left in the refrigerator and several sausages. Hana brings these out to Koerner who wolves the entire plate while she watches.

"I don't know how they found out I had Jewish ancestry," he says between mouthfuls. "It was generations ago. Who figured they would research that far back?"

"You wanted me killed," Hana says. She's not interested in his ancestry or who sold him out. There are far more important questions to be asked. "You were my doctor. I trusted you."

Koerner practically licks his plate clean. This doctor of psychiatry has become an animal. "I'm glad things turned out the way they did," he says. "You've done well for yourself, Hana. A girl your age. I always knew you were brilliant."

"A girl with no future."

"Things were different then. Your grandfather is an insistent man."

"Excuses!" Hana raises her voice then immediately lowers it when one of the children moans in their sleep. "They were going to kill me, and you knew it."

What can Koerner say? Nothing.

"You could have told my grandfather to go fuck himself."

"He would have found another doctor."

"You could still have told him to fuck himself. A man would have. A good man."

Again, Koerner can't reply. He's run out of excuses and begun to weep.

"My grandmother, Herr Doctor." Hana is crying herself. But she has to know everything to go on with her life. She wants all of the answers now even the most painful ones. "Did she sign off on it? Did she know what was going to happen to me?"

Koerner sets down his empty plate. His fingers are trembling. He is either having trouble breathing due to his asthma or his emotions have got the better of him.

"I don't know," he says. He coughs. He wheezes. "I didn't ask. Your grandfather handled everything. Him and your uncle. Walter. And their attorney. I can't remember his name."

"Walter?"

Why should Hana be at all surprised? Even so, her breath catches and her body feels stricken by an electric shock. She can just imagine the gleam in Walter's eyes when he saw on the medical sheet the check mark in the square meant a life was about to be taken. Hers.

They were all against me, she thinks. *All of them. Maybe not my grandmother. I pray not her.*

"What about Sigrid?" Angry, but in control, she presses on.

"Sigrid?"

"Herr Haefner's crippled daughter. She was gassed the morning I was saved by Herr Haefner. How did that happen? Under whose order was she killed?"

"Not mine," Koerner insists. "I wasn't involved with the selections. That was T-4, the SS. Though, I suppose, Herr Haefner had to have given his approval. I'm sorry, Hana. That's just the way things were." He coughs, splutters. "In those days."

"Yes, in those days," Hana says. "Before Dachau."

She is sick to her stomach. Looking upon this man, this Jew. Yes, no matter how many years you have tried to hide it, you are still a Jew. And what, in the end, does it matter, if you can't even be a man?

"Hana?"

Hana spins about, startled by the soft voice calling her name.

"Monica, what are you doing out here? I asked you to stay in bed."

"I was w-worried," the little girl says. Feet bare and now filthy with mud, she clasps Hana about the waist. She eyes Koerner who is shadowed in darkness. "Is this one of the m-men the SS was g-going to shoot?"

"Yes," Hana says. "But he can't stay here."

"Why not?"

"He's sick. He might make you sick. And the men of the SS might come back looking for him."

"Oh."

But Koerner is such a pathetic shape, his coughing and sneezing causing his body to rock back and forth, that Monica, at least, takes pity on him.

"Can we b-bring him something for his c-cold?" she asks.

"No."

"To eat?"

"No. He's already eaten. He has to leave. Now."

Hana pulls Monica into her side as Koerner rises on unsteady feet.

"Can't I at least rest the night?" he begs.

Hana is torn. It doesn't help that Monica is so kind and innocent that she would offer the lion who is eating her a more choice spot to munch.

"I'll get s-something from the k-kitchen," she says. But as she turns to hurry back to the house, she pauses and looks back. The stranger who has escaped Dachau has moved out of the shadows so that she can now see his face more clearly. It is one she recognizes. It makes her smile.

"Herr Doctor Koerner," she says, "it's you."

"It is? Oh."

Koerner's eyes dart with guilt from the girl to Hana. The inference of what Monica has just said does not strike Hana right away, not until Monica has bolted from the barn to get food for the man who was also her psychiatrist.

When the realization hits, Hana is on Koerner in a heartbeat, grabbing him around the throat and forcing him back against a barn wall. Small as she is, her strength is augmented by her rage. Koerner doesn't stand a chance.

"You were going to kill her, weren't you, swine? She was your patient, too!"

Now Hana has become an animal.

"Children! What kind of man kills children!"

Koerner is so weakened by his days in Dachau and by his illness that he has no chance against her. His cheeks have gone the pallor of death, his eyes have rolled up and he is gagging for breath when Monica returns.

Hana doesn't know her child has come back with a plate of food until Monica yells, waking up the other children. One by one, they call out to her. What is going on? What is happening? We're scared.

Only then does Hana back away from Koerner, gasping for air, clenching and unclenching her fists, her nose leaking, her eyes running. The only words she can utter are, "Out! Out now! I don't care if you die!"

Koerner does leave, thanking the child, grabbing the food, mumbling to himself that life is terrible.

Hana would collapse, but she can't. Bracing herself on Monica's thin shoulders, she heaves until she can slowly bring herself some measure of calm. Even then, she takes a while to think of something to say, to find an explanation for how she has behaved, for what she has done to that poor man.

"He took the food?"

"Y-y-yes."

"Good. Good. You did a good thing, Monica. I'm sorry. I'm so sorry. I'm sorry."

"It's okay," Monica tells her. "It's okay, Hana. It's okay, Mama."

"Mama?"

Monica smiles, nods. Hana is overwhelmed.

"Mama? You called me Mama? Oh."

That night, she sleeps in the barn beside her daughter.

* * *

A gunshot wakens her in the morning. More than one keeps her from going back to sleep. Besides, the children have heard the same loud, familiar, frightening noise.

She is curled up in Monica's bed. It's a good thing they're both small. Monica's head is resting under Hana's chin so that the first thing Hana smells in waking is the lilac soap in Monica's hair. When the barn door opens with a bang, she sits up with a start bringing Monica with her.

"What's going on? Who is it?" she calls.

It's Haefner. Early morning light filters into the barn. He's dressed in a modest suitcoat. Apparently, he was preparing to drive into the city when the shooting changed his plans.

"It's the SS," he calls. "They're back. They found the escapee. One of them, at least. I think they killed him."

"Oh?"

Hana doesn't dare look at Monica. Why should she feel the slightest guilt or remorse, she wonders? But she does.

"Stay here," she tells the children. "Wash up. I'll make sure Frau Hartenstein brings you breakfast. If I'm not back, start your lessons. Sara, you can be the teacher today."

211

Hana is hardly dressed to meet the SS. She is still wearing the blue dress she wore yesterday, now rumpled and mud-covered. Her hair is unkempt and she smells unwashed.

"You should clean up," Haefner tells her. "Stay out of this. Let me handle it."

"Handle what?"

"Gretchen."

"What about her?"

Hana is utterly confused. Exhaustion probably has a big role to play in that. She hardly slept this past evening. Fear. Guilt. She is feeling all of it and doesn't understand what Haefner is telling her as he pulls her toward the house.

"She's dead," he says.

"What? Dead? Gretchen?"

"Last night some time. I found her in the kitchen this morning. I think the escapee was robbing us, she stumbled in on him, and he killed her."

"Where's Frau Hartenstein?"

This is all really too much. First, Koerner breaks into the barn, fleeing the nightmare of Dachau, frightening the children. Then Hana sends him out into the night, having nearly killed him, a sick helpless man. Now this.

"I advised Gertrud and Alfrieda to stay home," Haefner says. "What with the SS up and about, I thought it safer if the staff stay away."

Dead. Gretchen. Hana still can't fathom it as Haefner ushers her into the house. Perverse impulse wants her to go to the kitchen to see the body for herself, to perform some sort of forensic inspection. Haefner advises against it.

"I called the police. They called the SS. Everybody knows how much you two hated one another. You'll be a suspect. The further you are from all this, the better. I'll make sure they understand who really killed her."

Who really killed her? But who could that be? Not the Dachau escapee. Not Koerner. He was in no shape to do anything. A different escapee? One of Koerner's cohorts?

Hana is like a puppet in Haefner's hands. She is too drained of physical and emotional energy to protest her innocence. She lets him guide her upstairs to her bedroom.

"Can I call Silke?" she asks. I need my Silke. "Or Otto? Do I need a lawyer?"

"Not if you do what I tell you," Haefner says. "And remember," he adds before closing the door on her, "you owe me. Again."

It is an hour before a pounding on the main door to the house awakens Hana who has showered, dressed in a slip but fallen asleep on her bed.

My God! The children!

By the time she is fully dressed in clothes that Haefner had laid out for her on her bed, the police have invested the entire house. The police. The SS. A heavy knock on her bedroom door is followed by an uninvited entry. A blustery local cop forces his way in, followed by Walter.

"Well, well," Walter says, "wherever you go, trouble follows."

"I didn't... I need to be with my children," Hana says. She tries to brush by the men but is halted by a thick hand on her arm.

"Not yet. The brats can wait." The local police detective ushers in two subordinates to go through all of Hana's possessions.

"Didn't Ernst tell you?" she says. "There was an escapee from Dachau. He was here. He was stealing from us and Gretchen caught him."

"Did you see this escapee?" the detective asks. "With your own eyes?"

Hana's not sure how to answer that.

"Yes," she says. She assumes the police will question the children. Monica will tell the truth. "He was hiding in the barn. I had no idea he was there. As soon as I found him, I threw him out. I told him he had to leave. He was jeopardizing the children."

"Yes. But not before you gave him this."

Walter has been hiding something behind his back. Now, having heard Hana's testimony, he displays a cloth napkin that Hana immediately recognizes. It had been covering the plate of food that Monica had brought to the barn. In the corner of the napkin are the monogrammed Haefner initials.

"One has to ask oneself," says Walter, "why an escapee with the SS on his

213

tail, would take the time to browse your kitchen, make selections, choose the proper plates and eating utensils and cover the whole thing with an elegant napkin. If I were he, I would go hungry first. I would eat mushrooms and berries, second. I certainly wouldn't engage in a physical battle with the lady of the house, who, by the way, shows no signs of struggle."

"We must assume," says the local detective, "that someone fed him. Perhaps before sending him on his merry way. A subterfuge. An opportunity to do what you've been intending to do all along. Kill the lady of the house."

Hana gazes at these men, knowing that they want to find her guilty. Walter wanted her dead years ago. Because of Doctor Koerner, he's been given another chance.

"I killed no one," Hana says. "I was with my children all last night, sleeping with them, because the SS put such a fright in them. Ask them. They'll tell you."

"They'll cover for you, for certain."

"No, they won't. Children don't lie. Not my children."

Hana is shivering despite the warmth of the morning. This is madness, made worse by the fact that she almost did kill someone last night. Koerner. But if the doctor didn't kill Gretchen, and Hana didn't, who did?

The answer to Hana is obvious. Not another Dachau prisoner on the run. Haefner. Who else could it have been? He wanted her out of the way as much as Hana did. His fourth wife. In which case, money will pass hands. Bribes will be paid. The case will go unresolved. But that won't be the end of it. Haefner won't let that be the end of it. Now she belongs to him completely.

Chapter Twenty-Four

May 1947

David would just as soon not have brought his father to the location where a grave has apparently been found. The Sorensen-Ziegler investigation has nothing to do with the McAuliffe's political agenda. But driving his father to Nuremberg and then driving back alone to the Haefner compound would take too long. He does, however, tell his father to stay by the car.

"This won't take long," he says. "It's hot. In the mood you're in, you'll have a stroke. On the other hand, we'll have a ready-made grave."

"Funny boy. Fine. I'll wait. Just keep in mind, if there's something here we can use. You know. Leverage. Let me know."

A gathering of U.S. military personnel has collected in a forested ravine on the Haefner property two miles from the main house. To get here, David has followed a dirt road apparently used also by the farm machines and by horses. Whoever was out riding this morning left behind a fresh trail of crap. From there, all David has to do is park where he sees all the other military vehicles. Muffled voices and a path lead him the rest of the way.

"Hey!" he calls to Major Adams who is in charge.

Adams looks up, waves him over.

Sunlight shines through the canopy of new leaves and budding branches but not enough to brighten the glade. Conversation is kept low, though an occasional dove shares its thoughts with the soldiers, several of whom are armed, not with rifles, but with shovels and pickaxes. The ground is hard here, covered in autumn deposit. A stream runs behind the milling crowd, gurgling onto some larger estuary. Unaware that the shade has prevented all of the winter ice from melting, David slips on a hidden patch and has to be kept from an embarrassing fall by Avi Kreisler.

"What a joke that would be," Kreisler says a moment after the fact. "Survive war only to be killed by leaves. The undergrowth can be treacherous."

"Like life."

"Like life, yes. An analogy worthy of a Harvard man."

A path has been worn down a short steep muddy slope to the bottom of the gully where the military work crew has already begun to dig.

"What led you guys to this place?" David wonders.

Adams' eyes never leave the deepening hole. "People are eager to help the American police. They have a lot of stories to tell."

"Stories, right. Rumors. Fiction."

"Yes, true," Adams says. "But sometimes life can be so crazy, what seems like fiction, or what should be consigned to fiction, isn't. It's all too real. The cadaver dogs can attest to that."

At the side of a hole that has been dug out of the soil, David proffers his hand to Adams. At the bottom of the hole are the skeletal remains of a human being. Tattered remains of clothes are still attached to the leg bones. As if an odd funereal gift to the departed, a dinner plate has been tossed in. Nothing else.

"We haven't touched the corpse yet," Adams says. "We're waiting for a forensics person to come out."

David crouches by the hole to take a closer look. "Any detail at all? Any clue who it might be? Male? Female?"

"Male," says Kreisler, standing beside David. "You get to know some things from years of police work. Maybe he was one of mine."

"Yours?" asks David.

"In the fall of '44, I organized an escape from Dachau. There were a dozen of us. We stole two trucks. The one I was in got a flat tire and we had to abandon it not far from here. The SS was right on our backs, so we split up.

I have no idea what happened to the others. Maybe this is one of the others."

"A victim of the SS."

David stands. Frankly, he doesn't see what the remains have to do with either the Ziegler-Sorensen case or the paternity issue involving his brother. He says so to Adams.

"Maybe so," Adams replies. "The thing is, this isn't the only grave."

The major points along the gully in the distance to where other soldiers are busy digging up other bodies.

"Dog's been busy," he says.

"Shit."

"My thought exactly."

David just stares at the disturbing labor that is being performed. He's seen mass graves before. At other concentration camps. Thousands upon thousands of people who had been forced to kneel or stand at the lip of a vast hole, then shot in the head so that they would crumple and fall onto the previous batch. A human foundation of death. Tens of thousands. Hundreds of thousands. Layers of people on top of each other. Covered with lime, covered in dirt. Men, women, children. Well, no, sub-humans.

In time, in some places, the SS exhumed and incinerated the remains in the hopes of hiding their crime. In other places, time simply ran out.

David is astonished. He takes in all of this unfathomable evidence and wonders aloud, "What the hell happened here? Who are these people?"

"Not escapees." Kreisler knows this. Not as a former police detective but as a former inmate. "Children," he says, placing a hand on David's arm. "Now do you think your pretty and sweet Hana Ziegler is innocent?"

* * *

At the end of the war, just days before Hitler commits suicide in his bunker, everyone is in a mad dash. It's just a scramble to survive. Former Reich leaders try to take on new identities, try to go underground. Some are caught. Some aren't. While men like Lieutenant Heinrich Wicker are gunned down at places like Dachau, others face criminal prosecution, lengthy prison terms, or the noose. A massive cover-up begins.

At Dachau, seven thousand prisoners are sent on a forced march to nowhere. Wherever the SS was taking them, supposedly the Swiss Alps, over a thousand didn't make it.

At the Haefner estate, Hana gets a frantic phone call from Silke.

"I've been raped!" she cries.

"Where are you? Silke, where are you?"

"At Dachau."

"I'm coming. Just tell me where you are."

"It was the Americans."

Hana doesn't know how to drive. She runs to find Haefner, but he has gone perhaps out riding a horse. His car is still in the garage. Hana has no intention of waiting for him. She has to get to Dachau now. She has to get to Silke now. Instead, she heads into the kitchen and yells at Silke's mother.

"Where's Vitor?" she shouts. "I need Vitor."

"Why, child? He's out in the fields somewhere."

"Is his car here?"

"Yes. How do you think we got here?"

"Do you know how to drive?"

"A little."

"Then let's go. Now!"

Fortunately, this happens to be one of those days when Hilda Schoenweis comes to help with the children. Hana leaves instructions, says a hasty goodbye to them, including a quick kiss on Monica's cheek, then rushes off with Gertrud Hartenstein at the wheel of her husband's car.

Silke is waiting for them in the infirmary, sitting alone, on a cot beneath a window, a blanket covering her hunched-up knees. Hana is on her hugging and kissing her before Silke even knows she's there.

"How are you? Are you hurt? Who did this to you?"

Despite everything she endured the night before, Silke manages a smile, surrounded by her mother and Hana. "You got here fast," she says.

"We would have gotten here faster, but your mother hit a cow." Hana hugs Silke as tight as she can. "Oh, I love you, Silke. So much. Tell me who did this to you. I'll kill them."

"Don't say such things," Gertrud warns her. "The walls have ears."

"I don't care. You said an American? He must have a commanding officer. We'll tell him."

"Not now. I'm too tired. I just want to go home."

Dachau is not so chaotic now. The Americans have taken over. An American flag flies over the German commandant's headquarters. There are tanks, jeeps, trucks of all sorts, dozens of American GIs. None of them pay much attention to two German women helping a third to a battered old VW. Except for one young man, an officer, handsome, who goes out of his way not only to approach the women but to hold open the door for Silke to get in.

"Hope you didn't mind last night," he says. He takes off his hat and offers an embarrassed grin. "Are you the mother?" he asks Frau Hartenstein. "Your daughter and I, well, we were both drunk last night and, well, you know. The war. People do crazy things. Is she okay? She seems okay. She was when I left. Are you, Fraulein?"

Silke is still dazed. She studies the young American officer's face with some puzzlement. "I didn't ask for it," she says.

"I know, Ma'am, Fraulein. It's just..."

"You raped her," Hana barks. She is not nearly as easygoing about the whole thing as her friend. "Are you going to do something about it? Tell your commanding officer what you did? What if she's pregnant?"

The stunned look on the American's face says it all. The thought has never remotely dawned on him. His face crumples. Whatever military training he had in the States, whatever education he received back home, whatever lessons he has been taught by his father, none of it has prepared him for this possibility.

"My name," he says. "Look. Here." He finds a scrap of paper in a wallet. It contains his name and an address in the United States. "Take it. If it happens, you know, just, contact me. Okay? We'll handle it. I'm sorry." Then he hurries away.

"*Feigling*," says Frau Hartenstein. Coward.

"Oh, well," says Silke.

"Give me," says Hana and takes the scrap of paper herself. Someday, she suspects, it will come in handy.

As Gertrud drives, Hana sits in the cramped back seat with Silke, still holding the blanket around her. "We'll feed you when we get home," Gertrud tells her daughter. "Dumplings and sausage. Then you sleep. Tomorrow we'll take you to the city to see a doctor."

"What if you are pregnant?" Hana asks her. "What should we do?"

Silke smiles, cuddles with Hana. "We?" she says.

"Of course, 'we.' Ursula can have a sister. The Americans have money."

"I don't want his money."

"It would be a way out of our financial troubles," Gertrud says. "Herr Haefner is a cheapskate."

"I said, I don't need his money. Herr Haefner's or the American's. I have made a decision, Hana," she says.

"You're keeping it."

"Of course. But that's not what I mean. I want to be a doctor. I want to study things like you do. I want to help people."

What more can anybody say? Good for you? Good luck with that? Silke is as stubborn as they come. Once she's made up her mind... In any case, Hana is very proud of her friend. She leans over and whispers in Silke's ear.

"Someday," she says, "I want to make love with you. Is that permissible, Herr Doktor?"

Silke giggles, causing her mother to glance at her through the rearview mirror.

"What will Otto think?"

"Otto will just have to accept it, that's all."

"Poor Otto." Then Silke becomes serious. She places a hand on Hana's thigh, squeezes gently. "To become a doctor," she utters very softly, "I guess, you must once in a while play doctor."

They arrive back at the Haefner estate quite pleased with each other. If Frau Hartenstein has figured anything out regarding the two girls in the back seat, she shows no hint of it. She beeps the horn for Hilda. Once, twice, three times.

"Maybe they went out for a walk," Hana says. She's suddenly very happy.

It's a nice enough spring day, and Hilda always says that a hearty constitutional is good for the young and the old. There are numerous paths that one can take into the surrounding country, though Hana has advised her former maid to avoid them while the land is still in such turmoil.

She looks about as she climbs out of the car, a worried twenty-year-old 'mother' just needing a single view of her kids at play to put her at ease. But she doesn't see them. She doesn't see anyone or hear anyone. Perhaps they're in the barn, deep into their studies. Eleven-year-old Sara can be a very mature teacher when she wants to be.

Hana's pace and her concerns grow as she approaches the barn, shouting, "Sara! Monica! Anatoly!"

She is just about to enter when she hears her name being called from behind. Two people are yelling for her. Hilda, first, then Silke's Ursula. Vitor Hartenstein also comes at a jog from where he's parked his tractor.

"They're gone! They're gone!" Vitor cries. "I tried to stop them."

Hana doesn't understand. Oh, she hears the words, all right. But they don't make sense.

"Children?"

When she bursts through the opening, all she sees are empty beds. They've been made up just as she has taught them. Blankets and sheets neatly tucked in, pillows fluffed and centered appropriately. Ernst has purchased each child a bureau in which to place their extra clothes. These are situated beside the beds. It is here that Hana first realizes something isn't right.

The drawers have been thrown open. Clothes are lying scattered on the ground. It's as if each child were in such a hurry to dress that they pulled out whatever they could and left the rest behind, a mess quite unlike them. Shoes, though, still laid out, heels only visible under the beds. They're still neatly arranged. Why? Why wouldn't they take their shoes?

Maybe the classroom. But before she can access the rear of the barn, Hilda intercepts her. Big, strong Hilda, who never cries, is crying inconsolably.

"The SS!" she wails. "They came. They just took them away."

"Where was Ernst?"

It still hasn't hit that deepest part of her brain that what she is experiencing is real. The children are here somewhere. She just can't see them.

Hana grabs Hilda by the arms. "Where was he? Where are they? They're just children!"

Hana will scour the countryside if she has to. She will abscond with the Hartenstein VW, even though she's never had a driving lesson, and she will drive wherever she has to go to get her children back.

"Why? Why would they take them? It makes no sense."

Hana releases Hilda but only to run into Vitor.

"For protection," he says. "They'll be all right. I'm sure. Americans won't kill them if they have children with them."

"Yes, yes, that must be it." Hilda is using the sleeve of her dress to clean her face. "Protection. Go to the Americans, Hana. We'll find them. We have to. Oh, the little ones."

Now. Now it is filtering through. Now that the barn is empty. Now that the schoolroom is empty. Now that the play area is empty. Now that there is no laughter. Now that there are no open books, no busy pens, no eager arms raised. Oh, now it's filtering through. No sweet embraces. No bedtime stories. No strudel with ice cream.

"Monica! Sara! Children!"

How will they do it?

Hana staggers out of the barn and falls to her knees clasping Silke around the legs. She would weep. Oh, she would wash away the world with a flood of tears. She would beg the Almighty for an answer, only something else is building up inside her, shoving out all other feelings. Rage.

Sigrid. That's who Hana visualizes now. Wheelchair-bound Sigrid. Sigrid who could have laughed and played and loved given the chance; who in just a few short hours had become a sister to Hana. Sigrid who, instead, had been wheeled into the back of a van to be extinguished.

How will they do it?

Hana buries her face in Silke's belly. The unthinkable world, in this way, vanishes.

CHAPTER TWENTY-FOUR

"Oh, God. What have You done?"

Gone? Taken? Kidnapped? Her own children? For protection? As a bargaining chip? No, no, it's worse than that. She understands that now even if the others do not. Much worse.

Mothers who have lost their most prized possessions would comprehend. Mothers with empty arms and empty cupboards and empty cradles. Mothers throughout history in times of war or plague would be kneeling right beside Hana. Like her, they would be raising their tear-battered eyes to the heavens, they would be stretching out trembling fingers to grasp the Divine around the throat, they would at long last be giving vent to what is truly in their hearts.

Forsaken by the unimaginable, they would be invoking God much as Hana does when she opens her mouth and screams at Him.

"Where are my children!"

Chapter Twenty-Five

Spring 1946-Spring 1947

I t is now up to the men. Two in particular. Ernst Haefner and his attorney Reinhardt Froeling. A third man, confined to a wheelchair, watches the first two complete their paperwork.

"You're sure she'll agree to this?" the lawyer asks, looking over Haefner's shoulder as he signs a document at his desk.

"Of course. It's a mere formality," Haefner says as he completes forging Hana's signature to a marriage license. "She wants to get married. She gave me permission just this morning. But fatigue, depression, since the children were taken. It's been more than a year, for God's sake. It's about time she gets over it. You know how women are. I've been more than patient. She loves me. She loves me for that."

"Hah!"

The laughter comes from the corner of the room where old August admires his son's duplicity.

"What's so amusing?" Haefner asks.

"Number five, that's what's amusing," his father says. "Herr Froeling wasn't around for the first three. I'm not so certain that love ever came in to play with you, Ernst, not to belittle your efforts."

"Shut up, Father." Ernst rises, hands the completed document to his attorney. "You will keep Otto out of the way?"

"Is Argentina far enough?" Froeling asks. "I do have business there. It will keep him busy for at least a year. By then, well, who knows?"

"Hah!" Another laugh from the corner. A little more whimsical this time. A little more annoying. "Four wives, and the only child my son ever produced was a cripple. But you'd know about that, Herr Froeling. You were there for that one."

"I said, shut up, Father. Wheelchairs can be very awkward going down stairs."

"I see. And you, Froeling, you're okay with this?"

As long as Attorney Froeling gets paid, he's okay with anything. Noncommittal, he says, "Marriage can be a good thing if the right people make it work. I've been married to the same woman for forty-three years."

"Children?"

"Five. Otto is the youngest."

"Well, there you go," says August. "I would call that a successful arrangement. You have heirs aplenty. At this rate, the Haefner wealth and property, earned over four generations of hard work and industrious money management, will end up in the hands of a Jewess. Well, at least you're in love, Ernst, yes. Finally. Does she return those feelings? Really, Ernst, really."

Haefner utters a sigh and shrugs when Froeling puts a sympathetic hand on his shoulder. "As hard as it may be for you to believe, Father, yes, she loves me. And I love her. And now that everything is legal, we will make you an heir. Will that make you happy, old man? Will that finally shut you up?"

Haefner walks past his father, signals to a nurse who has been waiting in the hall outside to come get the family patriarch. But August has one last thing he just has to say before his son sallies forth to procreate.

"You just better hope she never finds out what you did to her children."

* * *

In the immediate aftermath of the disappearance of Monica, Sara, and the other Dachau children, Hana suffered a complete breakdown. The events of 1945 might as well have occurred during the Dark Ages. 1946 entered the same way, one dark room leading to another. Had this been 1939 all over again and had Haefner lost his patience with her as he had with Sigrid, she could well have ended up back at Hollenschloss.

For more than a year, while Haefner sputters, fumes, pleads, and ultimately conspires, she can hardly lay pen to paper. All desire to work, to study, to research is gone. Ernst tries to be a good husband.

The Allied prosecutors have not yet come down on the industrialist Haefner, so he takes her everywhere. To the Bodensee. To the mountains. Even to Paris and Zurich. His travels have not yet been restricted. Perhaps he has friends in America. Powerful ones who keep the legal dogs at bay. He buys her whatever he thinks her heart desires. Not clothes or jewelry, but scientific equipment. He takes her to symposiums and lectures as far away as London and Rome. Any tidbit of information he comes across in the international press in her field of study, he cuts out and shares with her. He has even contacted some of the top men in genetics and brought them to Bavaria to dine at his house so that they can meet his prodigy.

These men are fascinated by her theories and, in private, wonder why she is producing no paper, no research, to support her views. The truth is that Hana has lost all interest in genetics, in anything. It doesn't help that Ernst is drugging her with sedatives to prevent the outbursts of hatred that pour from her lips when no one else is around to hear them. Still, he keeps trying. He does love her.

What sustains her are the women in her life. Now that Otto has disappeared, his copious letters from Buenos Aires never reaching her, she depends entirely upon four women. Silke's mother force-feeds her. Her loyal maid Hilda spends as much time at the Haefner estate, as she does working for the Zieglers. And Ilse has become a true grandmother. She and Hana spend a great deal of time in her greenhouse. It is here that Hana can relax, try to find her way back to the world.

"You're only twenty-one years old, Hana," Ilse says. "During the war, entire families were wiped out."

"My children are still alive. I know they are. Somewhere. We just haven't found them yet."

Ilse doesn't believe that for a minute, but she can't convince Hana

226

otherwise. As they clip and snip their flowers, Ilse suggests Hana try the one thing that may cure her. Motherhood.

"Have your own children," she says. "At your age, you could have as many as you want."

"With Herr Haefner?"

"He'll provide for them. Do you think your grandfather was my first choice? To look at me now, you wouldn't think it but I could have had any man I wanted when I was your age."

"I believe you, *Grossmutter.*"

"God bless you for saying that. But girls of our station had to take into consideration other things besides looks. I only wish...well, if you had someone else in mind, that would be one thing. But you don't. Do you?"

Hana is good at keeping secrets, about whom she loves, about who is on her mind every day, every hour. She never mentions the letters she found buried in the soil either, written by a lover who did find and still finds Ilse desirable. Nor the letters written by her mother to her grandmother. Louis Marksohn. Oh, she definitely hasn't forgotten what she read in those letters. Nor her own crayon creations. She sees no point in revisiting a painful past nor of reopening wounds that have apparently healed. Nor does she wonder anymore about whether or not her grandmother ever loved her. She does now, and that is enough.

But she does think about children all the time. Her children. Where are they now? What happened to them? Are they in the custody of the Americans? Surely, if that were the case, they would have mentioned Hana to them. They would have been reunited by now.

Oh, how frightened they must have been. Hana can't get the image out of her brain. Defenseless against a world that views them as unworthy of life. But they were so worthy, so full of potential. Wonderful, gorgeous flowers.

How will they do it?

If a thought could kill, if a vision of what may have been could permanently destroy a soul, that is the nightmare she is constantly trying to ward off. By gas. By injection. By starvation. Oh, please, have it done quickly.

Hana's greatest place of refuge is Silke. Silke is her eyes and ears, her arms and legs. It is Silke who braves desolated and ruined Germany to try to find out what happened to the children. From Frankfurt to Munich, driving with her father Vitor, she has been visiting adoption agencies and resettlement agencies to look for the missing children.

She has been delivered of a second child by now, Charlie McAuliffe's daughter, Charlotte, but that doesn't stop her. Her mother Gertrud and Hilda Schoenweis can take care of Silke's little girls while she's away. Ursula and Charlotte are in the best of hands. It is Hana who needs her help, and Silke won't abandon the effort. Her English is improving, and she will even confront Eisenhower if that is what it will take to get answers.

Ernst has also been digging into the mystery. "I'm contacting anybody I know who can help," he tells Hana. "You've seen me on the telephone. You've heard my conversations."

They're eating dinner. Winter has settled over Europe, a cold one, which does not help the thousands of Germans who are still living in internment camps, still homeless in early March 1947. Certain types of food are very scarce. The Americans won't share. But Haefner manages to stock his kitchen with whatever his family needs, and Gertrud Hartenstein is a wonderful cook.

The house is lonely, though, occupied by three people: Hana, Ernst, and his father August. They sit around the table, often in silence, forcing Ernst to take the conversational lead. Tonight, it is a touchy subject he chooses to broach. He is trying to work his way into the subject gently.

"We could adopt other children, of course, Hana," he says. "There are so many others who are homeless. We have a big house. There's plenty of space, and we can certainly afford it."

"What about the trials?" Hana asks. "Aren't you afraid of being sent to jail? Who knows how long that could be?"

"That's right, Ernst. What about the trials?" August wonders. With a nasty gleam in his eye.

Haefner pooh-poohs the trials. "Froeling will handle that. I'm not concerned. We industrialists contributed to the war effort, yes. But what choice did we have? I'm a small fish."

August grunts affirmation.

"Which is another reason to consider adoption. It's a matter of image, you see. I'm a man of principles. I'm a man who cares." Haefner lays down his fork. "But, Hana, don't you think we should try to have our own child first? Having a baby will make you feel so much better. I've talked to your grandmother about it. She agrees."

Hana chews thoughtfully on a carrot, dips it into her lemonade, and takes another bite. It's certainly not a subject she hasn't considered. Otto is a man with whom she would be happy to raise a child. Whenever he comes back from wherever he went. But Ernst? The thought sickens her. What would happen if their child were born like Sigrid? What would Ernst think then? *How will they do it?*

It is Silke she would like as a partner, raising her children, maybe someday having her own. Looking up from her plate, she says, "When I'm better."

"Yes, and when will that be, my dear?"

She doesn't know.

"I think before the trials," he continues unperturbed by her dispassionate response. "You do know that your name has been raised as well as mine, my love. Ridiculous. Absurd, I know. But rumors persist. Witnesses. Who knows what they think they saw? It may be difficult, even for the finest defense attorney, to get an acquittal if experiments with children are brought up."

"Experiments!" The notion that she would ever hurt a child is so horrifying, Hana drops her fork and pushes away from the table. "How could you say such a thing?"

"It's not me saying it," Ernst insists. "Days like these, people turn on each other. They look for scapegoats. Witnesses remember things they didn't witness. 'What did she inject those children with? I don't know, but it was something.' That's what they'll say. But if you're with child, then you have everyone's sympathy."

"I never hurt my children. I never did."

Whatever Hana thinks of Haefner's reasoning, August is amused by it. He applauds the effort. "I always wanted to be a great-grandfather, Hana. That would give me such pleasure."

The phrase 'fuck you' is on her lips when suddenly she drops to the floor in a dead faint. Her head hits the table first, spilling her drink, then the chair before attaining the carpet. All is silence except for August slurping his own glass of lemonade. Ernst rises from the table only after a moment. He waits to make sure Hana isn't going to get up before he slides his hands beneath her and scoops her into his arms.

"To bed?" August says.

"Yes."

"The lemonade?"

"Do you care?"

August continues to eat, unfazed. "Not at all, my boy. Just make sure you find the right hole this time, all right?"

* * *

"Someday you'll learn to drive, right?" Vitor begs of his only daughter, his only surviving child now that Georg has died for the Fatherland two years ago.

Silke is a madwoman at the wheel on far too many occasions when Vitor is trying to teach her the rules of the road. At night, close calls become a bit more disconcerting.

"We have to make sure we get to Otto before his father finds out he's come home," she says, gripping the wheel, taking a curve that tosses her father against the side of the car.

"You're driving faster than his plane. Slow down or he'll be finding us parked against a tree."

Otto wired her from Buenos Aires. Though his telegram had been sent a week ago, she just received it an hour before. All it said was a date and time. She has a half hour to get to their agreed-upon rendezvous to pick him up, hopefully long before Reinhardt Froeling has a clue his wayward son has fled the Americas.

"He's probably already landed in Zurich," Silke says. German civilian airfields are not yet up and running. She does let up on the accelerator though. "He's supposed to meet us at Herr Haefner's cottage on the Bodensee."

"Why all the secrecy? The Gestapo doesn't exist anymore."

"Otto wanted it that way. He'll tell us when we get there."

"If we get there, my darling. Watch out for that truck."

The Haefner summer retreat on the Bodensee, Lake Constance, is built in the chalet-style on a forested slope looking down on the cold waters of the lake that borders Germany and Switzerland. Whether or not her reckless driving is the reason, Silke arrives before Otto. This only worries her more.

Up here, on the slopes of the Alps, winter stays longer. Silke wraps a thin woolen coat around her and crunches through two inches of newly-fallen snow to the cottage, her father by her side. Vitor's VW is the first auto to form tracks in the snow. There are no footprints.

Silke is accustomed to the Alpine cold. But at night the temperature can drop precipitously and she had been in such a rush to leave her house, she hasn't dressed properly.

The wind exacerbates the cold. Blowing off the lake, it rustles her blonde hair, which she has allowed to grow longer because Hana likes it when it flows down her back. Charlotte, her baby, has blonde hair, too. Does she resemble her American father? Who knows?

"How can you smoke?" she asks her father, who has brushed snow off a porch chair and sat down. She is stalking the deck watching the lone road into the retreat.

"I'm calming my nerves," he says.

"I wish I could. Where could he be?"

As Silke paces, she ponders a telephone conversation she had that morning with Hana.

"Ernst is getting impatient."

"So? Leave him. How many times have I told you?"

"I can't."

"Why, for God's sake, Hana?"

"Because I can't."

231

'Because,' Silke thinks, 'he has something on her.'

Then, at last, headlights.

"There! There!" she cries. "It's Otto. He's here!"

She leaps down the steps, slips, and slides in the snow, but still manages to throw herself into his arms knocking him back into the car in her anticipation. She gives him a peck on the cheek but little opportunity for him to give her one back.

Otto has become a handsome young man several years older than Silke. Tall, slender, well-suited to the American-style clothes he has adopted, he still wears a bright sunburn from his days in the tropics. Dressed only in a brown suit coat, he has gone from summer to winter in a matter of hours. He isn't alone.

"Hans," he says pointing to the driver of the car with Swiss plates. "It isn't easy crossing the border if you're German. They ask for so many papers."

"But you made it," Silke says as her father comes up to shake Otto's hand. "What's going on?"

Otto has taken off his hat. A puff of his breath forms crystals that fall lightly on Silke's face. Otherwise, the cold night air doesn't seem to bother him.

"Well," he says, "I found out why my father hustled me off to Argentina. I thought we were buying property. But we're not. We're helping this secret outfit move Nazis out of the country. I'm not supposed to know that."

"Shit, Otto, I'm sorry."

"Yes, well, guess who one of those former Nazis is we're trying to help get away. Hana's uncle Walter. I saw the fucking documents. I wasn't supposed to."

"Walter. That pig."

"Ursula's father."

"A fact she will never know." Silke gives Otto a reassuring hug.

"Come on." She's in a hurry, pulling him by the hands to her father's VW. "Hana will be excited to see you. She doesn't know you've come back."

"How is Hana?"

Otto lets his Swiss driver leave. Then he, Silke, and Vitor get into the VW,

Vitor now grabbing the wheel.

"She's still struggling," Silke tells him. "It's awful. What happened to those children."

"Do you think...?"

"Of course. But she refuses to. And Herr Haefner, that swine, keeps prodding her to get married and have children. For whatever reason, she allows him to get away with this. I think she's given up on life, and I don't know what to do."

"I love her."

"I know you do, Otto. So, get her pregnant."

Silke has never been one to bake what she can bite right into. Otto is astounded by her candor.

"We'd have to get married first, wouldn't we?" he says.

"Oh, Otto." She pats his cheek. "Am I married?"

"That's different. I'm not going to..."

"Rape her? No one's asking you to. Just...be a man."

Vitor drives. He doesn't let his eyes wander off the road. He knows his daughter all too well. He just pretends not to. "What about Herr Haefner?" he says. "They're as good as married."

"That's something we'll deal with when the time comes," Silke tells him, and she sounds quite confident in the utterance.

As they drive through the late winter evening, heading for the Ziegler estate, Silke lays her head back against her seat. Marriage is a thing she hadn't considered for herself since her days in the BDM. Marriage to her is nothing more than a political arrangement, an obligation to the Reich, a contractual process between two people who might very well hate one another. Absent of romance and passion, unconcerned about family and the actual well-being of the children, marriage becomes something akin to a handshake between lawyers.

How does she feel about Hana? Their friendship is a complication she had never expected, the powerful feelings engendered, the confusion. It was hardly unusual for BDM girls on bivouac, when Frau Zoeller and Frau Goedeler were asleep, to sneak into the forest. Girls, of course, were not supposed to do such things, to explore youthful sexuality with each other or with Hitler Youth boys. But nature will out even under the most dire of circumstances. Perhaps because of them. Beautiful teenage Silke was the object of the desire of several boys and girls, but she had never allowed herself to get that carried away. She was a good girl, after all. Catholic. All the more reason now for her to consider her feelings for Hana. This was different. This was important.

Hana tried to seduce her some weeks ago at a time when they were both quite vulnerable. An innocent attempt. An impulsive attempt. Worthy of a giggle at the time, embarrassment for both of them. Haefner was away on business. Hana was alone in her bedroom, lying on her bed half-asleep, half-drugged. Silke had come to see her for two reasons. First, to console her over the loss of the children. And, second, to tell Hana that she was indeed pregnant with Charlie McAuliffe's baby.

Haefner was too wise to leave pill bottles around, so when Silke opened Hana's bedroom door, she assumed that her friend was merely drowsy or in one of her deep depressed moods. She stood beside the bed, whispering her name, got Hana to open her eyes.

"Silke?" Hana said.

"You okay?"

"I'm alive."

"I've got good news." Silke lifts her skirt and tells Hana to rub her belly. "I'm pregnant."

"Pregnant?"

"Yes. With Captain America's kid."

While the exciting news doesn't launch Hana out of her drugged stupor, it does lift her spirits. There is a distinct gleam of happiness in her eyes for Silke, and she lets her hand reach out and sweep over Silke's bare belly.

"You're sure she's in there? I can't feel anything."

"It's too soon. I missed my period. You do know what that means, don't you?"

"Of course."

Well, no, not really. Shamed to say, no woman in Hana's family had ever instructed her in such things, and her own biological reading had been far more technical than, 'Ooops, I've got a loaf in the oven.'

"I'm happy for you." Hana doesn't stop rubbing. "I think I want a baby."

"You're too young."

"You're young."

"Not as young, or as naive, as you, liebchen."

Hana sighs. Her mind is swimming with thoughts of babies, of Silke. "Does it feel nice when I do that to you?" she asks.

"I guess. Walter isn't quite so gentle. Of course, you would know that."

Hana has lifted herself up on an elbow and is watching her hand as it glides over Silke's belly. "I would kill Walter if I got the chance," she says.

"Don't."

"Okay."

"I mean it."

"Okay."

Hana leans forward. "It's just..."

It's as if the circular motion of her hand over Silke's torso has caused her to go into a trance. She isn't even hearing what Silke is saying. She is in Berlin's National Gallery and can't help reaching out toward the work of one of Germany's masters. Signs warn her not to touch, but she can't help herself. She is in her grandmother's greenhouse so intoxicated by the aroma of a flower, she must stick her nose inside its petals. Silke's bare flesh is a work of art Hana can't keep from kissing.

"Hana," Silke says. Hana pays no attention and kisses Silke again. "Hana, maybe you shouldn't."

Silke has to gently push Hana away as her friend's hand grazes her lower belly in a way that almost makes Silke regret the push. Hana comes fully awake now, cheeks glowing, fingers trembling from the touch of flesh to flesh, realizing she has crossed a line she is not sure either of them wants crossed.

"I'm sorry." Hana is mortified. She sits up. Silke's smile is an attempt to put Hana at ease.

"It's okay. I don't mind."

"I wasn't thinking. I couldn't..."

"Hana."

"I love you so!"

Hana blurts out her emotions with the tact of a child, causing Silke to take Hana in her arms and cradle her. She understands. When everything around you is violence and you have lived a life unloved, you offer your heart to whomever will accept it. And Silke is not in the least bit averse to lending her heart in return.

Remembering all of this, she blushes when she realizes Otto is staring at her. That is another thing, she thinks, they will all have to deal with.

By the time they reach the Haefner estate, it is nearly midnight. They probably could have waited until the next morning to pay Hana a visit. But something tells Silke that they shouldn't wait, that Hana needs her tonight. In fact, as Vitor drives down the private road and onto the circular drive, Silke is suddenly struck by a fear she can't account for. There are lights on downstairs but none on the upper floors.

"Maybe we should wait until tomorrow," Vitor says.

"No. Tonight. Come on. Both of you."

Silke races ahead through the snow. The front door is unlocked, and she pushes inside to complete silence.

"Hana! Hana!"

The echo is not a good sign. A hollow house is an empty house.

"Try the parlor," Vitor suggests. His wife does the cooking, but she'll have been gone hours before. So will the rest of the house staff. In the evening, Herr Haefner wants to be alone with his 'bride'.

The three interlopers hurry into the dining hall where they find the table still set, though with plates empty or half-eaten. There is a stain on the tiled floor from where someone dropped their dinner drink. It has already turned a viscous pale yellow.

They find August in the back hall between the dining room and the kitchen where the elevators are located. His chair has drifted away from the opening and come to rest against a cabinet of fine porcelain dinnerware. His head has lolled to one side. But when Otto shakes him by the shoulder, the whole body collapses forward onto the floor.

"Oh, my God, he's dead."

Otto stumbles back against the cabinet. Vitor kneels beside the corpse and verifies what Otto has said. He makes the sign of the cross.

"This is a bad place," he says. "A house of the dead."

It better not be. Silke hurries back out into the foyer, then takes the stairs two at a time. "Hana! Hana! We're here. Hana!"

Down the unlit second-floor hallway, she rushes, heart-pounding, fear building, anger mounting. If what she suspects is true, she will kill tonight. At long last, she will become what Hitler wanted.

She bursts into Hana's bedroom, and at first, due to the dark, can't see anything. The window is open. A cold breeze is blowing in. The curtains are billowing. Then, eyes adjusted to the dark, she sees a figure lying on the bed.

"Hana! Oh, God, Hana!"

Right behind her comes Vitor, then Otto. Otto finds the light switch. Flicking it up, he reveals Hana lying fully clothed on her bed, it would seem, fast asleep. Silke has cradled her friend's head in her arms and is whispering to her.

"She's alive. She's okay. Just asleep, thank God. He didn't kill her."

"No, he didn't."

In their focus on the figure lying in bed, none of them has seen Haefner quietly sitting in the dark near the closet. He may well have been sitting there for hours, hands resting on his lap, just watching the lovely sleeping figure. Who can say? Vitor has worked for the man for many years and never seen him look so beaten, so old.

"I do love her," he says. The room is frigid from the open window, but Haefner hasn't moved to shut it. Vitor does.

"I know none of you believe that," Haefner says. "I know she doesn't. But I couldn't do that to her. I've done a lot, but that I couldn't do."

"Drug her. Rape her. Get her pregnant," Silke shouts at him.

Haefner doesn't deny any of it. "My father was right," he tells them. "Four times a failure. What right do I have to be loved by anyone, especially by this one? Such an angel. Such a mind. I could see it right away. Even when she was so young, even when they were going to kill her, I knew. I saw. I had to have her. It was the first time I have ever really been in love."

"Your father is dead," Otto says. Haefner doesn't blink. "This doesn't bother you? Downstairs. A heart attack?"

"I am like a stone," Haefner tells them. Then, for the first time, he looks up at his guests. "Many years ago, your father drew up my will. I want you to change it, Otto. I'll instruct you in the morning, if you have the time."

"If I have the time?"

"Let it be, Herr Froeling," Vitor advises.

Otto nods, fighting his anger. Then Vitor lifts the unconscious Hana off the bed. "I think we'll take her, sir," he says, "if you don't mind."

Haefner is too filled with remorse, self-pity, call it what you will, to move. After Otto and Vitor leave, taking Hana with them, Silke remains only to grab some of Hana's clothing before she heads out.

"It was you who killed Frau Haefner, wasn't it?" she asks from the doorway. "And your father?"

Haefner merely shrugs. Just a flick of the hand is the only indication that he is still in this world. "By the way," he says, "on the way out, don't drink the lemonade."

Chapter Twenty-Six

May 1947

Before revealing what they have found to the person they consider responsible, Adams and David have decided to complete the exhumation of the gravesite. It's a single hole into which a number of bodies have been cast. Eight remains have been discovered so far.

"All children," Adams says. "Now, why would you do something like that unless you were trying to cover something up?"

"There's got to be another reason," David says. "Another motive."

"You've read her file. You've read the testimony of witnesses. This nurse, Dora Voss. She saw hundreds of pages of statistics, not only of children, but of the male prisoners. The work of an obsessive-compulsive mind. Even Kreisler heard stories. 'Little Daughter.' 'Little Monster' is more like it. And Ziegler, her uncle, he kept a file on her. We found it where he was hiding out. She was bat crazy from the get-go, and she killed him to keep him from spilling the beans on her."

David still isn't sure. As the little bodies are retrieved and brought out into the light...one, two, three, four, five, six, seven, eight...he can't help thinking about his sister Peggy. He remembers hearing his father use similar words. Bat crazy. Obsessive-compulsive. 'God only knows what she'll be like as an adult.'

"It'll be cruel if you don't warn her in advance," he tells Adams.

"That, my naive friend, is just the point."

Avi Kreisler says this standing over the sheet-covered remains of a child who seems to have been killed or tossed coldly into the mass grave wearing a Star of David pendant. Weeping, Kreisler takes the Jewish pendant from the dead child's corpse, puts it to his lips.

"A killer such as this," he says, "deserves no mercy."

David had told his father that they wouldn't be long. But, in fact, it has taken four hours to recover all the remains. The only thing that keeps Harold McAuliffe from suing the planet for the delay is the fact that this new evidence will foil Hana Ziegler's attempts at bribing him and ruining Charlie's political future.

"If that isn't a smoking gun," he tells David as his son returns to the car. "We won't have to do anything now. Your mother will be quite pleased. Let the American government hang her, and Charlie skates."

"Yuh. Maybe."

Still, David can't forget Copenhagen and the Hana he knew back then, befriending Peggy in a way no one else ever had. He is quiet the entire two-mile ride back to the Ziegler mansion, trying to shut out his father who doesn't stop babbling.

'This is Charlie's mess,' he's thinking, 'and he's dragged us all into it.'

He is not looking forward to this next interview with Hana. She, of course, can refuse to answer any of his questions. Her lawyer Froeling never leaves her side, the father of her baby, her protector. Who can blame him? And Silke Hartenstein. God, what a beauty. What a mistake. Charlie really fucked up this time. Fubar, fucked up beyond all recognition. More complications. More deviousness. More secrets. What a world. Is anybody innocent of anything?

Harold is ready to pounce the moment his car parks. Avi Kreisler has stayed behind. The last time David saw him, the Dachau survivor was uttering a prayer for the dead and said he wanted to stay with the children for a bit longer. Just as well. Having two screaming adversaries yelling for Hana's neck is two too many.

But Harold is not prepared for what happens next. It isn't Hana or Silke who greets him at the front door, which he has been prepared to barge through for his "Aha!" moment. It is Ilse Ziegler. The sight of the elegant German woman he's been having an on-again-off-again affair with for the better part of two decades stops him cold.

"Ilse?"

"Harry."

For the first time in his life, Harold McAuliffe is at a loss for words. He appears to be a bumbling freshman meeting a blind date far above his status.

"Hana told me you had come. I had to see for myself. What, not even a hug?"

Words elude McAuliffe. He is fortunate his son is there to take Ilse's hand and give it a gentlemanly shake.

"Frau Ziegler," David says. "You probably don't remember me from Copenhagen. I was much younger then."

Ilse smiles, nods. "Oh, I remember. For some reason, my clarity around that holiday is as sharp as ever."

She moves out of the way so that the men can enter. The scenario in the house has changed since David, his father, and Major Adams were last there. David wonders if the others notice it, but there is an obvious sexual divide. Intentional? Maybe.

With the exception of Otto Froeling, the far side of the parlor into which they have entered is occupied entirely by females. Pregnant Hana sits beside Silke Hartenstein. They're holding hands. Otto stands behind them. Once Ilse has let the men in, she takes her place standing to Hana's right. David also recognizes Hilda Schoeneweis and Gertrud Hartenstein, a formidable duo perched like mother eagles to the left. Husband Vitor, like some vigilant goat herder, stays in the outer room, an interested but passive non-participant.

'Ah,' David thinks, 'a set-up.' Clever. But for what?

"Well, Ladies," Adams says. He removes his hat and makes himself comfortable while the two McAuliffes remain standing. "You'll never guess what we found."

The major has determined a strategy. Faced with an opponent who has brought in the reserves, he has decided to attack right up the middle.

"Did you know there is a cemetery on your property, Fraulein Ziegler?

241

Or is that Frau Haefner?"

"Draw your own conclusions," Hana replies. She glances up as the man in question, Ernst Haefner, stumbles in, tipsy, but, by being the fourth male, creating a sexual balance of sorts.

"Fraulein," Haefner says. "Twas ever thus."

"Are you certain, Herr Haefner?" Otto eyes the man whose feelings for Hana disgust him. "There is a marriage license. My father was gracious enough to tell me about it while I was away."

"An adroit man, Reinhardt. Clever. Duplicitous. Even in regards to his own son. Well, he was an attorney, after all. And my father was no better with me. No, no marriage license. No certificate. No consummation. *Mea culpa*. The whole thing was a forgery from the outset."

"From Hollenschloss on, you mean," Hana says. She tries to avoid eye contact with him, but she can't control her temper which is rising. "Don't talk to me of sons. Talk to me of daughters. Crippled ones who didn't meet your standards." At this, Hana doesn't just level Haefner with her stare but turns it toward Harold McAuliffe, too. "Sigrid. What about Sigrid, Ernst? Tell me about her. No? No explanation? And you, Mr. McAuliffe? Innocent? You have a daughter, don't you?"

"Be quiet about Peggy," Harold says. "You know nothing."

"Nothing? You think so?"

Hana needs no lawyer now. No protector. No defender. She rises, carrying her baby inside her. This is a moment she has been building towards for many years. Unplanned, but here it is. She is holding something in her clenched fist as she moves out from the side of the women to the side of the men. She stands halfway between Haefner to her right and McAuliffe to her left.

"I know what Ernst did to his daughter," she says. She is twenty-one. She is small in stature. But an eruption is brewing, and even Adams keeps an intimidated silence. "Killed her. Had her gassed so he could have me instead. You, my grandfather, Doctor Koerner. Erase this check mark. Put it in someone else's paperwork, and there you go. One girl lives. The other dies. Simple as that."

Haefner bursts into tears. Hana ignores him and turns to McAuliffe.

"I've been writing your daughter for many years," she says to him. Her voice now is suspiciously calm. Harold senses a trap.

"I'm aware," he says. "You mailed them to an incorrect address. They always ended up with us."

"She never got them."

"No."

"None of them."

"That's right."

"You had her institutionalized. Like I was."

"Well, I hardly..."

"And you didn't see fit to bring them to her yourself? Didn't you ever visit her?"

"That is none of your concern."

His own eruption building inside him, Harold advances toward Hana with the intention of grabbing whatever document she is holding so firmly in her grasp. She pulls away. He approaches. She moves to confront David.

"She's interrogating me, David," McAuliffe says, his voice rising. "You see that? You're the lawyer. You see what she's doing? This is absurd. The criminal attacking the integrity of the court. The strategy is obvious."

"But you didn't answer my question, sir," Hana says. As McAuliffe's composure wanes, hers becomes steadier. "You never visited her, your own daughter. Why?"

McAuliffe is flustered. He stumbles for an answer. "We did. Many times. Her mother and I. David was away at law school. Then the war. But we visited. Just ask my wife."

"Oh, sir, but I did."

There. Hana utters a sigh. Her baby has just unleashed a series of kicks that almost distract her. She has to place a hand on David's arm to stabilize herself. She's feeling a little dizzy and would ask Silke to get her something to drink. But now is not the time. The trap has been sprung, and Harold McAuliffe has stuck both feet right into it. She opens her hand and gives David the wire she received earlier that morning from Portland, Maine.

"How to say this, David," she says to him gently. "Believe me, I didn't want to have to do it this way."

"What way? What are you talking about?" Harold says. He steps forward, tries to intercept the wire, but his son holds it away to read for himself.

"You see?" Hana says. "The difference between my grandfather and your father is trifling really. One consigns his granddaughter to death. The other—"

"You had her lobotomized!" David screams.

In a sudden frightening spasm of violence, unlike anything he has ever exhibited in his life, David hurls the wire at his father and charges him. "You had her fucking lobotomized!"

Adams has to intercede, grabbing David from behind, pulling him off his now flailing thoroughly shaken father.

"Lobotomized, for the love of Christ! Why?"

"Her doctors," Harold stutters. "David, please, calm down. They said. They said it would help her. They said it would make her better. You saw how she was. You saw how she behaved. They screwed up, not me."

"Oh, my God." David clutches his head. It is better than clutching his father's throat. "You had her fucking lobotomized, Dad. And you didn't tell me. You didn't even tell Mom. You just—"

David is so beside himself, he has to leave, he has to get away from his father. He spins about and pushes away from Adams.

"David, please..." Harold would go after his son, resolve things, but Vitor Hartenstein comes to stand in his way and won't move.

"Sir, I wouldn't."

"You'll pay for this, you little...bitch!" Harold shouts at Hana. It is all in vain now, and he knows it, looks up when an unexpected voice tells him otherwise.

"No, Harry," this someone says, "**you** will. Pay, that is."

The voice belongs to one of the women. Low. Composed. Familiar to Harold, as it should be. In the past, he has loved hearing that voice whisper sweet nothings in his ear when his wife Lizzie was away. Now he is ashamed to look her way.

CHAPTER TWENTY-SIX

"She said it wasn't about money."

"It is now," Ilse says.

Ilse takes Hana's hand. "Sit, dear. You've done your part. Let the rest of us take over now. I happen to know through personal experience that Harry has a generous account with the Bank of Maine."

* * *

"We have a plan, Hana and I," Silke says from the couch. "And you can help."

"You mean, I'd better help."

"I think you'll want to when you hear what it is. I'm sure your son Charlie will be pleased. Politicians being politicians."

Shaken off his pedestal, Harold has to find a place to sit down. He's not ready to hear anything just yet. It is into this renewed silence that Adams reasserts himself.

"Well, then," he says, "I suppose you've satisfied whatever was going on between the two of you. Any further negotiating can wait. I'm the father of two daughters myself. Which makes it painful for me to remind you that we still have two murders to resolve. Plus, eight."

Haefner has been holding a glass of wine. He sets it down on the mantle above the fireplace, trying desperately to appear sober.

"Eight?" he says.

"That's correct."

"You said something about a cemetery."

Hana has expended a great deal of emotional energy exposing her past. Now she turns a worried face toward the American army officer.

"I did. About two miles from here off a dirt road. Down in a gully, surrounded by forest. If it hadn't been for the dog, we'd never have found it."

Adams, in plunging ahead, never takes his eyes off Hana. He doesn't doubt Haefner's guilt for a moment in crimes for which he may never be punished. And he feels no sympathy for Harold McAuliffe and his poor parenting skills.

But Hana is someone else. A Marie Curie with a dark, perverse past? His fellow officer McAuliffe is sympathetic. Maybe McAuliffe's in love. He may even be right. A young girl twisted by war. But does that excuse murder? Not in Adams's view. Did he just see her flinch? Did she just give herself away? In that case, time to go for the jugular.

"We found the remains of eight people. Children," he says.

Hana gasps. "Eight?"

"Does the number mean something to you, Fraulein?"

"Oh, God!"

Hana's sudden outburst startles everyone except Adams. This is just what he expected, just what he hoped to see. Hilda leaps to her rescue as Hana trips over her own feet and crashes to the floor. Silke's up, and Otto rushes from around the sofa. While Ilse bends to help her granddaughter, Frau Hartenstein pushes Adams aside.

"You did this to her. You Americans. Shame on you."

"Cemetery. What cemetery?" Hana rises with the help of the other women. "What are you talking about? My children? Where are they? Are they here? Did you find them?"

Hilda has hurried to the kitchen to fetch Hana something to drink. But Hana no longer exists in the moment. She can't see the glass held upright in front of her.

"If you found them, I want to see them," Hana says. "Monica. Sara. Oleg. Anatoly. All of them. Where are they?"

Adams intentionally pauses. He has neatly stolen her thunder. From the victorious prosecutor of Ernst Haefner and Harold McAuliffe, an admittedly clever accomplishment, she has become the hapless defendant on the verge of spilling her guts.

Despite the chaotic response to Hana's collapse, Adams takes it all in stride. 'Nice acting,' he is thinking, 'but it doesn't fool me.'

"You really want to see them?" he says.

"Officer, don't," Silke pleads.

"No, Fraulein, if she wants to see them, she ought to have that opportunity. All of you should. You're Germans. You all share some of the guilt." He

246

stands aside then and gestures toward the door. "Outside. I've ordered them brought here before we take them for autopsy."

"Autopsy?"

Hana hears the word but it doesn't quite register. In her mind, she is seeing all of the children, alive and well.

"Listen," Silke tells her. She is holding Hana up, whispering into her ear. "Listen to me. You've suspected this all along. Be brave. I'm with you. We all are. Do you hear me?"

If Hana does, she can't answer.

"It is why Herr McAuliffe is going to help us," Silke reminds her. "Remember?"

"Help? Us?"

With Silke on one side of her and her grandmother on the other, Hilda and the Hartensteins behind, Hana manages the long walk to the main drive where the eight bodies have been arranged in the backs of two military trucks. They have been placed in body bags. At the first truck, Adams steps up and then offers his hand to help Hana.

"I would ask you to identify them," he says, "but there's nothing left to identify. Bones. But you can tell they're children. We'll know more about them after the autopsy. I mean, about how they died."

At first, all Hana can do is crouch beside the closest body bag. She is shaking. Adams has prevented Silke or any of the other women from accompanying Hana into the truck. Her tears fall on the canvas container which could as easily be carrying someone's camping equipment or golf clubs. She is afraid to take the final step, to reach for the zipper. Sobbing, she is taking too long.

"Should I?" Adams finally offers. "If you can't." And so, he does the honors himself, grabbing the zipper and throwing open the body bag as if it were a highly anticipated Christmas present. Then he lifts the cover exposing the body. "Look, Fraulein," he insists. "Take a look. Tell me what you see."

It is with the greatest difficulty that Hana complies. Behind her from the ground, Silke is telling her everything will be all right, everything will be all right. But will it?

Hana wipes her eyes with her sleeve, opens her mouth, tilts her head, and braves a peek inside.

Adams is wrong about one thing. The remains aren't all bone. Some human tissue is left. Hair on the skull. Certain unique features that, even in death, tell her whether or not this person was a boy or girl, short or tall. Plus, there is something, a token, a necklace Hana remembers giving to this particular child on the day she stopped stuttering. 'I am the best,' it says.

"My Monica," Hana whispers.

"Pardon?"

"My daughter."

Hana collapses on top of the girl. She hugs her as if by embracing the body she will restore her to life. Monica will sit up. She will open her eyes. A smile of profound happiness will appear on her face, and she will say, without the slightest hint of a stammer, "Mommy, where have you been? We've been waiting for you for so long."

Adams has not gotten the response he was hoping for. The grief is overwhelming. There is no terror at having been found out. No admission of guilt. Only a sorrow that remorse can't explain away. But still, he thinks she is putting on an act. Her weeping: please.

"Your daughter," he says. "Did you notice her skull? There's a bullet hole in it. A bullet hole! Go on. Look. Right there. See? Someone put a pistol to this child's head, to your daughter's head, and blew her away. Look at it! And all the others."

"Stop it, Major."

"Lined them all up. One at a time."

"Major, stop it."

"Then...bang!...eight times!"

"Major!"

"Down they go. Into the ground. One at a time. Without even a kiss good night."

"Major!"

Adams looks up. He is panting with the effort, furious that he has been interrupted. By whom? Who dared to order him to stop just when she was about to confess?

"Oh, for God's sake! Kreisler!"

Of all people, he thinks. If anyone should want her confession, it's the survivor from the camps. But instead, the former Jewish detective climbs into the back of the truck and takes Hana in his arms.

"Kreisler, what the fuck?"

"She didn't do it, Major," he says. "Leave her alone now. She didn't do it."

"Are you crazy?" Adams says. "What the hell are you doing?"

"Listen to me. Listen to me," he says, not to Adams but to the young woman he is holding in his arms. His tears fall beside hers. "You didn't do this. You didn't do any of it. I know this now. I'm so sorry, little one."

Hana continues to clutch her dead child, but at least her tremors are subsiding. She is listening.

Kreisler says, "It was a cold winter morning. We were packed into the boxcars like sardines. As soon as they opened the doors, *'Rouse! Rouse, Juden!'* The dead just dropped to the ground. The rest of us who were able formed a line-up. I'd seen it many times at many camps. To the right, you live. To the left, you die. Mengele was there, the monster. I saw him."

"Yes, yes," Hana whispers.

"You remember?"

"Yes. You were there?"

"Indeed. And you know who else I saw?"

"Who?"

Kreisler holds Hana like a father would hold a child. He never married, has no children of his own, so this will do for all the hugs he has missed in his lifetime.

"I saw you. I only just now recognized you here in the back of the truck. You got into a fight with another woman, much bigger than you."

"Gretchen."

"She punched you, kicked you. All you were trying to do was save some of the children. Twins, as I recall it." Kreisler turns his glance to Adams. "This is true, Major. With my own eyes, I saw it."

"Saw her trying to grab up a couple of twins for her own experiments is what you saw, Herr Kreisler."

"No, no," Kreisler insists. "You haven't heard the whole story." Taking Hana's chin in his hand, he turns her face towards him so she can see the truth in what he is saying.

"A man came to your rescue," he explains. "A suicidal thing to do with the SS guards all around. You disobey orders, you get shot. But I heard him say something to you. And the look on your face. This man, it came to me, was your father."

At last, Hana releases the remains of seven-year-old Monica Baranowski so that she can grab instead onto this man who knows the truth.

"Oh, you saw," she says.

"And I saw how they carted you away unconscious and how Mengele gave the children to you rather than to this Gretchen. The one good deed in his life."

"My father? It was him? He called my name."

Kreisler nods. "They would have killed him then and there for daring to break ranks, but I, occasionally insightful and rash, yelled, 'Herr Doktor, please don't shoot. He's my twin."

"Your twin?"

Kreisler chuckles. "Well, you live in the camps long enough, you all begin to look alike. Mr. Skin, meet Mr. Bones. I saved your father's life that day. And today, maybe, I save yours."

Chapter Twenty-Seven

May 1947

"Case closed? I don't think so."

Adams is not a heartless or stubborn man when faced with certain evidence. Secretly respecting Kreisler, he has become convinced that Hana Zeigler is no murderer, just another victim of the Nazis. But someone killed Walter Ziegler and someone killed William Sorensen. And Sorensen is an American, so his murder can't go unresolved. Adams is convinced that the killers, one male, one female, are here on the Haefner estate right now. But what can he do? So much drama for one afternoon.

"Tomorrow," he tells everyone. "We reconvene here. One of you, two of you, killed an American. Either you'll confess, or I'll hang these murders on all of you. Understood?"

It is an evening of unusual weather, early in the season for thunder and lightning. But the thunder is loud, the lightning flashes scary and the rain comes down with such intensity that it appears to Hana that a guilt-ridden God is trying to cover up His failure to protect eight children. By the time the storm passes, the graves and every other bit of evidence against the Almighty will be washed away.

Kreisler has dinner that night with the Hartensteins. Vitor and Gertrud's house is tiny in comparison to that of August Haefner and Friedrich Ziegler, but the supper table is large enough for the two Hartenstein parents, their daughter Silke, granddaughters Ursula and Charlotte, Ilse Ziegler, and her pregnant granddaughter Hana.

"Our idea is a beautiful one," Silke is saying. "Think of all the unwanted children there are in Germany today, those who will never be adopted. Hana now stands to inherit both the Ziegler estate and the Haefner estate. We convert those and, *voila*, a home for the unwanted."

"It makes me happy to think that some good may come of all this insanity and unhappiness," Ilse says. "My greatest regret is, well, I think you know what that is, my dear."

Hana kisses her grandmother's cheek. "Maybe this was God's will all the time."

Thunder cracks. Lightning fires the sky. Kreisler snorts. His appetite fully recovered, he is eating Frau Hartenstein's baked quail, shot by her husband, with the zest of Robinson Crusoe.

"You don't believe in God anymore?" Hana asks him sitting across the table.

"Yuh, yuh, yuh, God. Pardon me if I hem and haw."

"I suppose I don't either. But, still, it's sad."

Hana glances to her left. Her god, or goddess, is Silke who eats with Charlotte in her lap and Ursula clutching her arm. Silke, who has decided she wants to be a doctor.

"What about science, Herr Kreisler? Do you think I'm wasting my time trying to find out who we are, where we come from?"

"Where we come from is no mystery," he says. "No, no mystery at all. It is rather a sordid tale that the Old Testament dances around." Kreisler chews, swallows. "This is a lovely meal, by the way, Frau Hartenstein."

"Danke, Herr Kreisler."

"Your daughter is quite a good shot."

"Me, Herr Kreisler?"

"I remember it from a magazine article." He stops eating long enough to give her an innocent smile. "Even Himmler paid you a compliment."

The fork and bird that are heading for Silke's mouth stop halfway from her plate.

"Herr Kreisler, must you?" she scolds.

"Avi, please. Why does everyone insist on calling me 'herr'?"

"Because you're interrogating us," Silke says. "I know what you're doing. After all this. How can you? It's insulting."

"My daughter killed no one," Vitor says in his Silke's defense.

"I'm only asking things that Major Adams will ask tomorrow. I apologize for my manner. I was never taught any. But, you see, the matter isn't closed. Not for him, and I don't want to see any of you fine people get into trouble. But I must be honest, for this is part of being the new man I've become. I agree with him. Two of you killed the American Sorensen and Fraulein Hana's uncle, the SS pig Walter Ziegler. By admitting it, you'll make it easier for me to help you cover it up."

"We don't need a cover-up, Herr Ziegler. Avi," Hana says. "None of us did anything."

"Hmmm."

Kreisler ponders this, takes another bite of quail mixed in with the mashed potato. "I hope dessert is as good as the main course," he says. "Then let me say this, if this is the line you wish to take. I am in a position to doctor passports. Yes, believe me, this is true. Even Honest Abe Kreisler is still dishonest when he must be. If things become unpleasant, if Major Adams persists and decides to charge you, Fraulein Hana, I can get you into Palestine. It wouldn't be easy. There are risks involved, but you'd make it with your child. You can raise unwanted children there. God knows, there are plenty enough of them in the world."

Hana shakes her head. "No, thank you. My family is here."

"Germany is a wreck."

"Even so."

"If he doesn't charge you with the murder of Ziegler and Sorensen, he surely will for the eight children. And for the woman, Gretchen. Perhaps even for Doctor Koerner."

"Even so. Otto will take care of me. I have faith in him. And he is the father, after all."

"Yes, yes. Of course."

"You may disapprove, Avi, but I've made up my mind to stay. No matter how long it takes, Silke and I will make it work."

Kreisler nods, lays down his fork, and heaves a sigh of satisfaction. "Then, perhaps," he says, "I should mention I am helping someone else with their papers at the moment. I've spoken of him before to you. The man who called your name at Dachau. The man I called my twin brother. Louis Marksohn. Your father."

* * *

"You're not going to do it, are you?" Silke asks her that night after the children have been put to bed. "Go to Palestine?"

They are sitting in the back seat of the Hartenstein VW. The violent part of the spring storm has passed, but rain continues to pelt the ground. It creates a curtain that keeps the world away, at least for a little while. The windows have also fogged up, giving Hana and Silke much-needed privacy.

"I'd never leave you, Silke," Hana says. "Shame on you for asking."

"You could."

Silke is worried and wondering why she is so worried. She and Hana are friends, yes? Very good friends. Bonded in wartime. Strengthened by all that they have experienced together. Friends forever, though Silke knows Hana wants more than mere friendship. Hana doesn't just love Silke. She is **in** love with Silke.

"Maybe I can convince my father to stay with us," Hana says. "I hope he will."

"He may have brothers and sisters who survived the war. You may have cousins, nieces, and nephews, a whole family. What if they all choose to go to Palestine?"

"Then I'll stay here with you. Fatherland. Holy Land. You're my land, Silke, my country. You and the girls and my Monica."

Silke heaves a sigh. Trying to push Hana away, convince her to emigrate, doesn't work. Hana is the type of woman who can forebear almost anything. She has had to. She is the bravest person Silke has ever known. Stubborn, resistant, full of love despite all of the hatred that has been flung at her. So, why should Silke be so intent upon denying her the love she wants most of all?

"You've chosen her name," Silke says. "Monica. What if it's a boy?"

"I don't know. I told Otto he could choose."

"Mmmm. Good luck."

Out of nowhere, it would seem to Hana, Silke places a hand on Hana's cheek and turns her face so that she can gaze into Hana's eyes.

Hana blushes. "What?"

Silke smiles then breaks into a fit of shy laughter. It is so typical of her to do this at the most serious of moments. "You're lucky I can't get you pregnant."

"God help us all," says a startled Hana. "So much for science." But if Hana's eyes could make it so, they would. It is Silke's gaze that is confused.

In the morning, after a quick breakfast, they all pack into Vitor's VW and head back to the Ziegler estate for the confrontation with Major Adams and Captain David McAuliffe. Hana half anticipates dozens of American MPs already there ahead of them, set to arrest her and haul her off to prison. Her stomach is pounding and it has nothing to do with her baby.

In fact, as Vitor drives along the wet asphalt and enters the estate grounds, Hana sees a great deal of activity. Three cars but also an ambulance. Uniformed and helmeted MPs are milling about, but they don't show her much interest when she gets out of the VW, followed by Silke and the Hartensteins.

Major Adams is nowhere to be seen, but Hana spies David smoking a cigarette by himself. She approaches him, wondering what kind of an evening he had with his father.

"Are you all right?" she asks him.

He crushes the cigarette out under his foot. "You mean my old man? Serves him right. You?" He glances at Silke, offers her a tentative smile, which she returns.

"I managed to get a few hours of sleep," Hana says. "What's going on here? Where's Major Adams?"

"Inside." David looks behind him at the men coming and going out of the front door of the house. "You up for surprises?" he asks. "Big one?"

"Surprises?"

"You didn't have any feelings for Haefner, did you? Hope not."

David turns about. "It's okay. They're with me," he tells a guard at the doorway. Hana, Silke, and her parents follow inside. "Apparently, he hung himself last night."

"Ernst?" Hana falters.

"You're sure you're up for this?"

No, Hana isn't. This is more than unpleasant. This was a man, after all, who did save her life.

"He's still hanging?"

"They may have just taken him down. We only got here an hour ago. That's when we found him. He left a note."

"A note?" Hana asks. She finds herself trembling. "Rip it up."

"Can't. It's evidence that exonerates you. It exonerates all of you."

As Hana is escorted up the staircase to the second floor and down the corridor that leads to Haefner's bedroom, she clings to Silke, not sure how she feels. Certainly, she had no love for him. But death piled upon death only adds to the tragedy that seems to surround her. Where does it all come from? Where does it end?

Adams greets them at the doorway into Haefner's bedroom. Haefner's body is carried out at that moment on a sheet-covered stretcher.

"Well," he says, "seems you're off the hook. Can't prove it was murder. Yet." He is holding Haefner's final statement, thinks twice before handing it to Hana to read. "Says he was responsible for the deaths of those eight children. Him and your uncle Walter. Says he poisoned his wife and his father and then shot Walter to try to cover his tracks. Finishes by asking God and you for forgiveness. Quite the fella, wouldn't you say?"

"You sound doubtful, Major," Hana says.

"Well, there is one glaring omission. If Haefner was the man, the driver, who was the woman who shot Sorensen and Ziegler?"

"Not me, if that's what you're thinking."

But Hana has to wonder. If not her…she… She hands the letter back to

Adams. But she is suddenly feeling dizzy, leans on Silke, thinking pregnancy isn't all that fun. She hopes to God Silke had nothing to do with Walter's death.

"That may be a mystery you're never going to be able to solve, Tom," David says. "Even if you did, what jury is going to find the killer of an SS officer guilty? Given the evidence you're holding right now? Would you?"

Adams hands the evidence off to his lieutenant. "You'd make a hell of a prosecutor, that's for sure. I ain't buying everything that's in that letter, you know."

"That's your problem. I quit."

David walks away from Adams accompanying Hana and Silke outside. While the rain has stopped, the sky is filled with gray clouds. No sun. Little warmth.

Before parting, David says, "I think you'll be okay now. I'm my father's attorney. Whatever you two have in mind, work it through me. I'll make sure you get what you need."

"It could be a lot," says Silke.

"Whatever. If my brother wants to be president, he's got to be generous."

At the door to the Hartenstein VW, he offers his hand to Hana and a hopeful smile to Silke. "I wouldn't mind being invited for dinner sometime," he says.

"Good to know." Silke returns the smile then climbs into the car beside Hana, who gives her friend a curious gaze.

"Are you leading him on, my dear?" she asks.

"Maybe," Silke says. "The world's an odd place."

* * *

In the days that follow, some normalcy returns to the Ziegler and Hartenstein households. Hana has abandoned the Haefner estate and has moved back in with her grandmother. As her due date approaches, she spends much of her time with Ilse in the greenhouse while Silke continues her studies and prepares to apply to the university.

"You found my letters," Ilse says one morning.

"You knew?" Hana, belly protruding, is embarrassed but no longer intimidated by the older woman.

"You weren't very careful returning them to their place," Ilse says. "Is that what caused you to write Harry McAuliffe?"

"No. I wasn't going to do anything with them until Silke got pregnant. I didn't mean to be nosy. I'm sorry."

"No need to be." Glancing at the other young woman poring over some biology textbook, Ilse, the Victorian aristocrat, understands more than, in the past, she would admit. "You love Silke, don't you?"

"Does it show?"

"Every time you look at her."

Hana blushes. She weighs the question in her mind as she tends her grandmother's roses. What to tell a woman who was born in the last century and who was raised believing that girls of her social rank married men of means and that was that?

"She means the world to me," Hana says.

"As she should, Hana. As she should. But..."

Shedding soft tears that are quickly snuffed out by a silk handkerchief, Ilse reaches for Hana's hand. "They say love conquers all, but they're wrong. It's the strong, the patient, who conquer love."

"You kept my letters," Hana says. "And my mother's. All that time I thought you hated me. But if that were true, if it was entirely true, you wouldn't have done that, would you?"

"I suppose not."

"Then we'll leave it at that, okay?"

"We'll leave everything as it is, *liebchen*." Ilse lets go of Hana's hand then and pats her granddaughter on the cheek. "Be kind to Otto, that's all I have to say on the matter. I'll never say another word."

"Absolutely no more words."

When Silke looks up from her reading at that moment and gives Hana and Ilse a smile, a key is turned in a lock. Hana will not speak of love again. Not now at least. As her grandmother said, 'patience,' and if Hana has learned anything, it is that.

They are still at work pruning and planting when a car pulls up outside. The children are with Hilda, and Vitor and Gertrude are still working at the Haefner estate, maintaining the grounds for the next owner. David and Otto have been collaborating to see that the forged marriage between Ernst Haefner and Hana becomes a real one and that Haefner's will, therefore, is complied with in full. Hana won't really need McAuliffe money at this point, but there was one other request Hana made of David that he is in the process of working on with the full cooperation of his parents.

The visit, then, is from someone else. At first, Hana's heart thumps with worry that Major Adams has followed through on his promise to find out who the mystery woman is. Instead, she sees Avi Kreisler get out from the driver's side of the car and hold the door open for his passenger.

The man who exits is barely recognizable. He is dressed well, in a suitcoat and tie, with new shoes and a homburg hat that he doffs the moment his eyes alight on Hana. Years in the camps have cost him many pounds that he has not put back on since liberation. His hair has turned white. His cheeks are hollow and he walks with a distinct limp.

Kreisler has to help him move forward but not far. Louis Marksohn has taken only two wary steps before Hana has rushed, in tears, into his arms.

"Father!"

She nearly bowls him over in her excitement. She can't utter any other words but merely blubbers against his chest.

"You see? I'm a man of my word," Kreisler says. "A few more pounds on him, he'll be as good as new."

Marksohn has no words either. What unimaginable horrors each one has faced alone is beyond expression. Father and daughter simply declare their unbounding love with tears.

"Don't leave me," Hana begs him at last. "Stay. Don't go to Palestine. Let me take care of you."

"I…I…I…"

"He has trouble speaking," Avi says, stepping in and offering Louis a tissue to wipe his eyes. "He suffered a stroke shortly after the Americans came. If

Eisenhower had been a day later, he wouldn't have made it at all. There are doctors in Palestine who can fix him."

"There are doctors in Germany," Hana says. On tiptoes, she reaches to kiss her father's unshaven cheek.

"He won't see a German doctor, and the Americans are sick of Jews asking them for things. Like a homeland. Palestine is his only option. He's going tomorrow, Hana. He's come to ask you to join us."

"But, I can't."

Hana backs away, eyes to the ground. She needs to think. She needs to sort things out. There must be an answer. Why must life always create impediments to happiness? Where have all those precious brain cells gone, Hana? Why can't you make things work? In desperation, she lifts her hands to caress either side of her father's face. His eyes are questioning. Hers are faltering.

"I love someone here," she says. "I can't leave them. Please. We can help you here."

Louis closes his eyes, opens them. His head is rocking back and forth. It is as if he is trying to say something but the words are imprisoned within.

"I...I..."

"Stay. I promise you a cure."

"I... I..."

At last, frustrated beyond measure, Louis glances at Avi, gestures angrily with his head, until Avi reaches into one of Louis's coat pockets and retrieves something. It is a locket. Avi hands it to Hana.

"Open it," he says. "Your father wants you to have it. As a going-away gift."

"No, I don't..."

"Take it or you'll leave your father an unhappy man. Go on."

Hana's fingers are trembling so much, Silke has to open the locket for her so that when the picture of baby Hana with her mother and father is revealed, they both see it together. Hana breaks down, clasping the locket to her heart.

"Oh, what did we lose?" she cries and tightens her hold on her father.

"I...I..."

Silke has to pry them apart. She says to Louis, "We'll come visit you. We promise. With your grandchild." She pats Hana on the belly. "No need for tears. See? How many more would you like?"

Louis seems to chuckle. He raises three unsteady fingers then reflects upon Silke. For a moment, it appears as though his mind is working up something to say. He may be ill. He may have suffered a debilitating stroke. But in his youth, he had been an actor, and people of the Berlin theater scene back in those days knew a lot more than they ever told anyone. He gives a nod and a smile.

'Ah, yes,' he seems to be saying. 'So, you're my daughter's lover, are you? Can hardly blame her.'

Then with all the effort he can muster, he utters the one word he is able to speak with such clarity that his meaning is unmistakable.

"L'chaim."

Chapter Twenty-Eight

December 1947

On a brisk winter morning, Hana and Silke bundle up the children, Ursula, Charlotte, and Monica, and head to Munich. They are not driving in the Hartenstein VW, which is far too small. While Hana could have afforded her own vehicle now that the Haefner will has been probated, the McAuliffes, with much fanfare and delight, purchased for her an American-made Buick Estate Wagon. It's not a luxury car, but it is large enough for a family that is still growing.

They're heading to the American airbase outside Munich because their family is about to add another member. Hana is excited, and not just because Silke is teaching her to drive and this is the first time she has taken the steering wheel out onto the speedy German autobahn.

"You're doing great," Silke tells her. "Ten kilometers per hour faster, and we'll get there next year."

"I'm nervous."

"I can see. But at least you're staying on the right side of the road. Don't let me rattle you."

Ever cognizant of numbers, Hana has made sure they have plenty of time to greet the Pan Am flight out of Boston. Fortunately, it didn't take a lot of convincing for Harold and Lizzie McAuliffe to agree to the terms Hana and Silke had set to let Charlie off the hook. '48 would be his year. Congress to Senate to the White House. And all it took was the completion of a few legal documents that David made sure were signed, sealed, and delivered with all due speed.

Hana would be happy to see him. He was accompanying the flight. Otto was on it, too.

It might be amusing to see if David flirted with Silke. For his part, Otto was content with his role in the Ziegler-Hartenstein household. He was a loving father to Monica and, as he stated over and over again, he was more than happy to share his sperm with Hana any time she wished. He would never leave her, and he would gladly spawn more Ziegler-Froelings so long as none of them were pure Aryans.

David may have felt he still had a shot at Silke, too. And Silke isn't averse to the idea, so long as he understands that his role must be exactly like Otto's.

"We'll see," she tells Hana.

"Just don't string him along forever. He is a nice guy."

"One of the best. God knows we might just ruin Charlie McAuliffe's life, after all."

As cautious a driver as Hana is, she gets them to the airfield just before three in the afternoon, twenty minutes before the scheduled landing. Enough time to feed the kids, go to the bathroom, and hurry to the waiting area.

Hana has never seen a large passenger plane like the Pan Am touch down. It's an exciting moment as the craft comes out of the clouds and, with a roar of engines, makes a perfect landing.

"That's it!" she shouts. "Come on, kids. Let's go meet our new aunt."

Peg McAuliffe.

Well, Hana wasn't going to let her old pen pal rot away in some upstate New York institution until old age ended her unhappy life. Everyone needs to know they are loved. Everyone needs a home. How do horrifying things like Holocausts happen without a million tiny holocausts going on every day in families across the world? Unhappy, ruined children grow up to be unhappy, ruined adults who vent their rage on the world. That is Hana's opinion. Genetics, yes. That is a factor, but so is the slap on the face, the curse, the locked heart, the slammed door, the threats, and the torture. No child should experience that.

As soon as David wheels his sister down the ramp, Hana is there with a smile, a kiss, and a present, a bouquet of her grandmother's flowers.

"Welcome home," she says. Then Peg is smothered with children who want to sit in her lap and ride the wheelchair with her.

Peg has brought her own gift for Hana. The operation to remove part of her frontal lobe has impacted her ability to speak clearly. Still, she tries to express her feelings as she hands Hana her gift. A drawing of two girls sitting on the branch of a tree, legs dangling down, sharing a laugh.

"For you," Peg says.

"You kept it all these years. Copenhagen." Hana can only stifle her anger by wrapping her arms around Peg and whispering in the other young woman's ear.

"Well," she says. "There'll be plenty of time to do more of that. You're home now."

"Home," Peg says.

"Absolutely."

And off they go, this family. One child who was supposed to be euthanized. Another molded to be a female robot. A third whose brain has been permanently damaged. One baby born of rape, another of systematic Nazi breeding. But they are as good a family as there is in Germany now. Anywhere in the world, for that matter.

'L'Chaim indeed,' Hana thinks. The unwanted are going home.

Epilogue

May 1947

The truth came out innocently enough. The furthest thing from either of their minds was to commit murder. They'd seen enough of it, experienced its horror too often and too close to home.

At first, it was a conversation.

"I overheard them talking," the first conspirator says. "Haefner was drunk as usual. Ziegler was scared. You could hear it in his voice. 'You're the one who allowed it to happen. Yes, well, you're the one who fucking shot them,' pardon my use of the word. Then there was the lawyer, Herr Froeling."

"What did you hear?"

"Argentina. I heard them mention Argentina. There's an American who can help."

"An American?" The second conspirator is curious but not overly impressed. "What of it? What did you expect those cowards to do? Run at the first chance, that's what. Let him go, is my attitude."

The two conspirators might have left it at that had the second incident not occurred. Just a week later, the second of the two makes a frightening discovery on the Ziegler property. A chance encounter with a fox leads to a chase, through a forest, around trees, up hills, and down hollows until a gunshot, narrowly missing the fox, digs up, instead, the top layer of a shallow grave.

"Bones, I tell you," the conspirator yells at his collaborator. "Human bones.

265

I don't have to tell you who they belong to, do I?"

Still, they have to make sure. Without alerting anyone else, they sneak out one dawn and experiment in the soil that a gunshot had uncovered. They don't have to dig far.

The shock is only exceeded by the rage that follows.

"You're right. It's them, poor dears," says the first. "It's Herr Haefner's doing."

"And that SS scum."

"Yes, him, too."

"We can't let them get away with it. We can't let him fly the coop and leave this on our consciences."

But what can they do? Alert the local police? Alert the American MPs? That is their intention. Until the American Sorensen arrives one day, and Walter Ziegler, after a quick change of clothes, joins him in the American's car. Then, there is nothing left to be done. The border to Switzerland lies a very short ride from the Haefner estate. In an hour, Hauptscharfuhrer Walter Ziegler will be home free, and all the harm that he has done, all the misery that he has caused, will go without punishment.

The two conspirators jump into their car and follow. One of them has brought a gun. Even then, they have decided that they will force the American at gunpoint to stop the car. They will force Ziegler out and bring him to justice. They have no plan to kill anyone.

The gap closes. They are doubling the speed limit while the American is driving at a more leisurely pace. Fifty meters back, the shooter checks the gun, makes sure it's loaded.

"What are you going to do?" asks the driver.

"Scare him. Pull closer. Get up beside him if you have to."

By now, the American has noticed the trailing car and has picked up speed. This means the driver must now accelerate. He is pushing his car faster than it has ever gone. The wind off the highway blows off his hat as the shooter opens her window.

"Pull over!" she shouts at the American. "Pull over!"

She exhibits her gun as a threat, not expecting the American driver to do the same. But when he raises his gun, what choice does she have? He fires. She fires. He misses. She doesn't.

She screams in terror as one bullet creases her companion's forehead while hers hits home. Blood and bone spray everywhere. In an instant, the American's car spins out of control and flies off the road into a ditch. It flips over and skids, coming to a sickening stop against a tree.

The driver brakes sharply, bringing his automobile to a screeching halt. He is out of the car quickly followed by the shooter. The American must be dead, but what of the other man, the SS man, the one they really want?

Down into the ditch they stumble, setting off an avalanche of debris. The shooter twists an ankle and yelps in pain before she catches a glimpse of a wounded man crawling free of the destroyed car.

"Children!" she shouts at him.

"What?" Walter Ziegler is bleeding, stunned.

"Children!"

She raises her weapon. The driver tries to stop her, but she breaks free.

"Children!" she shouts one last time before her gun discharges. Perhaps it is an accident. Perhaps her rage causes her finger to move in such a way she will come to regret it later.

But in the moment, in her fury, all she can think about is the dead. Sigrid Haefner. The eight innocents mowed down because they are perceived as a threat. The thousands of others euthanized or sterilized or dressed up as soldiers and sent into the front lines to die for a cause already dead. And, of course, her own son Georg.

After Gertrud Hartenstein spits in Walter Ziegler's face, she hands the gun to her husband Vitor.

Acknowledgements

I began my writing career after I took my last college exam. With a college notebook, several sharpened pencils, an eraser and a pencil sharpener, I began to write a science fiction novel called *The Third World*. That was nearly a half century ago. Skipping ahead some forty-eight years, I would like to thank the remarkable people behind Level Best Books who finally recognized someone who had a modicum of writing talent: Verena, Shawn and Harriette. Thanks forever. Every good writer needs an honest editor to bring the best out of his or her creation. Mine has been Stacy Donovan. Honest and affordable. You can't beat that. Writing is easy. Marketing is horrible. My publicist, Mary Bisbee-Beek, is opening doors I never could. The quintessential professional you want on your writing team. I am computer illiterate. Kristen Weber has created a professional web site that makes me look like a genius. (We'll be in tocu, I'm sure. A lot.) I have many friends I'd like to thank, but I don't want to make any of them jealous by forgetting someone. Maybe the next book. But I did promise the casting couch (For Carol). Lastly, I would like to thank the one person who never gave up, who survived the hundreds of rejection slips and always found a reason to go on. Me. Tip o' the hat, lad.

About the Author

Born in Portland, Maine, Mr. Clenott graduated from Bowdoin College before setting down roots in Massachusetts. The father of three children, he currently works for an anti-poverty agency. His previous published works include *Hunting the King, Devolution,* and *The Hunted.*